KU-296-286

Small Worlds

Praise for *Open Water*

'*Open Water* is tender poetry, a love song to Black art and thought, an exploration of intimacy and vulnerability between two young artists learning to be soft with each other in a world that hardens against Black people' Yaa Gyasi, bestselling author of *Homegoing* and *Transcendent Kingdom*

'A short, poetic and intellectual meditation on art and a relationship between a young couple' Bernardine Evaristo

'An exciting, ambitious debut . . . While an elegance of style is a hallmark of Azumah Nelson's storytelling, there is bold risk-taking in his choices too' *Guardian*

'Hands-down the best debut I've read in years' *The Times*

'An unforgettable debut. Azumah Nelson's poetic brilliance, his ability to balance the general and the specific, the ambient and the granular, makes for a salient achievement. It's Sally Rooney meets Michaela Coel meets Teju Cole' *The New York Times*

'An emotionally intelligent and tender tale of first love . . . what makes it remarkable is its bracing and nuanced exploration of Black masculinity. An abundance of cultural references are framed through the perspective of a Black British male – one seldom seen in modern British fiction. It is worth questioning why, and whose stories get to be told. Thankfully, Azumah Nelson has told this tale of art, love and Black identity. And what a gift it is' *Independent*

'A tender and touching love story, beautifully told' *Observer*, Ten Best Debut Novelists of 2021

'A lyrical, modern love story, just 200 pages but brilliant on music, art, race and London life; I enjoyed it hugely' David Nicholls, bestselling author of *One Day* and *Sweet Sorrow*

'This is an amazing debut novel. It's a beautifully narrated, intelligently crafted piece of love that goes deep, then goes deeper. You should read this book' Benjamin Zephaniah, award-winning poet, playwright and novelist

'A beautiful and powerful novel about the true and sometimes painful depths of love' Candice Carty-Williams, *Sunday Times* bestselling author of *Queenie*

'*Open Water* is a very touching and heartfelt book, passionately written, which brings London to life in a painterly, emotive way. I love its musical richness and espousal of the power of the arts – pictures, sounds, movement' Diana Evans, Women's Prize-shortlisted author of *Ordinary People*

'Caleb Azumah Nelson has become quite the thing in literary circles this year with his novel, *Open Water*, a tale of two Black artists who fall in love against a beating backdrop of music, politics and race. It's already one of the bestselling debuts of 2021. The novel has drawn comparisons to Sally Rooney's *Normal People* and Michaela Coel's BBC series *I May Destroy You*, and is currently being turned into a TV series' *Sunday Times*

'*Open Water* encapsulates what it means to fall in love, explores what it means to move through the world whilst Black, and explores the beautiful melding of the two. I will always remember it and I will always return to this novel. A stunning piece of art' Bolu Babalola, *Sunday Times* bestselling author of *Love in Colour*

'*Open Water* is a beautifully, delicately written novel about love, for self and others, about being seen, about vulnerability and mental health. Sentence by sentence it oozes longing and grace' Nikesh Shukla, editor of *The Good Immigrant* and author of *Brown Baby*

'A poetic novel about Black identity and first love in the capital from one of Britain's most exciting young voices' *Harper's Bazaar*

'For those that are missing the tentative depiction of love in *Normal People*, Caleb Azumah Nelson's *Open Water* is set to become one of 2021's unmissable books. Utterly transporting, it'll leave you weeping and in awe' *Stylist*

'A book about Black bodies and strength, vulnerability and fear, with a magnetic romance woven throughout that entrances the reader'
Evening Standard

'This short debut novel is both a sweet, painful love story to savour and an account of what it means to live in fear in your own city, to be viewed simply as a Black body and never truly seen. Azumah Nelson's prose is intense and lyrical, with a pleasing scattering of musical references' *New Statesman*

'A debut already attracting awards-season buzz, this shattering love story about two Black British artists is a compelling insight into race and masculinity. You'll remember this author's name' *Elle*

'A short, sharp poetic burst of a novel; it crystallizes the torments and heat of young love brilliantly' Andrew McMillan, award-winning author of *Physical*

'*Open Water* is a powerful portrayal of the way that systemic violence can make a person forget softness and vulnerability. It exposes the failure of language to encapsulate feeling and illuminates the love and the anger that rage around the edges of everything' Jessica Andrews, award-winning author of *Saltwater*

'*Open Water* is about defiance, mourning, art and music. It is an ode to being a full human being in a society that does not see you that way. It is about clinging to love in a world heavy with injustice and violence. There is not a wasted page' Rowan Hisayo Buchanan, award-winning author of *Starling Days*

'A once-in-a-blue-moon kind of read, a truly remarkable debut from a gifted young wordsmith . . . The novel is at once a celebration of Black love and Black art and expression. Thoroughly unforgettable' *Buzzfeed*

'*Open Water* has a delicate, painterly quality while packing a real emotional punch. Caleb Azumah Nelson is a real talent' Olivia Sudjic, author of *Sympathy*, *Exposure* and *Asylum Road*

'A stunning debut novel . . . Written in a unique second-person style, and with profound insight into race and masculinity, it's a tender love story you won't forget' *Red*

'*Open Water* bristles with intelligence and sensuality . . . an irresistible debut with the promise of greatness' *RTÉ*

'*Open Water* is the most mesmerizing read. Caleb Azumah Nelson writes voice like a young Baldwin, placing himself both inside and outside the world he describes. *Open Water* drew me in, hypnotized me and left me, a few hours later, both devastated and a little high. This is the kind of novel which doesn't let go' Jan Carson, award-winning author of *The Fire Starters*

'Lush, urban, Black, British and beautiful' Inua Ellams, award-winning playwright and poet

'Exquisite' Kayo Chingonyi, award-winning author of *Kumukanda*

'Set to the rhythms of jazz and hip-hop, *Open Water* is an unforgettable story about making art and making a home in another person. In language bursting with grief and joy, Caleb Azumah Nelson has written the ode to Black creativity, love and survival that we need right now' Nadia Owusu, author of *Aftershocks*

'A brilliant debut whose gentleness and joyfulness are as profound as its examination of the cost of living in a racist society' Megha Majumdar, author of *A Burning*

'In this achingly tender and intensely moving debut, two Black artists fall in and out of love in South London. Featuring a stunning opening chapter, vulnerability, loss, masculinity and longing are covered. Written in a second-person narrative, this is a majestic debut' *Cosmopolitan*

'A hotly tipped new voice in British fiction' *Metro*

'Azumah Nelson's impressive first novel is tender, lyrical and all-consuming . . . A truly exceptional debut' *Booklist*

'One of the most beautiful novels I've ever read, impossible to put down even as it made my heart ache. Just stunning' *Refinery29*

'Considering the ways identity shapes experience, *Open Water* is a soulful meditation on art and love' *Culture Whisper*

'Extraordinary' *Woman & Home*

'Gorgeous' *Marie Claire*

'Caleb's debut is soulful and poetic, celebrating and
exploring the varying emotions of a blossoming romance
while offering an insight into race and masculinity' *Heat*

'A riveting love story . . . written in lyrical and
propulsive prose, a searing debut' *Kirkus Reviews*

'Azumah Nelson's writing is so accomplished it's hard to
believe it comes from a debut author . . . A raw and unvarnished
look at what it means to be Black and British' *Scotsman*

'Caleb Azumah Nelson's debut novel is an intimate, London-set story
of two artists falling in love, learning to show tenderness to one
another in a society that's anything but. Azumah Nelson writes with
grace and poignancy; it's a memorable first novel' *Tatler*

'Stunning and soulful . . . Sally Rooney fans in search of their next stirring,
socially conscious romance, look no further' *Chicago Review of Books*

'Lyrical . . . this emotionally rich debut tells a budding love story
against backdrops of Black culture, joy and pain' *Entertainment Weekly*

'Azumah Nelson's elegant, poetic debut novel, uniquely written in the
second person, features two unnamed artistic Black characters living in
London: a twenty-something photographer and the dancer/student he
is drawn to. As they fall in love, their relationship is tested by
communication struggles, issues of race and Black masculinity' *CNN*

'We were awestruck by the lyrical power of Azumah Nelson's prose.
Boldly written in the second person, his poetic novel bursts with
incisive thoughts and observations about modern society that
reverberated with us long after we set the book down. A celebration of
the Black voice, a meditation on the power of art, and a hardhitting
commentary on the realities of systemic racism, *Open Water* is mostly a
love story that's like nothing else we've ever read' Apple Books

By the same author

Open Water

Small Worlds

CALEB AZUMAH NELSON

VIKING

an imprint of

PENGUIN BOOKS

VIKING

UK | USA | Canada | Ireland | Australia
India | New Zealand | South Africa

Viking is part of the Penguin Random House group of companies
whose addresses can be found at global.penguinrandomhouse.com.

First published 2023
004

Copyright © Caleb Azumah Nelson, 2023

The moral right of the author has been asserted

The permissions on p. 260 constitute an extension of this copyright page

Set in 11/13pt Dante MT Std
Typeset by Jouve (UK), Milton Keynes
Printed and bound in Great Britain by Clays Ltd, Elcograf S.p.A.

The authorized representative in the EEA is Penguin Random House Ireland,
Morrison Chambers, 32 Nassau Street, Dublin D02 YH68

A CIP catalogue record for this book is available from the British Library

ISBN: 978–0–241–57434–8

www.greenpenguin.co.uk

MIX
Paper | Supporting
responsible forestry
FSC® C018179

Penguin Random House is committed to a
sustainable future for our business, our readers
and our planet. This book is made from Forest
Stewardship Council® certified paper.

For Mum and Pops,
for J and J,
my own Small World

Black faith still can't be washed away

– Solange

From my heart, that's the making of me

– Dave

PART ONE

Two Young People in the Summertime

2010

I.

Since the one thing that can solve most of our problems is dancing, it only makes sense that here, following the shimmer of Black hands, raised in praise, the pastor invited us, the congregation, to pray, and we allowed that prayer to make space, allowed ourselves to explore the depths and heights of our beings, allowed ourselves to say things which were honest and true, God-like even. Allowed ourselves to speak to someone who is both us and the people we want to be, allowed ourselves to speak quietly, which is a call to give up the need to be sure, and ask, when was the last time we surrendered? When was the last time we were this open? And before we could try to answer, the drums start off, sudden and sure. A thick bassline follows, getting to the heart of things. The pianist plays secret chords from the soul. And before the intro is done, the choir magic themselves to the stage, and there's a microphone in hand, and a grin as the leader steps down, singing her prayer: *I'm trading my sorrows, I'm trading my shame.* She sings these words, knowing that if we're in this room, then we've probably known sorrow, probably known shame. We know death in its multitudes, but we're all very serious about being alive. And since the one thing that can solve most of our problems is dancing, we turn our mourning into movement. We breach the borders of our rows, spilling into the aisles, making our way to the area in front of the stage, making our way into that space.

I see my father, up ahead, amongst the congregation, his body free and flailing and loose. He's waving a handkerchief in his hand, like a beacon, as if to say, *I am here.* He's going and going and then we watch as Pops slows down a little, like he's misplaced a part of himself. A quick search for my mother. He finds her with ease, and signals. She waves him off, but he won't have it, making

3

his way back to where we are standing, coaxing her out of the row, their soft hands in a tender embrace, pulling her close, lips to her ear, *you're safe here*; not just in this building, or this church, but in his arms. I gaze at my parents, and see that a world can be two people, occupying a space where they don't have to explain. Where they can feel beautiful. Where they might feel free.

I nudge Raymond. It's a joyous, brotherly laugh we share. I know that, like me, his faith is a daily wrangle, that he's had to build a church elsewhere in order to know himself. We share the same small motion, a little two-step on the spot, because despite everything, the music is undeniable. I've only ever known myself in song, between notes, in that place where language won't suffice but the drums might, might speak for us, might speak for what is on our hearts. In this moment, as the music gathers pace, looping round once more, passing frenzy, approaching ecstasy, that prayer taking flight, *I'm trading my sorrows, I'm trading my shame*, I'm pulled to nudge Raymond again, to try to say to him, *I wish we could always be this open, wish we might always feel some of this freedom*. I don't know I have the words. But since the one thing that can solve most of our problems is dancing, it only makes sense that here, when our parents signal for us, we join them.

Long after the church service, long after the day has lost its shine, the sun a soft glow, we make the short journey to Uncle T's, who helps us carefully load his speakers into Raymond's back seat, showing us how to snip a wire with pliers, strip it bare with our teeth, twist it into the speaker, his warning to bring them back intact a distant echo as we drive down to Tej's flat near Walworth Road. Pulling in, I see Adeline, having known her so long I know the way light holds her neck, know her rhythm even when she's still, and seeing the space between us, I go towards her, allowing a smile to emerge from the depths of my being, allowing our cheeks to meet during a tender embrace, and on separation, ask her, *when was the last time we did this?* Before she can say, *it's not been that long since we partied*, Tej's door swings open, and soon, we are not just one or two, but many. Soon, we're rowdy in conversation, allowing ourselves to say things which are honest and true, Godlike even. Soon, from indoors, we're hearing music we recognize, we're breaching the borders of rooms, spilling into the garden, making our way to the area in front of the decks, making our way into that *space*, plastic cups in hand, held high above our heads, like beacons, as if to say, *we are here*. Many of us gathered have long lost our faith but we do believe in rhythm. We do believe in the ability of a four-minute cut to stretch time until it is unrecognizable, each second its own forever. As Charmz's 'Buy Out Da Bar' is wheeled up once more, this action its own nostalgia, its own prayer, wanting to be the person you were just moments before, I'm thinking, I wish we could always be this open, in tender motion, shoulder to shoulder, heart to heart, *energy energy, gimme that energy energy*.

We're already nostalgic for yesterday, so soon it's grime cuts that Adeline spins from the decks. 'Too Many Man', 'I Spy', '21 Seconds'. 'Pow!' begins to play, a kick drum starting off, sudden and sure. A thick bassline follows, getting to the heart of things. Eerie chords ring round the garden. Before the intro is done, Raymond magics himself next to me, calling for the song to start again. There isn't time for what I want to say to him before the song starts fresh, the intro bare and empty of words, leaving space for us. The floor clears, bare and empty of bodies, a circle forming around us, something possessing Raymond and me as we push the edges further towards the confines of the garden. Look, I'm trying to tell you what it means to be in the eye of a moshpit: a small, beautiful world in the midst of chaos, free, amongst flailing limbs and half-shouted lyrics. Soon, after the fifth or sixth reload, we begin to tire. Soon, we're disappearing into the night, four abreast down Walworth Road, in search of food. Soon, it's Bagel King, the only place we know that's open forever. Soon, it's Raymond with an arm around my shoulder, mouth to my ear, saying, *you good, yeah*, and I nod into the space he makes. Soon, it's an arm wrapping around my body from behind, and I know

5

it's Del. We've known each other so long she knows the way light holds my neck, she knows my rhythm, even when I'm still. Soon, it's a cappellas and phone speakers, and since the one thing which might solve most of our problems is dancing, an easy two-step on the pavement.

Soon, too soon, it's time to split. Those who are together disappear into the night, pulling even closer. Those single long for the knock of knees on a journey home, a brush of skin on the doorstep, the invitation inside a free yard. We're young and often struggle to express just what it is we need, but I know we all value *closeness*.

That's what I'm thinking as Del and I take the night bus back towards Peckham – Raymond has disappeared into the night, so it's just me and her. Asleep, her soft cheek resting on my shoulder for the short journey. Off the bus, down her road, a gentle light on her doorstep, like a beacon. It's the quietest it has been all evening. I gaze at her. Thrust my hands into my pockets, breaking the gaze with a glance at the ground, before stealing another look. She smiles at my shyness, and I smile back. It's here, when I'm with her, I know that a world can be two people, occupying a space where we don't have to explain. Where we can feel beautiful. Where we might feel free.

Del's lips make a brief home on my cheek, and we pull each other close. We give no goodbyes – we know death in its multitudes, and goodbye sounds like an end – instead, after our embrace, the soft pounding of fists accompanied by, *in a bit*, which is less a goodbye, more a promise to stay alive.

2.

A few hours later, sunshine sneaks through a split in the curtains. It's too early, even before I've checked the time. Ray's bed is empty, unmade. I will myself up and out, knowing I have to get to work. The world wobbles for a moment, then rights itself. Downstairs, Ray is laid out across the sofa, bottle of beer in hand, as if the party never stopped.

'Bit early for a drink,' I say, nodding to the bottle.

'Bit late for you to be waking up.'

'Touché. Where's Mum?'

'Out.'

'Where's Dad?'

'Out.'

Football highlights play on the TV screen. I know Ray has the capacity for conversation, or watching the highlights, but not both, so I briefly abandon this effort, instead heading to the kitchen, checking the fridge for food. Most of the Tupperware on the shelves contain meals Mum would've laboured over, something heavy and home-made, the sort of food which might fill the house with longing for a whole day, the sort which you might quickly devour, only to enter a strange stupor in which you can do nothing but nod and say how wonderful that meal was. Aware this is no condition in which to work, I keep looking for something lighter, finding a brown paper bag nestled in the fridge door. Inside, two patties. I heat them, and plate one for me, one for Ray. When I return, he swings his legs off the sofa, making space for me. We eat, quick, each bite a little too hot, but still, we eat.

'What you on today?'

Ray shakes his head, shrugs. 'Don't even know, you know. Might check Deb.'

'Deb? Don't you mean Tej?'

'Nah, I'm in her bad books.'

'Why?'

''Cause I keep going to see Deb.'

'You're looking for trouble, man.'

'Me? Never,' he says, the grin boyish and unconvincing. He slumps back in the sofa, letting out an almighty yawn. 'What you saying?'

'Working. Actually, I need a favour.'

'If it's money, I haven't got it.'

'No – I need to borrow your suit. For prom.'

Ray screws up his face in confusion. 'Swear down your prom is tonight?'

'Yup.'

At this, Ray transforms, becoming our father, his chest puffing out, the tone of his voice low and sure.

'You young people, all lastminute.com business, you like it too much!'

Raymond needs no excuse to continue but he takes my laughter as cue, beginning our father's favourite monologue of *'When I was your age . . .'* At my age, eighteen, Pops had already moved from Accra to London, had already started to build something of a life for himself, and often lets us know. Raymond grows more extravagant and absurd with his tone and gestures and content, until we're both falling about laughing, trailing off into a silence which isn't uncomfortable. From outdoors, we hear the patter of feet, balls bouncing, children making their way to spend their summer days in the park. Ray takes a swig from his bottle, considering, before asking, 'You going with Del?'

'It's not even like that.'

'Sure.'

Del and I have known each other since early years, even before the times our fathers would go to the Gold Coast bar and drink spirits, straight, hoping this sort of dumb courage might have brought them closer to something spiritual, closer to themselves.

The way we know each other, it's different from seeing someone across a room, sharing a brief, coy smile, perhaps playing it cool and waiting for them to approach you, or asking a friend for an introduction. We have time. Over a decade now, since that day on a primary school trip to the farm, when I left my packed lunch on the long-departed coach. I was too ashamed to say anything. We weren't friends but she could see I was holding myself awkwardly, while everyone else unpacked their sandwiches. *I have extra*, she whispered – her father was always scared what he gave would not be enough – and, sitting together, as if we had done so many times, she unpacked the contents of her lunchbox, enough for a sandwich, some fruit and a doughnut each.

There's a trust between us, built from the time we've spent together: in our early years, racing each other up and down the same patch of playground until our legs could no longer carry us; taking trips to central in our early teens, her deep laughter the spine of our days, from Marble Arch to Oxford Circus to St James's Park – Del, the soul and spirit of the group, our glue, until she grew tired, and then, with our secret signal, what became known between us as her double wink – she can't wink, only blink, her eyes scrunched for a moment – we'd split, heading back towards Peckham, playing games to keep our tired bodies awake on the bus home. Nowadays, it is she and I, whenever we can, because it's easy, because we want to, because we can. Recently, when her aunt is out, we'll dig through her father's records. We've known each other so long, I know her go-tos, depending on her mood: Bill Withers's +*'Justments*, for tenderness; *Bitches Brew*, for its beautiful looseness, its courage; *Curtis*, when she needs to move. We've known each other so long, I know when she hears a sequence or phrase which pleases, her features will soften, taken by something like wonder. We've known each other so long I don't know what name to give to this knowing.

'Don't be mad when someone else makes a move, that's all I'm saying. Man, if you're not on it, I might have to see what she's saying.'

My body tenses before I have a chance to speak. The boyish grin is back.

'See? Don't wait, bro. *You young people, lastminute.com.* Do you want a beer?'

'Nah, I'm good.' Ray leaves me for a moment, leaves me with these feelings. When he returns with a beer for him, a juice for me, the clink of the bottlenecks, a deep swig from us both, Ray points at the screen, begins to tell me about the Ghanaian football team's prospects in the upcoming World Cup. I nod along with his commentary and try to stay present, and still my mind drifts elsewhere: somewhere with Del, perhaps at hers with a record playing, something slow and warm and beautiful, where it's she and I, and the time we have together. But Ray, always the brightest in every room, brings me back with ease, letting out a roar as someone scores on-screen, beginning to explain how and why the goal occurred.

As he speaks, I begin to realize that this kind of time with Ray is limited. It's summer now and September will come and then I'll be away at university. He'll stay and I'll go. I lean forwards in my seat, asking him questions. I cheer at the screen when he does. I ask more of his romantic escapades and laugh at the absurdity of his stories, let myself be warmed by his contagious grin.

I bask in my older brother's shine.

3.

Because it's summer, and we're young until September, I'm not the only one starting their day late. As I cut through the estate, a man who could be my mirror tries to shut the door softly, winces as it lets out a small bang. He sees me seeing him, and shrugs, smiling, as if to say, 'What am I to do?', before adjusting the collar on his overshirt, walking off with a slight and beautiful lean to his steps. I follow his path, passing a group holding up the wall in an underpass, trying to decide which motive to touch tonight. I hear one of them insist on a party in Deptford. They gently rib and tease until the truth spills: he only wants to go because his crush will be there, he's tired of waiting, he's hoping to make a move. Calls from the chorus of 'Why didn't you say that then?' Because it's summer, and we're all young until September, they'll do anything for their brothers, blood or otherwise. Onwards, past the multisport area, where the footballers have arrived early, taking up the whole small pitch, one young man controlling the ball with such a delicate touch, as if it is his and only his and the rest of the players are borrowers. Past Uncle T's where, because it's summer, dub rattles glass, a whistle cuts through the narrow gap in the window. I catch a glimpse of his soft dreads, pulled up in a bun, revealing a kind face and a mouth full of gold. He sings like he's singing to a lover at dusk, but I know it's just him in the room. Bob Marley's 'Waiting in Vain'. I raise a hand in greeting, and he calls back, and in that moment, memory, image and possibility slide across one another. As in: Uncle T singing to an old lover; my father in his twenties, trying to decide at which end of London to party, to find freedom; me in a few years, trying not to bang the door of a stranger I've made the night familiar with. What becomes of time when summer arrives?

★

We're sure my Auntie Yaa has the largest Afro-Caribbean shop in Peckham; in south London, maybe. Just off Rye Lane, head to the high street, on the corner, just before the library, and you'll find her there. She stocks everything that people, away from home, trying to build something here, need. Yams and plantain and kenkey and fufu powder, garden eggs and okra and Scotch bonnets, dried fish by the box, Supermalt by the crate. For her, for many of us, food is not just sustenance but memory, nostalgia; a way to quell longing, a way to build new foundations. Auntie sends stuff back home too, allowing people to ship pieces of themselves for their loved ones to hold. There's a regular, Dorcas, who once a month will send a box of cereals and confectioneries back to her sister in Ghana, ginger snaps and Weetabix and Tetley tea. Dorcas always says she was responsible for the shopping, so she hopes it will feel like she never left. Before sealing the box, she places a photo of herself atop the food, so it is her smile which greets her sister on arrival.

At the door, you'll find Uncle D, who is no blood relation to anyone and yet related to everyone. He's a joyous man in middle age, always wearing aviators with clear lenses. I've never known if he's officially employed by the shop, but early afternoon, you'll find him shuffling and sweeping, pointing out items to customers, smiling and laughing. Come evening time, a Guinness in hand, a bottle or two a day. I would say he's the shop's security but the one time when he might've been called into action, when Ray's friend Koby ran into the shop, breathless and begging for somewhere to hide, and a few minutes later, several boys came in, demanding we hand Koby over, Uncle stood broad and tall but Auntie shooed him away. Instead, she asked after each of the boys' parents, then enquired about *them*. Who was doing what at

12

school, who had scored the winning goal in the match that week-end? Auntie understood that anger was a necessary emotion but often it was misdirected; and its misdirection was how the death we knew in multitudes multiplied further, and much of this misdirection emerged from not having *space*. She held this brief court and sent them home with shea butter for their hair, meat pies for their hunger.

I'm manning the counter when Del wobbles in, flushed from the heat. She balances the case of her double bass against a free patch of wall and, making her way through the small maze of tables, comes towards the counter. A chain with a tiny pendant – her father's – swings from her neck. The light has made her eyes wide and open, a slight smile on her features. She's beautiful. I want to say this to her, but outside of song and film, I've never heard this spoken. Still, in the moment, I'm closer to her, perhaps because I'm closer to myself, closer to knowing how I feel about her.

I must be staring because she asks, 'What?'

'Nothing.'

She doesn't push, instead taking a place at the counter. I undo the cap on a bottle of Fanta, half the bottle over ice. She drinks, deeply, before spinning in her seat to face the shop as I see it. There's a couple with eyes only for each other, their hands clasped in the middle of the table; another pair play cards, seemingly locked in stalemate; and a woman, pen in hand, scribbling into a notebook. 'Peace on Earth' by Ebo Taylor trails us in the background.

'What do you reckon is going on there?' I ask, quietly.

'He messed up and she's finally forgiven him.'

'How do you know it was him?'

'*He* always messes up. Don't be offended. Just how it goes.'

'Whatever. And the others?'

'I reckon . . . they're friends. About to move in together. Winner gets the largest room. And that woman is . . . writing a story.'

'About?'

'Two young people in the summertime.'

'Sounds like us.'

'Might be.' She shrugs, smiling. 'But everyone's younger in the summertime.' She swings round to face me, as Auntie Yaa emerges from the back room, and I am briefly forgotten. They hold each other's faces in soft palms; greeting like sisters. Auntie Yaa lost her parents in similar fashion to Del; a mother who didn't make it through childbirth, a father who held on for as long as he could, but eventually lost the battle with his mirror. Auntie Yaa and Del, they are held together by some unknown I could never know.

'And how are you?'

'I'm fine, Auntie.'

'Have you heard yet?'

'Not yet.'

'You will.'

My and Del's heads dip. We've both applied for music school. Even with a student loan, it will only be possible with a scholarship, which, with each passing day without news, seems less and less likely. Only a handful are available. It feels arbitrary to rely on a small group to decide whether we are good enough, when, until this point, much of our judgement relied on *feeling*.

Del and I mostly jam with a group on evenings and weekends. We've been doing so for the past few years. We are told it's jazz we're playing but if asked what that means, we'd probably point to each other and shrug and grin. It's not that we don't know, it's just that we don't know how to explain this strange expression of improvisation, where we enter a space and lean into the unknown. Theo usually starts us off, something quick and sure, the knock of his drums a call to attention. Del will follow, her thick bass notes like walls, building a place for us to move into, and I'll dart inside this house she has made, sneaking notes through with my trumpet. All of us local, we converge wherever we can be housed: in school rehearsal rooms, music studios someone has slid us the keys to, or usually, someone's kitchen or garage. One time, we crammed into two cars and drove a little further south, to Beckenham Place Park, with its grounds which sprawl endlessly. It was spring and new life seemed to be blossoming, everywhere. Everything was possible. We dragged our instruments, deep into the wooded area, and formed a circle, sending sounds into the trees. Just before we started playing, someone placed a recorder in the middle of our small gathering, not because we didn't think we would remember, but because we didn't want to forget.

As we were playing, my fingers slipped, an odd note coming from my horn. The mistake didn't go unnoticed, but we continued on. It made me grateful for the freedom to be in that space, to make a mistake; and how that mistake might be beautiful to the right ear; how Del heard that odd note and followed with her own, adjusting her thrum; how the rest of us followed that twist and shift, surrendering to whatever unknown we were going towards. It was there that I noticed I only really knew myself in song. In the quiet, in the freedom, in the surrender.

Afterwards, as we trailed back to the cars, spent and yet still so full, we said things like 'I didn't know I needed that' and 'that was a spiritual experience.' We – Del and I – have been trying to tap into that spiritual now, to have optimism, faith. But the wait is hard. Especially when, on the other side of that wait might be us going separate ways, an idea we've never broached, always assuming, somehow, we'll be close to one another. Neither of us want to ask what happens then; if these last days of school, of summer, are the last days we'll have to be close.

As if she knows what's on our hearts, Auntie Yaa says, 'The wait will be worth it.' She shuffles away and Del glances at the clock.

'I better dip too,' she says.

'So soon?'

'Said I'd jam with Theo and them man. Only came to see you.'

'Wait!'

'Yeah?'

15

'Are you . . . are you going to prom with anyone?'

'Erm . . .' She gazes down, considering how to say what she needs to. My heart breaks a little in the silence.

'Someone already asked you,' I say, not accusation, but fact.

'Yeah. Johnny did. Yesterday.' Johnny, a guitarist, often jams with us. Somehow, having shared these small intimacies with him makes what I'm feeling worse, but I say nothing of this to Del. And what is there to say? 'That's cool,' I say.

'I just assumed as you hadn't asked, you'd made other plans—'

'Yeah, no . . . erm . . .' I shrug. Neither of us can meet the other's gaze.

'And anyway, it doesn't really mean anything, does it?'

'No.' I wonder if either of us believe that. There's another pause that neither of us want to go towards. Del diverts elsewhere.

'We'll have fun. You owe me a dance, anyway.'

'Huh?'

'Your cousin's wedding? You refused to dance with me.'

'I didn't refuse, I was too drunk.'

'Whatever.' She lets out an exhale, as if not realizing she had been holding her breath. 'I'll erm . . .' She looks down once more, before meeting my gaze. 'I'll see you later.'

'Yeah,' I nod. 'In a bit.'

She turns away from me, fetching her double bass on the way out, turning to give a wave before leaving. I gaze into the mirror nailed into the wall by the side of the bar, wondering if it will give me answers. Something has changed, shifted between us; or maybe, it had always been this way, just we've chosen now to see it.

4.

'Told you not to wait, man,' Raymond says, adjusting my collar, pulling my tie in tight. I let out a heavy sigh. I feel like I've lost something. Ray sees this and tries not to fill the space, but spin me away from it. 'No matter, bro. Prom night! Don't come home unless,' he begins to count out on his fingers, 'you're drunk, you lipsed someone, or both.'

My boy, Nam, hears from his date the girls are getting ready together, so he comes over to mine. He invites Jeremiah, I invite Jimmy. They invite Tony and Kwame. Soon, a group of boys on the cusp of something – not quite adulthood, but that place between, where anything seems possible – converge in my living room. Soon, we're teasing Jeremiah about the purple velvet suit he's chosen, poking light fun at Kwame's decision to wear his afro in pigtails. Soon, we're revelling in our excitement, trying to beat away any nerves. Soon, my father is passing out beers to each of us, because these are moments in which he thrives, where he can care for those around him with ease. He perches on the edge of the sofa, his own drink in hand, something stronger, telling joyful stories of parties in his twenties, those nights which never seemed to end.

Mum asks each of us to shuffle in so that we fit in the frame for a photo. I wonder what she sees in this moment, what she wants to commit to celluloid, what she might want to hold, forever. I know that I am eighteen, the same age she was when she arrived in London. I wonder, then, if this is a nostalgia for a time my parents never knew, that period between childhood and adulthood skipped, responsibility coaxing them away from carefree.

★

17

Pops has a friend at a local taxi agency, so he books one we can all fit into. As we're leaving, he shakes my hand with a slightly closed fist, slipping a twenty-pound note into my own. From the doorstep, Mum only holds her face, and smiles. As the taxi slides through London, we pass scores of people spilling out of pubs and bars, or queuing for concerts, or just on their way elsewhere. It's hard not to see this energy, and for my quietness to become excitement. By the time we've hit central, the radio has been switched to Choice FM, and we're loud and boisterous and beautiful, listening in as the DJ spins back to the nineties, to garage, music our fathers swear by. 'A Little Bit of Luck' spins into 'Booo!'. By the time Craig David's 'Rewind' is wheeled up, on air, for the third time, we are threatening to spill from our seats, calling for the DJ, who can't hear us, to *play it again, play it again*.

On arrival, we follow the stream of people and sound, that same excitable sound present in the car, the throb of energy. We emerge from the lift into a large space, as the DJ, who we spot immediately, his face contorted in concentration, tries to mix 'Party Hard' into 'Migraine Skank'. A few weeks earlier, Ray and I, as we like to do sometimes, had gone song for song into the early hours of the morning. He played a nine-minute cut by DJ Gregory. The sounds were unmistakable: this was where 'Migraine Skank' had snipped its pounding drums, the pulse of a bassline. Raymond explained something I already knew but didn't have the words for: that when you sample, it's not just sounds you're repurposing, but *feeling*. You're taking whatever was present in the room on recording, or whatever was on the heart of the artists in those moments of conception. So here, now, on hearing the lyrics from Gracious K and knowing the DJ Gregory tune, a joyous loop which goes round and round, deepening the feeling, when this is mixed with the throb of energy in the room, with screams and whoops, the pounding of feet, the irresistible call to move, our spirits threaten to leap from our bodies. Joy emerges in its multitudes.

★

Somewhere between 'Next Hype' and 'Talkin the Hardest', I tap Nam, asking for the toilet. He points in the general direction of a side door. In the corridor, there's a queue. I spot a sign for another, and follow with confidence but I'm quickly lost, somehow on the floor below. I turn back round—

'Hey.'

Del, a few metres in front of me. I try to play it cool but the words tumble over themselves, twisting my tongue into a knot which spools into silence. Up above, we hear the insistence of kick drums, the rattle of a bassline, cheers and whoops from all on the dance floor. We gaze upwards, before turning back to each other. I don't know how to hold myself in these moments, where the magic of language fails to manifest itself, but she has always made it easier. I look at her and she looks at me. Memory, image and possibility all fold in on each other. We're not just occupying this moment, but all those we have spent together, all those which might unfold. The gaze holds. It's just us in the corridor. No one comes, no one goes.

After a moment, she reaches up for my shirt collar, and, where it had been crooked, plucks it straight, pulls it down, tugs it into place. Flattens with a tender palm. She's close to me, as close as can be, her hand sliding from my shoulder to rest on my chest. It's just us in the corridor. I open my mouth to speak, not knowing what I will say. She leans even closer as if to better hear what is not being said.

'Oi, oi!'

We separate as a small group march down the corridor, cheering the discovery of a bottle of spirits. Lucy loops her arm through Del's as she reaches us, insisting she join. There's a tiny wry smile on Del's face, to acknowledge the break in proceedings. Her hand falls further, her fingers briefly grazing mine; a squeeze, and she is gone.

By midnight, the party is beginning to wane; emotions are fraught, and some begin to cry. We've known each other for the better part of seven years. This is *all* we've known. We hold each other, close, as the music stops and the lights go up. We're all seeing each other here, really seeing each other, the fullness of our lives apparent in this moment of strange grief. We continue to hold each other, heads buried into shirts, tender palms gripping forearms, insisting we'll link up, insisting we'll keep in touch. Insisting the only thing between us is love.

There's a desire to keep the party going, to bring an after-party into existence, but I can see, as we're coming down in the lift, that this might be the end of the night. We emerge on to the street, holding out our arms as black cab after black cab passes us. Eventually, one stops, then another. I spot Del speaking to her date. It's the first I'm seeing them together all night. He's saying something and she's shaking her head. He steps towards her, and she steps back, holding up her hands. Another cab pulls up, and I hail it down. Nam appears beside me, climbing in, as do Jimmy and Delilah. There are two spots left. I make my move.

'Who else is going Peckham?' I call out.

'Me,' Del says, recognizing something in my voice. I hold open the door for her. We squeeze in, six of us, pooling together what we have to make it back to our small worlds. I'm opposite Del. It may as well just be us in the taxi. It's as if we're back in the corridor, holding hands, our gazes wide and honest and open, locked together in this moment of strange grief; knowing that, even with the insistence that we'll link up and we'll keep in touch, everything is changing.

The cab stops at Peckham Rye. We're all so tired, the split is quick, Del and I heading towards Commercial Way. Rye Lane is still alive, pockets of people drinking on the street, heading towards a party or perhaps coming from one, deciding whether to continue on. We continue on, cutting into a residential area, the world quietening around us. At some point, our hands graze each other; I've walked her home countless times but we've never held hands; finding the link between fingers, I don't let go. I think about pulling up short, turning towards her, hoping she would turn towards me; that her hand would rest on my chest once more, and she might feel my heart race; that I wouldn't have to house what I feel for her anywhere, because she could feel it; that—

'This is me,' she says.

'Ah yeah,' I say. 'So it is.'

A small, wry smile appears. 'You still owe me that dance.'

'Here?'

'Why not?'

'Why not,' I say, returning her smile. 'Erm – where's the music?'

'Oh – well, I mean, I'd say you should come in but my aunt's home, and you know what she's like—'

'Say nothing,' I say quickly, not wanting to ruin the moment. I pull out my phone, scrolling through the few songs I have saved. 'If I Ain't Got You' plays softly into the night. Del feigns disinterest at first; a shake of her head, a bite of her lip. She's shy and I am too, but the music pulls us together. I hold my hand out and she gazes at it with wide, curious eyes, long enough for the thud of my heartbeat to fill my ears. Long enough to consider if she actually will take it. And then she does, hand in hand, the distance closing until her head rests on my chest. She looks up at me and her gaze is direct. It's an easy two-step. Nothing else matters.

5.

'We met on a beach,' Mum says, before turning back to the mirror.

It's Sunday afternoon, the day after prom. I slept through the morning, only waking up when my parents returned from church and began to blast gospel music. The day has taken on a desultory quality; there's nothing to be done, really. I finish school this week, so there's nothing to prep for. I float around the house, from room to room, looking for purpose; looking for something to distract me from the memory of last night, of Del and I, hand in hand on her doorstep, her head on my chest, an easy two-step. I look for distractions, worried the memory of our closeness might consume me, might become all I'm interested in. I float, going from room to room. In the kitchen, the sweetness of stew, jollof on the way, the rice cooking low and slow. To the bedroom, where my phone lies, empty of messages. To the storage room – which is really a tiny cupboard into which we throw everything which evades category – and that's when I see it, the gloss of a printed photo, catching the light coming through the doorway. Standing in the corridor, I study the image, the paper bent at the edges, but otherwise intact. It's a group photo, taken on a beach. If I had to guess, those in the image might be sixteen or seventeen. There are some I don't recognize but many I do: my Uncle David, Uncle Kweku, Auntie Georgina, Auntie Rebecca, Auntie Comfort, Uncle James. And cosier than the rest, as if in their own small world, Mum and Pops.

I find Mum in her bedroom. For her, it's not only a day of faith but a day of care. Mum works full-time, as a receptionist at a school in Bermondsey, often going over her hours, always looking out for the children. Sunday is an opportunity to slow down, to take care of herself.

When I come in, she's washed and dried her hair, a patterned scarf tied around the edges of her scalp as she prepares to oil a dense afro, a tiny shock of grey nestled in the front. From her window, as if watching a TV with the sound off, Raymond and Pops washing the car, deep in discussion, Raymond gesturing from Pops to himself, tapping his chest several times, Pops nodding in agreement. I'm holding out the photo and Mum is letting her story dangle, teasing me. I encourage her to carry on.

On summer days, she says, they would pile into a *tro-tro*, her brothers and sisters and some friends, some family, making the short drive to Labadi beach, where they'd let a boombox send sound across the sand, let summer make light work of time, the days gone so quick, yet in the right circumstances, stretching on and on. The beach was one of those places where time would stretch, the men masquerading as boys, amateur gymnasts in the sand. They were more coy, laughing and pretending not to watch.

'That day,' she says, gesturing to the photo, 'the boys started a game of football. Your father was clearly one of the best and he knew it. He was flashy but effective. It was like watching a dancer, the rhythm. We met eyes and I couldn't look away. There was *something* there.'

She pauses, reaching into the cupboard. Not finding what she wants, Mum points to the wide-toothed comb on her bedside table. I pass it to her and she continues.

'I didn't know him then,' she says. 'He was the brother of my brother's best friend, Kweku. Your Uncle David and Kweku were in a band, a three-piece that would perform on weekends at parties and weddings and, when they could, art spaces. From what I gathered later, your father would tag along after them everywhere. He didn't play any instruments, but he loved the music.

'Anyway, when the game broke up, we all ran towards the lip of the ocean, splashing about in the water. I was one of the last to make it down. Everyone was already knee-deep, but your father was letting water lap at his ankles, holding himself awkwardly, as if the water might reveal something he was not ready to tell. He caught me watching and shook off whatever it was, walking into the water, that beautiful, clear water.' Mum pauses now, taken by the memory. She shakes her head, saying, 'The water is shallow, until it is not. Before I knew it, your father was up to his neck in the deep end, his feet scrabbling for ground where there was none. I swam towards him as he was thrashing around. *Calm down*, I said. Which is easier said than done when you think you're drowning! I took his hand and said, *I got you*. I pulled him back towards shore, into the shallows where we could both stand. He was suddenly very shy, asking me if I wanted anything to eat, anything to drink. I said, he didn't have to do all that. I didn't want what I had done to feel like a transaction. He shook his head, saying, *no, no, I've got you*.'

Mum pulls her hair into two big bunches, and it brings her face into full focus, her eyes wide and wistful. She's somewhere between memory and the present, somewhere between then and now. From outside, we hear Raymond's and Pops's voices carrying, escalating, some disagreement being had.

'We were friends for a long time after that. We were always together. After school, parties, gatherings. The beach, we would return to often. And then I moved to London. He used to write me letters.'

The shock must show on my features because Mum grins, saying, 'Oh, he's very romantic. Charming. He knew I had his back and he always wanted me to know he had mine. His letters would arrive, on blue airmail paper, and I would have to work hard to decipher his scrawl. But the reward was worth it. It lifted my spirits.'

'And then?' I ask.

'And then, he joined me here, in London.' Mum pauses, swallows. 'It was very difficult when I first got here. I was glad I had your father. He always knew how to make me laugh. It was contagious!' And, as if on cue, outside, their argument warps, shifts and we hear their laughter, like a chorus, like they might be the same person. Mum begins to laugh and so do I. There's more I want to know but as the laughter settles, I see it's not just joy Mum is holding but melancholy too. I don't push, instead coming round to where she stands, putting my arm around her. She leans into the hug, and we stay like this, mother and son, holding on to our joy, our melancholy, our love.

6.

It's the last day of school. The air vibrates with something large and unknown, something which shimmers and shines, something which excites and terrifies. In our final assembly, a teacher had stood and insisted that this was not the end, but the beginning. That we had the rest of our lives ahead of us, that from this moment, anything was possible. Though we're young and often so sure we know what we want, sure we know ourselves, these moments are sobering. In the times we didn't know ourselves, we always had each other; when faced with the unknown, we could lean back into the familiar, knowing each other's hearts, knowing each other's intimacies. So, knowing how valuable this is, we all insist, once more, that we'll link up, that we'll keep in touch, that the only thing between us is love. After we've scribbled messages into yearbooks, after the frantic energy of not wanting to let go of each other begins to settle, Del and I find ourselves in our usual spot on the edge of the school fields. I discard my tie, as a slow bead of sweat darts from my forehead, blesses the grass. Del has rolled up her blazer like a pillow, inviting sunshine to graze her face. A tiny portable speaker tries its best with *Kind of Blue*. Where it fails, we fill in the gaps, knowing the record so well, knowing the beautifully odd notes, the flourish of an extended solo, the mastery of it all.

'I need an ice cream,' Del says, her eyes closed.

I gesture in the vague direction of the school gates. 'We could go shop.'

'I don't wanna move, though,' which is another way of saying, I don't want this to end. I don't say anything to this, instead reclining on the grass. Del opens one eye to spy on me, and seeing I've joined her, unrolls the tightness of her blazer, so I might lay my head down on it too. We lie in opposite directions, our cheeks close enough to touch. I can feel her deep and slow breaths. I can feel her life. Miles and his group play on. We're halfway through 'All Blues', someway into Coltrane's meandering solo. There's one more track – 'Flamenco Sketches' – and that will be it.

I close my eyes too. I think of how the track I can hear playing was recorded in one take, and what faith this would've taken, what it might mean to fall forwards into the vastness of possibility. How it might feel like the fear I feel now, but what beauty might lie on the other side. I don't know how to say this to Del, so I let the music fill in the gaps where I have failed, and, knowing each other so well, Del occupies this quiet with me. After some time, as 'Flamenco Sketches' starts up, we let our hands graze each other, and, finding the link between fingers, don't let go.

'Hey,' she says.

'Yeah?'

'Tell me about the spot.'

There was one afternoon when Auntie Yaa's was particularly chaotic, when orders were coming through at a pace I struggled to keep up with, and lines snaked through the shop, but there was this feeling that arrived early and stayed, a feeling I couldn't shake, something beautiful, a pull towards what I was doing that I did not want to refuse. After my shift, I described this to Del, and she told me it was not something to ignore. I confessed that, from time to time, I thought about running a place similar to Auntie Yaa's. And ever since, she insists that I tell her about this dream, again and again, not because I don't remember, but so I won't forget.

So today, I tell her what I always do: I want a place for us. On the menu, food from home: waakye and red-red, fresh fish and meat stews. There would be a space for dining, and a space for more casual gathering, where people could grab and pick at food, eat happily with their hands if they wish. I would have long tables where families could gather, platters spread at intervals, or where friends could come together at the weekends, for no other reason than to talk, to talk about it all, to laugh and cry and everything between. I want a bar where people might drink and drink together, or enjoy their solitude. Art hanging on the walls, music always playing. Live music evenings and weekends, small reminders that it is a place where people could express themselves. I want to build a place where there's a sense of freedom which isn't attached to anything else, that doesn't come as part of a transaction. There would be no catch. Just a place for people to eat and drink, to plot and breathe. To be. A place we could call home.

I open my eyes to steal a glance at her. She's smiling, content. The music trails away and it's silence we're left with. Without saying anything, she stands and helps me up. We gather our bags and begin to walk.

At the school gates, I ask, 'What you saying tonight?'

She points at her head, the afro threatening to snap the hairband. 'Trying to get this under control. But I'm free after, if you are.'

'Cinema with Mum.'

'Ah yeah, of course, it's Friday.'

'But tomorrow? Football's on. Auntie Yaa's having a little gathering. She's closing the shop and everything.'

'I'm there.'

'Cool. Well,' I shrug.

'Yeah,' she says.

The air vibrates with something large and unknown, something which shimmers and shines, something which excites and terrifies. We don't say goodbye – goodbye sounds like an ending, and we don't want this thing to end. Instead, after we separate, the soft pounding of fists accompanied by *in a bit*, which is less a goodbye, more a promise to meet again.

7.

Every other Friday evening, Mum and I seek refuge in the cinema. We'll usually hit Peckhamplex, taking pleasure in being able to make the short walk there. This is our time and always has been. Raymond showed no real interest, happy to stay in with Pops and watch Friday night football.

Mum tells me this is the place where she sought solace when she first arrived in the UK. She struggled to feel at home, but in the cinema she always felt less lonely, seated in a room full of strangers, with nowhere to go but the world on-screen and her imagination. It felt less like she was retreating into herself, and more like she was going forward, expanding her world. Even when she found the church – she says she always had her faith but it took her some time to find a church she trusted – the cinema remained a mainstay, a place she would return to. As I grew older, it became a regular thing for us. We would package up little snacks in cling film, biscuits and cakes, sometimes indulging in a box of popcorn from the concession stand. For the length of whatever film we saw, we would hold still, and watch and listen, feeling what the film-maker was trying to communicate, often feeling something open up within us.

Now Raymond is around more, having just finished up a marketing internship (and currently out of work or, as he likes to say, *funemployed*), he and Pops will drive down to Norwood, to the Gold Coast bar, to watch the football, knocking back spirits which might imbue their own spirits with something else, some dumb courage. After the film, Mum and I will hop on a bus and join them. It's almost an hour but we'll cram into a two-seat on the top deck, and talk. We'll start with the film. Today, we saw Spike Lee's *Do the Right Thing*, which felt like summer in the city, where everything is of urgency, everything on the brink. Mum says she liked it because it didn't shy away from depicting the wholeness of a community, not unlike ours in Peckham. We're about to start on the finer details, when out of the window, I spot Del walking down the street, plastic bag swinging in hand. I twist in my seat, hoping to catch another glimpse of her before the bus rounds the corner, but the angles are off, I miss her.

'What will you two do if you have to leave each other?' Mum asks, careful and tender.

'*If* we have to . . . we'll work it out.'

After a few moments, I ask what I've been thinking since I found the photo in our storage room.

'You had to wait for Pops when you moved over here, right?' Mum nods. 'What was that like?'

I don't know what it means to move from one place to another, to make a home for yourself; to try and build a life from uncertainty. To have to do this alone, away from the people you love. I don't know how this feels, so sometimes, like today, I ask. There are the things I know: working an eight-hour shift, only to have to travel to another; the rain soaking her while she waited at a bus stop; the sickness which gripped her, a combination of both exhaustion and longing for what she had left behind. Today, I'm asking her what it means to wait. I'm asking her about the gaps where language fails us. I want to know because those stories are the making of me. I ask more of her, and my mother's face, an open sky, darkens. Usually, the water is a kind threat, the sheen on her eyes like a glimmer, a sad glint. Now, tears trail down her face. I put my hand on hers. I ask her what she needs. She shakes her head and smiles.

When we get off the bus, making the short walk to the bar, she is immediately composed. We join Pops and Ray on our usual table. She entertains them both as they drink and drink, growing louder, more boisterous, pulling others from the surrounding tables into their debates. It's like watching two mirrors try to produce the best image. She ensures we order lots and everyone eats more than their fill, which is both hospitality and practicality, trying to care for us all, while lining the stomach of the drinkers.

When it's time to go, in a practised action, she retrieves the keys from my father. In the car, with the dull hum of the engine as a lullaby, Ray and Pops are asleep in minutes. Mum presses Play on the stereo, letting gospel fill the car, quietly singing along. *He is a miracle-working God, he is alpha, he is omega, he is a miracle-working God.*

I smile at her, and she smiles back. Even though I struggle with my faith in church, I can recognize Mum holds her faith close because she is here. Because she emerged from that place of waiting, where surviving the conditions she was being asked to endure was nothing short of a miracle. When I ask more of Mum, of the time she came here, the problem isn't that she doesn't remember. It's that she cannot forget.

8.

A roomful of Ghanaians hold their collective breath as the ball is placed down for a free kick. There are several ideal routes here: from the right-hand side of the pitch, the ball might be curled into an area where almost every player has converged, meet a head which will guide it towards the goal, or, perhaps, it is glanced by a forehead, a knee, a foot, ricochets about the space, gaining some frenetic energy, each player willing it towards their desire. There is one ideal outcome, for us in this room, and that's for Ghana to score. It's 1–1, in the quarter-finals of the World Cup. There's no time left – they've been playing for a hundred and twenty minutes – and so if there is no separation after this play, they will go to penalties, on the other side of which lies euphoria or heartbreak. Somehow, it's worse to have made it that far, played a whole match and then some, before having to put all your faith in a penalty shoot-out, the ability to go one on one from ten or so metres away, and succeed. So, here, in this room, we're praying. Del beside me, Jimmy and Jeremiah close by too. We're squashed in by the door. There's barely enough room to breathe. Raymond, seated in the eye of the crowd, is excitedly explaining something, perhaps along the lines of why he loves this game: for its plotlessness, its meander, its sudden turns. On-screen, in the penalty box, the tempers of grown men fray as they push and shove, trying to gain position. The whistle is blown. The commentator, prophesying, says, 'It might just slip away from Uruguay here.' The ball is lofted in. It meets a head early, flicked skyward. It stays in the air, hovering, seemingly not wanting to come down, until it does, and there's chaos. Uruguay's goalkeeper rushes out, arm extended, missing the ball, which meets the foot of a Ghanaian player, heading goalward only to be cleared off the

35

line, met with a forceful header from a Ghanaian, so sure of what he wants – that is, to win – but the ball is cleared off the line once more.

And then, the game stops. There's outrage. I squint at the screen, trying to understand what's going on, replaying the last few moments in my mind, thinking it would take a miracle to have stopped that last powerful header. The replay is shown on-screen too, and there, I see it: the Uruguayan player has slapped the ball away with both hands. In the room, there are shouts and protests, which only quieten after the red card is shown, after the ball is placed on the penalty spot, after Asamoah Gyan has taken his walk back. As he begins his run-up, Del turns away from the screen. Jimmy and Jeremiah lean in. I hear the intake of breath, I hear prayers. I hear a roomful of Ghanaians, far from home, willing someone they are bound to in a way that is too complex to explain, bound to them in a way they might not necessarily know, but can *feel*. Gyan completes his run-up and skews the kick slightly, the ball meeting the crossbar and finding a new home in the crowd. We all groan. Next to me, Del deflates. There's not much to say. There's a brief rally as we head towards penalties, led by Raymond and a few older men, but something has been lost. That spirit which possessed the room has been damaged. We can see it in the players too. Adiyiah – so much pressure, he's only twenty – misses one, giving Uruguay the advantage, which they jump on with their next spot-kick. And then, the game is over. There's chaos. There's a roomful of Ghanaians protesting what they cannot change. The heartbreak is extreme. It's only the second World Cup Ghana have been to, but we were all so sure, all believed, somehow, they would go all the way.

*

Later, after we have consoled each other, after Auntie Yaa has begun to pour spirits and insists we all eat our fill, long after the sadness has begun to ebb away, replaced by music, Ebo Taylor and Pat

Thomas, that highlife which is both sweet and melancholic, long after we have danced, since it is the one thing which might solve most of our problems, long after we have begun to tire, I walk Del home. We both hesitate on her doorstep. Neither of us speak, not wanting to address the thing between us, its awkwardness, its uncertainty. I think to myself, lean into the unknown. I think, now is as good a time as any. It's just us. I go to close the gap between us, when her aunt magics herself into the doorway.

'Are you coming inside?'

It's more courtesy than invitation. I shake my head, and after a quick, close hug, our separation, a promise to see each other soon, tomorrow if we can manage it, I make the short walk back to mine, exhaustion pulling me down. Long after I've made it home, night singing its whisper, and I'm going towards its song, my phone begins to ring. It's Raymond.

'Yo, bro. You good?'

'Yeah.' There's a pause, a slight rush of static. 'Yeah, man. Beg you let me in, I've forgotten my keys.'

'Calm. You at the door?'

'Not even . . .' Another pause. 'I'm on the corner.'

'All right, lemme come down now.'

I leave my room, carefully taking the stairs, knowing where they creak, where they groan. Split the door open slightly, and I don't know what or why, but I'm pulled outside. I tap my pocket for my keys, and hearing the jingle, step out into the night, closing the door behind me. The moon is full, at its roundest. The night cool and still. After a few steps, I see Raymond, seated on the pavement, head between his knees, rocking a little, as if summoning the strength for action. I join him on the ground.

He turns towards me, his eyes bleary, his mind in a haze, and before I've spoken, says, 'I'm all right, you know.' He raises his head, skywards. 'Just had a few, went Gold Coast, went Naomi's for a drink-up, then went Tej's—' He heaves, twisting his head away, aiming for the gutter. Nothing comes. He continues.

'Went Tej's, had a little talk – we're good now, we're all good now. Nothing to worry about.' He smiles, more at himself than me. 'Nothing to worry about . . .' He kisses his teeth and tries to stand, and wobbles. 'Help me up, man . . .'

'Nah, chill for a bit, sober up.'

'It's *cold* out here, bro. Talking about summer, this doesn't feel like summer.'

Even I laugh at this. I unzip my hoody and drape it over his shoulders.

'You not cold?'

'Think you need it more than I do.'

'Love, bro. Love.'

Head between his knees once more. I rub the broadness of his back, trying to encourage whatever he needs to get out to emerge.

'I'm all right, you know. I'm all right.' A sigh. 'Don't you feel scared?' He turns towards me, and the gaze is direct, sure. 'Every-thing's changing. Don't you feel scared?'

'Every day,' I whisper.

He shakes his head. 'Feel like I'm just floating. Like I'm in an ocean and just floating. I just want it to take me away, to take me somewhere. Tired of just . . . floating. *Etomi*, Stephen. *Etomi*.'

We both laugh, sadly, knowing in Ga this word means tired. But not the kind which sleep might solve, no; the translation is to be tired to the depths of your being. His face contorts and I know he's about to cry. I slide my arm across his shoulder as he heaves and keens and groans. He cries until there's nothing left. Wipes at his face with the back of his hand.

'You ever seen Pops crying?' I shake my head. 'Me neither. Thought he might cry at the football today, you know. Yo, I think I gotta pack this ting in,' pointing to himself, shrugging, grinning. I don't follow. He seems annoyed at my confusion, before some recognition flicks in his mind.

'The drinking, man . . . it doesn't even feel good. Is this what he feels? That's what I'm trying to figure out.'

There's more silence. The moon is full, at its roundest. The night cool and still. I stand, putting out my hand. 'Come, man, let's go home.'

'You know what,' Raymond says, as I pull him up. 'I reckon I've seen Pops cry one time. Do you remember? That time. That night he tried to leave.'

He says it so plainly he might be describing a meal he's eaten. I know the night he's talking about. It's a memory forged from a secret that only we share – we being Mum, Pops, Ray and me. Pops had been drinking, drinking spirits straight, hoping that sort of dumb courage might have brought him closer to something spiritual, brought him closer to himself. Mum never liked it when he drank, and that night took exception; and this objection had turned into an argument; and this argument grew vicious, until my father, imbued with that dumb courage, had told my mother, *I don't need you*. There was a silence, in which he said it again, twisting in a knife he'd slid into her in plain sight, she too shocked to protest or defend herself. He'd made a grab for us, stronger and quicker than any of Mum's attempts to stop him, urging us to *come on, come on*. We made it as far as the pavement in our pyjamas and socks, before we found our voices, began to protest. We sat on the kerb. The moon was full, at its roundest. The night cool and still. There was silence unlike any I've known, that could've gone on and on, had Pops not interrupted with, *I don't need you two either*. He turned his back on us, and walked off into the night. I don't remember how long he was away for, or when he returned, but Ray isn't asking me this. He's asking if I remember, us seated on the pavement, our skinny frames huddled together, staring at our father as he seemingly tried to sever a connection, to walk out of his own life. Raymond is asking if I remember. Try as I might, I can't forget.

9

Onions, garlic, tinned tomatoes, peppers. Onions, garlic, tinned toma-toes, peppers. I repeat the ingredients Mum needs to myself, wishing I'd written them down as she had suggested. *Onions, garlic, tinned tomatoes, peppers.*

As I cut through the estate, the sweetness of stew drifts towards me, something I've tasted before. I look and see a woman through a window, her hair wrapped to protect from steam and smell, hovering over the stove, wooden spoon in hand, lost in her own thoughts.

On our last trip to Ghana, when I was fourteen, long after my parents had lost their parents, Mum gathered with her sisters and brothers in the kitchen of their family home, in West Legon, the suburbs of Accra. They set to work on preparing a meal, while A. B. Crentsil played in the background, those sweet and melancholic songs; the music scored by their own conversation and laughter. When I wandered into the room, I felt I was intruding, but my uncles and aunties didn't even break their flow, continuing to confer on the fate of a cousin, whose wife, through some high level of sleuthing, had come to understand her husband, the cousin, had taken a mistress in Kumasi, in another city. Mum sat me down on a plastic stool next to her, and set me to work, peeling the purple skin from garlic to reveal its hard, pale flesh, while my uncles and aunties laughed, almost in disbelief at this man's situation, the tale spinning itself into something larger, until it was said the man had several different families in Kumasi, Tema, Cape Coast, and was making the trip to the Volta region twice a week too, the tale spinning itself into something larger, until it fell apart of its own volition, the absurdity proving too much, all of us unable to contain our laughter. A quiet fell, interrupted only by the sputtering of onions in the pot, the dull thud of knife against board. They lost themselves in their own thoughts, remembering how, as children, they would do this, surrounding their mother, their own aunts and uncles, listening to tall tales being spun, perhaps someone asking for the music to be turned up, sharing the same small motion of a little two-step on the spot, the music always undeniable. They would remember these moments, times their hunger was sated, because how could they forget?

Now, when my mother is in the kitchen, I pull up a chair or stool, or plant myself on the countertop, or offer to lend a hand, preparing onions or garlic or peppers, frying the meat in a heavy pot for stew, or washing and chopping leaves for a salad. I play music from before – some A. B. Crentsil, maybe George Darko or Ben Brako. I listen to her tell stories, often of how she and Pops would party on Saturday nights, back in Ghana, at Nick's house – Nick's place was always free, his dad worked for the World Bank – how they would pack into the smaller house on the compound, everyone responsible for organizing something. For Mum, it was always the food. They'd have drinks too, and Pops and Nick would handle the music, wires trailing between each room, trying to spread the music from a single record player. If the year was 1978, then they were listening to Ebo Taylor, Pat Thomas and, of course, Fela. Nick would also import records from America: the Stylistics, Aretha, James Brown, and one more whose name always escapes her. Mum begins to hum, and I know it's Al Green, and she nods when I say so. I listen as she tells me of eating and drinking and dancing into the morning, how they *really* danced, how *good* they looked. What a special time it was, she says, trailing off into a quiet contentment, a tiny, sad smile on her face.

I watch her mind drift and mine moves towards a memory: I am young, five or six, and I'm handed a plate of kontomire stew – a hearty, spinach-based dish – with rice. I've already protested, knowing we had this meal the day before, and the day before that, maybe even the day before that. I'm handed the plate but I am elsewhere, wherever plantain is being fried, wherever someone is hovering over the stove, tending to jollof. I'm handed the plate, and drop it. Mum snaps, not because she's angry but because something in her is already broken. I'm five or six, so I don't understand that we're making meals stretch. I don't understand that they've already given Raymond and me the biggest servings, and that now mine has to be replaced, they will have to sleep with their hunger, which is not to sleep at all. I don't understand that away from the view of her children, Mum took my father aside, saying, '*Homo ye mi. Etomi.*' Hunger has taken me. I'm tired to the depths of my being.

★

Outside, Pops mans the barbecue, trying to will the coals from red- to white-hot. He's two or three drinks in – I can tell from the grin on his face when he sees me. Today, I indulge him, pulling up a plastic garden chair, letting him pour me a measure of something brown, adding juice, so it's sweetness we're drinking, not bitter. He can hear the music drifting from inside – by now we're making our way towards the Temptations, Isley Brothers, Earth, Wind & Fire. I listen to him tell stories, of how he and Mum would party on Saturday nights, back in Ghana, at Nick's house – Nick's place was always free, his dad worked for one of those big places: United Nations, if Pops remembers correctly – and on Saturdays they would pile into the smaller house on the compound, everyone responsible for organizing something. For Pops, it was always the music. There would be food and drink, but the music was his only real concern. He and Nick were like magicians, able to miracle music from a single record player into every room. If the year was 1979, or maybe 1980 – he waves away this detail, doesn't remember so well – then they were listening to George Darko, C. K. Mann and, of course, Fela. Nick would also import records from America: Tina Turner, the Supremes, Stevie Wonder, and one more whose name always escapes him. Pops begins to hum, and I know it's Eddie Kendricks, and he nods excitedly when I say it is him. I listen to him as he tells me of eating and drinking and dancing into the morning, how they *really* danced, how *good* they looked. *What a special time it was*, he says, trailing off into a quiet contentment, a tiny, sad smile on his face.

Pops says, he always thought that was what he would do when he arrived in the UK: DJ, send sound across rooms, encourage people to gather, to come together and look good and dance. But perhaps it wasn't meant to be. He turns away from me now, and is still, as if something has pulled his attention elsewhere.

Another memory: I am young, five or six. My parents have been arguing again. They're tired of making meals stretch. They're tired of struggling, of striving for more. They're just tired. I hear the snippets from behind the closed door, my mother's voice saying, *Homo ye mi. Etomi.* Hunger has taken me. I'm weary to the depths of my being. My father's reply is short, sharp, tight. The voices rise, louder and louder, until there are heavy steps, and my father emerges, appearing beside me, taking my hand, calling to Mum, *we're going for a drive.* This we do, winding through the night, street lights slashing through the window at intervals. We pull into a side street, and he kills the engine, telling me he'll be back soon. Out of the car and I am alone.

A woman greets him at the door. She is not my mother. They are happy to see each other, like old friends. As he enters the house, a click of the car lock, more for his reassurance than mine, because it can be opened from the inside. I clamber into the front seat and search for company in the fuzz of static. What I now know to be Otis Redding's 'Try a Little Tenderness'. Funny what we remember, what palaces we build to house these fragments. At some point, I grow hungry. I grow tired. *Homo ye mi. Etomi.*

I want to get out of the car, and walk home, to where I might be fed, where my mother is waiting with her embrace.

Outside, Pops mans the barbecue, trying to will the coals to go from red- to white-hot. I've never seen my father cry, but he looks close. The water is a kind threat, the sheen on his eyes like a glimmer, a sad glint. I wonder what fragment has bled into his day, wonder what wound of his I cannot see. What might haunt him. I wish I could ask. I wish we could be that open.

10.

Because it's summer, it's easier to shed a funk, to keep myself in the present. Time drifts, unmoored from the world, with no destination in mind. Auntie and I close up shop early and sit, roadside, drinks in hand, watching our small world. Many of the neighbouring shops have had the same idea; men and women stand on the kerb, holding plastic cups close, or eyeing their opponents in a game of dominoes, or trying to make plans to be elsewhere, perhaps dreaming of going back home. I ask Auntie Yaa if she'd ever return, if she would ever make her way back to Ghana. She takes a sip from her Supermalt and, with a little smile, shakes her head. Gesturing to her shop, the street, the people, she says, 'This is my home now. Besides, what would you do without me?' We both laugh and continue to watch our small world. Because it's summer, a young man on a tiny BMX bike winds his way through pedestrian traffic, a young woman balancing on the bike pegs, her palms on his shoulders. A pair of older men opposite us sit on the edge of the pavement, cans of beer tucked between their legs, holding rolling papers like spread hands, sprinkling tobacco and a little extra. The way light clasps to our skin at this hour makes us all look beautiful. I want to commit this moment to memory, but Del's not here with her disposable camera, and the camera on my phone wouldn't do it justice. Instead, I concentrate on rhythm. I concentrate on the patter of chatter in a group arguing about the football, the memory still fresh and raw. I concentrate on the head nods taking place in praise of Hugh Masekela's 'Riot', those jubilant horns spilling into the street. I concentrate on Uncle T magicking himself on to the road, with his dreads tied, his shirt open a few buttons more than usual, asking when Ray and I will return his speakers. I dodge his question and he turns his attention to Auntie Yaa; they play their game:

'Good evening, beautiful,' he says.

'Mr Tony. How are you?'

'Me, I can't complain. How's business?'

'Same as always. A labour of love.'

'You put so much love into this place and the people. You do it proper. When are you gonna let me love you proper?'

'When you're ready to be serious.'

At this, he laughs, and turns on heel, bopping away. I watch her watch him, seeing that she takes pleasure in their dance. I'm about to be cheeky and ask Auntie Yaa about her love life – a question she so often swerves – but because it's summer, and we're in London, at the top of July, the sky thunders. Moments later, a light shower. Auntie Yaa raises an open palm, in quiet reverence of hot rain. It comes harder and we seek shelter under the short awning of the shop. When it settles, I hug Auntie and we part ways.

Because it's summer, it's easier to shed a funk, to keep myself in the present. There's a jaunt to my step as I walk home along a tree-lined street. I spot Ray's friend Marlon and raise a hand in greeting. He's in his own small world, attention elsewhere – he hasn't been the same since the previous summer, when his father passed, quietly, too young – but when he does spot me, he crosses the road and envelops me in a hug. The sky has quickly cleared, and the way light reaches through the trees makes us both look beautiful. It's a quick catch-up, he's on the way to work, a night shift at a warehouse, but he's having a drink-up tomorrow night. I'm working at Yaa's the day after, but because it's summer, it's easier to say yes. As we part ways, I text Del, asking if she'd like to go, asking if she's free to link tonight. And because it's summer, I stay present. *I am here.* I don't worry about what has been or is to come, because right now, everything feels possible.

II.

'They always do this, man.' Ray circles the supermarket car park once more, peering in every direction for a spot.

'Lemme just hop out and you can swing round, come get me.'

'All right, yeah, I'll meet you out front.'

There's chaos in our household, as there always is before our parents make their yearly pilgrimage back home, to Ghana. I try to stay away from the madness but have inevitably been pulled in, picking up last-minute items from the supermarket, or ferrying documents to and from the Ghanaian Embassy, where the only reward for hours spent in the sweltering room is a brusque line of questioning, a stamp in a passport. To go back home is not to go on holiday. If you are to go on holiday to Ghana, then you must quietly pack your bags, catch your flight, and on landing at Kotoka international airport, tell no one you are there. You must stay in a hotel, or with a trusted member of the family who doesn't receive many visitors. You must ask the driver you hire – it's a driver, taxi or *tro-tro*, a van converted into a bus service, if you're trying to get around – not to take certain roads, for fear of being spotted, or that your longing will breach its borders. You must go as if you are a visitor, rather than returning to the place you were born. Otherwise, to go back home is to try to close an ever-widening chasm. With every year that passes, the bond between my parents and Ghana begins to weaken. When they go back, they are treated like foreigners who have suddenly realized their heritage and are making a big return. They are expected to care for everyone, in monetary form or in gifts. To go back home is to wrangle with who you are against who everyone thinks you should be. It must be a strange feeling, that this place my parents have longed for, a place they used to

49

call home, could also reject them in their current form, could ask them to be someone else.

Still, amidst the chaos, there is excitement. Mum will see her sister who has become too old to travel safely. Pops will link up with his brothers, washing down *kyinkyinga* with Supermalt and Guinness. They never knew that period between childhood and adulthood, so this is an opportunity for them to let go of responsibility, to be carefree. Knowing this, Ray and I pick up the extras from the supermarket. We make the trips to the embassy. We stand in the living room with our eyes closed, as the pastor from our church makes a home visit, praying for a safe trip for them.

When their taxi arrives to take them to the airport, we wheel their bags out, loading them into the boot. They'll be gone for three weeks. Pops pulls us in for a quick, sharp embrace, slapping our backs, reminding us not to wreck the house. Mum explains what meals are in the fridge: the jollof rice is fresh, should be eaten soonest; there's meat stew in both the fridge and freezer, kontomire too. If we need anything, she says, Auntie Yaa is never far. She's going and going, beginning to err towards worry, and I have to remind her, 'It's OK. We've got this.' She hugs us both, and we promise, out of habit, to be good.

We wave the cab away, exhaling, not realizing we had been holding our breath.

'All right, well, I'm heading out,' Ray says, rubbing the fatigue from his eyes. 'Gonna go see Deb.'

'Don't you mean Tej?'

'Nah – I gotta go tie things up with Deb, *then* go make it up to Tej.'

'Looking for trouble, bro.'

He flashes a quick grin. 'Always. I'll be back later on.'

'In a bit.' We pound fists, and with a jangle of keys, he's gone.

I check my phone. Midday. I send Del a text, checking in. It's the anniversary of her dad's passing, and then a few days later, it'll be her birthday, which also happens to be the anniversary of her mum's passing, that connection severed moments after childbirth.

She's away with her aunt, in Milton Keynes, where Del has more family she doesn't really know. For them, Del is more than a mirror of the sister they lost. She's a reminder of their endless grief; Del's presence necessitates a confrontation of their loss, which they aren't ready to do, and so they hold her at a distance, not out of cruelty, but for self-preservation, worried when they crack open the grief, it might be so immense it will consume them. Del's quick to say her family are always kind, always cater and provide, but mostly, don't engage past a few sentences. The times she spends away with them are often lonely. Whenever I've questioned why she insists on returning each year, she says there's a sense of obligation but curiosity too; these are her only living family members, and however distant, they hold stories and histories which concern her, and would otherwise go untold. She hopes, one day, to prise open the bunched fists of their hearts, to hear the people her parents once were, and then to know the intimacies of the family's grief; a grief which Del carries around, whole, like a guiding force; but rather than closing her off, the grief broke and breaks her open. Her life is informed by loss but because she's lost, she loves and loves freely, openly, with all she can. I've seen it first-hand, in what she gives to her art, how she holds her double bass, the quiet intensity with which she plays; what she gives to her friends, the space she makes for people to be honest, to be themselves. What she gives to me, how the feeling of freedom I have with her lasts long after we've separated. How each moment must be made the most of. *Life is too short to be holding back*, she'll say. Del loves, freely, openly and deeply, because now it's just her. Since her parents passed, she's all alone, and so those closest to her are more than friends, they are family. Those closest to her are more than wants, they are *needs*. Especially those like Nam and Jeremiah and myself, who knew her from early, from before the loss, can help her keep those memories alive, while also forging new ones, here, now.

My phone buzzes in my hand. I check the message from Del: *It's OK. Missing you.*

★

The days pass in a strange haze while I wait for her. I wake up late, trawling through my shifts at work at Yaa's, trying to make it to the end of the week, when I'll start my time off. And then, faced with the vast openness, I begin to float. Most days, I kick ball in the park with Nam, maybe Jimmy and Kwame, in the swelter of July, August not far. We set down jumpers and bags as makeshift goalposts, chasing each other around a short patch of grass until we're past tired. One of us will go to the ice-cream van, and realizing this won't sate our hunger, we head to Morley's on Rye Lane, or if we're willing to stretch, take the 484 bus to Nando's in Camberwell. One night, we end up at Nam's, where his mum sizzles chicken in a pan, the fragrance of lemongrass and jasmine so sweet it moves my spirit.

I see more of Ray too. He's supposed to be looking for work, but instead puts most of his energy into patching things up with Tej. This involves inviting her over one night, after we've spent the early evening with Pops's sound system turned up loud, letting the bass beat against the walls, singing and shouting until we are hoarse. While they debate what they'll have for dinner, I try to slip away, to give them some privacy, but Tej beckons me back, asks what I might want. We choose a takeaway from our local Chinese, eating until we've eaten too much, slumped in the plastic chairs in our garden, passing a joint between us, Tej telling me of Ray's drunken antics, spinning tales until they collapse under the weight of the absurdity, until we're all giggling like children. Usually, Ray is the brightest in any space but Tej has her own shine, and I see how they encourage a glow from one another. Amongst the teasing and quick quips, there's care too, his reassuring hand tucked against her hip, her wandering gaze always finding his. Our evening stretches on and on, chorused by our laughter, and we all end up falling asleep on the sofas while *You Got Served* plays on the TV screen.

I've taken to napping, mid-afternoon, just after lunch – to make time move – and I'm somewhere else, in some deep slumber, when the doorbell rings a few days later. I stumble to answer. It's Del.

'Hey.' A smile, then some confusion. 'Were you asleep?'

'You're back.'

'Yes.'

'You're early.'

'I can go back, if you like.'

'No, no . . .' I blink in the glare of the sun, trying to clear a haze. I see the short distance between us, and cross it, pulling her into my arms.

'Happy birthday,' I say.

She pulls away and grins. 'Are we partying or what?'

*

There is a space, which opens up of its own accord or by instruction. Usually – as is the case today – there is a rapper or MC or DJ, pointing to a congested part of the crowd, large or small, gesturing for us to *open up. Open up. Hey, hey. You guys didn't hear me? Open up.* The gap widens and we grow closer. Wider still. Closer still. Pressed up against familiar and foreign. There is a space, now. We have opened up. Del's hand in mine. Nam next to us, Jeremiah not far, Kwame lost in the small crowd of the club, which tips and sways but the space holds. *Hey, hey. Run the tune one time.*

And here, as the song starts, there's another space, or maybe the space takes on a different shape, and the hats begin to skip and swing, the click of a snare, such fantastic motion, the vocal sample cut and pitched just right, a sound thrumming at the deepest parts of us, and we all begin to skip and swing, our bodies moving, such fantastic motion, and we're there, almost there, when the beat drops, and maybe we would've been surprised the first time we heard it, the thud of bass sat atop a kick, but today, we're pressed up against the sound, broaching the space, bumping against familiar and foreign, expression, presence, present, all of us, hands raised, as if to say, *we are here.* Nothing else matters here, except Jeremiah bumping against a stranger, Nam and Kwame finding each other, a flick of the shoulders, a nimble tap of the toe, left, right, left, right, Del's hand in mine, a hug, a warm embrace. Nothing matters here, except the DJ, as we pass frenzy and approach ecstasy, pulls the track up once more, as we occupy this quiet space, willing to wait. Nothing matters here, except us growing closer, still.

We spill from the club, looking for something to eat, and, deciding on kebabs, we send Jeremiah in, hoping he'll remember our order. Nam lights a cigarette. I don't really smoke but take a few pulls, if only to keep me sharp. We talk and talk, excitedly reliving the night, wanting to forge new memories from the feeling which thrums in us all, now. Jeremiah returns, handing food out. We eat sloppily, trying to walk somewhere less congested, trying to find a cab back. We stick out our hands, as one passes, another, and another. No luck this evening, so it's the meander of a night bus, all the way back from central. Off the bus, we all separate, but Del and I, arm in arm, down her road, a soft light on her doorstep, like a beacon. Nothing else matters now. It's just us. It's the quietest it has been all evening. I gaze at her, and hesitate slightly. But I don't know what I could say which would be sufficient for the way I feel. She closes the gap between us, her lips making a brief home on my cheek, a close pull, our separation—

'You don't have to go,' she says. Her hand gripping my arm, tender yet firm.

'OK,' I say. She looks down at the ground, before meeting my gaze. It's so quiet. Just us. The jangle of keys, and her door is open. I follow her inside.

12.

We're falling deeper into summer. Early in August. Ray behind
the wheel of the old Ford he inherited from Pops. My arm
stretched out the window, palm open, trying to hold the warmth
of the world in my hand. Both of us singing Lauryn Hill's 'Doo
Wop' at the top of our voices, the music beating against the walls
of the car, the walls of our chests. Inching through traffic as half
of London seeks refuge from the stuffy heat of the city, making
for the seaside, families heading to Margate or Broadstairs, clusters of friends going towards Brighton, hoping not just to see the
water but a decent night out, Botany Bay for the couples, hoping
for a few hours of peace. Ray and I are heading towards a family
function that Pops, back from Ghana, insisted we attend, the first
Holy Communion of his cousin's daughter, in east London.
Emerging from the dead zone of the Blackwall Tunnel, I pull out
my phone to text Del; she texts back with the speed of someone
who had been waiting for a message; we go back and forth at a
pace, exchanging updates. Ray notices my smile and pounces,
asking, 'Who's got you smiling so sweet?' I try to hide but my
smile widens. Ray leans forwards, his gaze questioning, my silence
teasing, until something falls into place, and the smile on his face
is just as wide.

'It's Del! What you telling me, Stephen?' He raises his eyebrows, inviting me to share details.

The memory comes to me in fragments: Del's birthday, back
to her house. That time between night and day, light dousing all
in an other-worldly haze. The quiet between us. Just me and her
and D'Angelo's harmonies filling the space. A clumsy shyness to
us both. Undressing as quickly as we dare. Hands grazing, a link
between fingers, her hand on my chest, her grip ebbing and

flowing like an ocean, a knot of her braids between my fist, her fingers splayed across my back. Stumbling to her bed, wrestling with each other, searching for skin with lips, clasping curves and edges. Our closeness making language useless. For a moment, our eyes wide and open and dark and beautiful. In between curves and edges, a throb, a hum, longing, desire. That place past frenzy, more akin to ecstasy, which neither of us know but is somehow in sight, the route to which might be this rhythm we're making. We making our rhythm, until she says, *I'm close*, and I know I am too. There's a shudder, a shake, an ah, a gasp, a hum, my head against the warmth of her shoulder. We make our rhythm, until the quiet comes, until we're elsewhere, in some small world—

'Stephen?' Ray, one hand on the steering wheel, his eyes on me, waiting for me to answer.

I say, 'I stayed at hers.'

'You stayed at hers or you *stayed* at hers?'

'I *stayed* at hers.'

'Woi! And then?'

'And then I went to work the next morning.'

'And then?'

'Now, I'm here.'

'Are you joking?' Ray groans, leaning back against the headrest.

'What's wrong?'

'Look, I don't know if you've heard, but I've retired. I'm leaving the game. Hanging up my boots. Settling down. Me and Tej have a real good thing going, you know. But the only way I'm giving up my life of chaos is if I get to live vicariously through you.'

'I didn't sign up for that.'

'You don't choose this life, this life chooses you. And as such, you can't just spend one night, bro. At least spend the day too, if not another night.'

'But I had work.'

'Call in sick.'

'Ray, you're moving mad,' I say, laughing.

'Nah,' he says, 'I'm just happy for you. Now you can stop moping around, all like *I'll never find anyone to love*.'

'I've never said that—'

'You don't have to. It's all on your face. All right, we're here.' Ray slides into an empty parking spot on a residential street, pulls up the handbrake. 'Do up your window, I want a car to come back to.'

'No one's stealing this car, Ray. It's *old*.'

'If it's so old, you can walk home.'

'Whatever, man. Let's do this.'

'Do you remember the plan? You go through the house, I'll go through the side door. Say hello to the fam but one-word answers only. Don't get pulled in. Meet you at the back of the garden. Stay for an hour. Make our excuses. Boom.'

'Got it,' I say, pounding fists with him.

'Remember what's on the line. There's football to be watched. A party to go to. Fun to be had. And now I gotta get you back to Del,' he says, the grin returning to his face. We separate, Ray pushing open the side door into the garden, while I ring the doorbell.

Inside, a throng of parents are engaged in animated conversation, happy to let their excited children shriek and scream in the confines of the house and garden. I shake the hands of several uncles I recognize but can't name, moving quickly through the hallway, towards the kitchen, where if memory serves, there's a doorway leading outside. That's where I find my parents, Mum raising a young cousin towards the ceiling, lowering, raising, lowering, the child giggling like they're on a funfair ride. Pops leans against the counter, a Guinness in hand, chatting to Uncle Moses and Auntie Kay, Moses his cousin on his father's side. Pops and Moses grew up in the same household in Ghana and, as such, are often reminiscing when they get together. I must be catching the last snatch of a memory when they spot me, their laughter at its tail; I offer a quick hello and try to slide by, but Pops stops me.

'Don't run away, Stephen,' he says. 'I was just giving the updates, how you're getting ready for university.' I nod, remembering Ray's advice.

'What will you study?' Auntie Kay asks.

'Music,' I say.

'With some business modules too,' Pops cuts in. 'Have to prepare for the real world, music won't offer much out there.'

I open my mouth, something sharp bristling on my tongue, but Uncle Moses comes to my defence.

'I'm sure there's lots you can do with a music degree. Besides, it's important they get to do things they love. We didn't get that chance.'

'Love won't pay the bills,' Pops says. Mum flashes him a glance and he clears his throat.

'All I'm saying is,' Pops continues, 'is you should do something that will give you a sense of stability. I've said, if you need experience, you can come assist me at the council office a few days a week.'

'But . . .' I shrug, 'nothing's really stable any more, we're living in a different time.'

Pops shakes his head. 'The world hasn't changed. You work hard,' he says, his voice harsh. 'You make *smart* choices. You'll do well.'

'Eric,' Mum interjects.

Uncle Moses and Auntie Kay exchange a look of their own, unsure what to say. Pops doesn't take his eyes off me, but I won't say anything more. In this quiet lull, I make my excuses, heading out into the garden, where Ray waits with two cans of Lilt, extending one towards me.

'What's wrong?'

I shake my head. He gestures with his can, prodding, not letting it go. I relay the conversation in the kitchen and he smiles kindly.

'I told you not to stop, bro. One-word answers only.' He sighs and takes a sip of his drink. 'Don't watch Pops, man. He's always at his worst at these functions. Feels like he has to be something more than he is, you know.'

I nod and we turn to survey the party: highlife music does its quick dance towards us, pumping out of two speakers at the base of the garden; older relatives have squeezed themselves into plastic chairs, balancing paper plates on their laps; teenagers and those in their twenties, even thirties, huddle in clusters, not wanting to be drawn into a conversation as I was: *What are your plans? When will you marry? When will you give me grandchildren?* An older generation exacting pressures, expectations those below them could never exceed.

Ray pulls me back towards him, asking, 'You heard anything about the scholarship? From the uni?'

'Not even.'

'You will. Hold on. There's a barbecue? Where'd you get that?' In front of us, a teenager holding a plate of food, pointing a slender arm in the direction of the kitchen. Ray follows the instruction, telling me to wait right there. Alone, the worry I had perhaps been holding at bay for months bursts through. It's like a fully formed thing, a shadow version of me, the voice my own, asking, what will you do if you don't get into music school? What will you do if it doesn't work out and you're left behind, left alone? How could you believe it could? What will happen to you and Del if you're separated? What will happen to *you* if there's no music, no rhythm to your days? I'm in danger of becoming untethered, the fear swelling in me. I fear I might float up, up, away, but Ray returns, his reappearance pulling me gently back down to the ground. He hands me a plateful of barbecue food, and we eat where we stand.

'Next year will be calm, whatever happens,' Ray says, between mouthfuls. He sets his plate down to take a swig of his drink, saying, 'I kinda admire you, you know. Just doing your thing. Not too worried by what might happen.'

'Oh, I'm worried.'

Ray laughs, shaking his head. 'You shouldn't be. Best musician

I know. Apart from Del, she's serious.' I kiss my teeth and he laughs again. 'Nah, seriously. You've got this. Playing it safe, it's overrated. Going to music school, being a musician, if that makes you happy, then . . .' He shrugs, taking another bite of his burger.

'I wish everyone saw it that way.'

'Sometimes you just gotta do stuff for yourself. You can't please everyone.' He shakes his head again. 'That's my problem. That's all our problems, all the men in our family. Why you think Pops is like he is. It's like we're all haunted by the same thing.'

'How do you mean?'

'We're all scared. That we might offend someone, or we might do what we want to do, and it gets snatched away from us. And I hear it! The world's a scary place. But fuck all that, Stephen.' His eyes glitter in the sunshine, the sadness in his voice competing with the spark I see. 'Don't be scared of being honest, being yourself. Or you'll end up like me.'

'I'm gonna say this one time and one time only,' I say. 'But I think you're pretty great, Ray.'

'Nah.' He looks down at the ground, sets his plate down. 'I'm inconsistent. I've got a lot of love but I don't keep anything for myself. And when I can't cope, I drink, and I can't drink without getting drunk, which, call it what you want, is a problem. But I'm working on it. Great, nah. But I'll get to OK. Ah, man.' He raises his face to the sky to hide his eyes. 'Was not expecting to go there this afternoon.'

I take a step closer, my hand to his forearm. 'You need anything?' I ask.

'No, but do me a favour, text Koby and ask if he needs us to bring anything over later. My phone's on charge.'

I pat at my pockets and come up empty.

'You seen my phone?' I ask.

'You probably left it in the car.'

Out front, back by Ray's car, I see my phone nestled in the crack of the passenger seat, but the door is locked. I make back towards the garden to grab the keys off Ray, when I spot Pops,

60

leaning against his own car, a little further down the road. His head boughed, the crown cradled by the shadow of a tree above. He's muttering to himself, a fresh drink in hand, this time something brown in a clear plastic cup. I take a few steps closer. He lets out a sigh, shaking his head. It's like he's wrestling with something I can't see, some version of himself.

When I'm close enough, I call out, 'Pops, you good?'

It's a slow turn of his head, as if he was elsewhere and my voice brought him back. He starts to say something – for a moment, I think he might continue our earlier interaction, or maybe the opposite, he might explain himself, might open up – but after a few seconds, he closes his mouth. A deep sip of his drink, a swallow. A raise of his eyebrows, a quiet nod of his head. In the past, this wall he puts up was less a deterrent, more an invitation to break through; this idea that if I cared enough, I would reach towards him. But Ray's words are rattling about my mind. I can't please everyone, I think, as I return my father's nod, and head back inside.

13.

A few days later, when we meet on the corner, Del magics a small, battered joint in hand, and I don't refuse. The crackle of a spliff lit in the seclusion of broad daylight. Del takes two easy puffs, passes it along. After the second inhale, I begin to cough and sputter. A kind amusement pulls at her features.

'Don't,' I say. She stifles her smile.

The last time I smoked, I was with Ray and some guys we'd known for time, from Sunday school at church when we were young. We'd met near the end of May, on one of those rainy spring days, having to shelter under the canopy of an enormous tree in the park. They had passed the single joint around the whole group, and when it reached me, after one puff, my chest burned something wicked. I tried once more but whatever was packed into the joint was too harsh. I'd sworn off smoking, yet here I am, trying to make time soft-bodied, trying to bend and stretch and pull; trying to make this time last, trying to bring myself some reprieve, to relieve the pressure of my father's disapproving voice pressing inside my mind. I try not to pull so much in, and the smoke becomes easier to ingest. We share the joint as we walk. By the time we reach JB's, I'm headless. We order enough food for several people and head back to Del's flat, grinning.

Time flattens, pulls, stretches, grins and glints in the face of our wanting. We eat, clumsily, messily, and posit theories about time and its shape. I think part of us hopes to understand more of the shape of the thing between us, whether that thing is time, desire, closeness, uncertainty. At some point, Del lights another joint and we lean out of an open window, a tiny breeze gracing our shoulders. We run through our favourite records, sliding vinyls from out of their sleeves, cueing up another before a song is done, letting the music surround us. Del loads up 'Let's Stay Together' and we two-step around her living room, crooning and grooving like we were there when the record dropped.

Then she plays us something neither of us have heard before. She holds up the sleeve, a leaving gift from our music teacher: J Dilla's *Donuts*. Del tells me what she was told of the album: Dilla made it with just a sampler and a record player, while on an extended stint in the hospital, suffering from lupus. His mother had to massage his hands as they swelled so he could continue working; breathing his all, his last, into this album, passing away three days after its release. Three tracks in, it's clear Dilla knew stuff many do not, will not: how to chop a sample into such small slices they are like notes on a piano, how to program a bassline so it sounds as if it had been plucked on an instrument; how to make your neck bob uncontrollably. Have you tried resisting a good beat? It's impossible.

Aside from all this, the music is beautiful and warm and full. Where some might hear error, I hear intention: honest feelings in a vocal sample or the stutter of a drum. Each new song surprises me, with the arrival of a bassline, a slight break, an instrument falling away to make room for us, the listeners, in the music. The playfulness, as if each phrase emerges with a sly grin on his face.

We're halfway through the record when 'Don't Cry' comes on. I recognize the sample immediately: 'I Can't Stand to See You Cry' by the Escorts. I go to tell Del, but from the excitement on her face, she already knows. On hearing the way Dilla has chopped the sample, and knowing the Escorts tune, a mournful lament which goes round and round, deepening the feeling, when this is mixed with the throb of energy in the room, with what has led us to this moment, our spirits threaten to spill from our bodies. Joy emerges in its multitudes.

The record quickly comes to an end. Neither of us say anything as the needle bumps, bumps, the vinyl still spinning, still wanting to play its song.

'Do you wanna play that again?'

'Yeah.' She pauses. 'Yeah I do.'

She flips the record and it's like we're hearing it for the first time, an unbroken loop, the moment becoming its own forever.

We make it back outside for my favourite time of day, golden hour swarming our senses. Pink intersperses with the blue and grey of the sky, like a beautiful storm is coming. What's left of the sun softly punches our faces, discouraging sobriety. A young girl passes us, hand in hand with her mother, the other hand an open palm, feeling for the light in the world. Del turns to me, the black of her eyes full and open.

'Stephen?'

'Yeah?'

'What happens if one of us doesn't get in?'

She's asking what will happen if we have to separate, if everything has to change.

'We'll work it out,' I say.

*

There's a heat between us which won't dim. Back inside, Del puts the record back on, while I twist ice out of its tray. We're happy to let Dilla loop, to let him occupy the space between us. I pour us both a glass of water and watch the ice try and disappear itself.

'Thank you,' she says, holding the glass to her forehead. A big T-shirt swallows her chest and limbs. I'm in shorts, hoping the night will cool us. Del taps at her phone, shakes her head.

'It's meant to be thirty degrees today . . . tomorrow . . . the next day.'

'Beach weather,' I say.

'I haven't been to the beach since . . . well, since my dad—' She pauses, as if trying to grasp at something just out of reach. She gets up from where we sit, padding to her room, returning with a leather-bound photo album, its insides bulging out. She opens to the middle pages, as if by memory, and points to an image of her, in her early teens, on the beach with all our friends. I remember the day they took the trip, being jealous I couldn't go too (it coincided with the christening of a cousin and Mum wouldn't hear anything of me missing the occasion). Water laps at Del's thighs, her hands gripping her hips in a joyful embrace, a grin on her face.

'That was the day of the car crash,' she says. 'My aunt got the call a few minutes after she took this.'

'Do you remember much from that day?'

'The silence. It was like when he left this place, so did she.' A heavy sigh as she tries to shake off the weight of the memory. 'I thought once he survived the first, he could survive anything.' The confusion must show, so she continues. 'There was another accident, when I was much younger, which was much worse.' She slides the T-shirt up and turns away from me slightly, to reveal two scars, twin bolts of lightning zigzagging down the corner of her back.

'I've never seen these,' I say, surprised I missed them earlier.

'Why would you have?' She smiles, acknowledging the shape of the thing between us, acknowledging our rhythm. She reaches across for my hand, pulling it to each scar, tracing each one so I might better know the making of her.

'We should go to the beach,' I say.

For a moment, she looks as if she might turn and flee. As if the heat between us might simmer and dim, our closeness disappearing in the process. But then she turns to me, her gaze direct and sure. She nods, saying, 'Let's go to the beach.'

14.

It feels too easy, that we could wake up the next day, earlier than intended, the air already thick with heat, and decide to carry out our plan to go to the beach. That we could pack a couple of towels, some food, some drinks, a joint wrapped in cling film hidden in a purse, head towards the train station, take the train from Peckham to Bromley South, where we wait impatiently on the platform, some sense of urgency pushing us, both of us on the brink, the train pulling up, finding seats, and only then beginning to relax, knowing Broadstairs is our final destination. Still, it feels too easy, even when ten minutes into our journey Del magics a pack of cards and we play War to pass the time – I lose every round – until we catch our first glimpse of the ocean, vast and endless. It's only when we see our footprints in the sand that we let go of this disbelief. We're early, so while it's not just us, it is quiet. We stick our cooler in the ground, making camp. We lay our towels down, and I go to sit but Del beckons me, towards the water, where it ebbs and edges on to the sand. We soak our feet in the ocean. Del produces a tiny bottle of rum and begins to speak in Ga. I've never heard her speak Ga but do not question. I am but a witness, snatching at phrases. *Miiŋa bo*. I am greeting you. *Me shwe bo*. I miss you. *Kaa fo*. Don't cry. She goes on, the conversation continuing, pouring a measure of rum into water at intervals. She goes on, until a small wave rears up from the water, clattering our chests. Del only smiles, her eyes closed, content, for now. After a few more moments, she takes my hand in hers and we make our way back up the sand, both knowing something has touched us, something *spiritual*.

⋆

This becomes our summer. We return to the beach, again and again, until we're going several times a week. Auntie Yaa can see I'm only coming into work to count down the time in which I can be with Del again, so halfway through August, with a knowing smile, she gives me the rest of the month off. We pull others into our arrangement, and eventually there's a little crew, driving down to the coast on any spare day. Raymond and Tej, Nam and Jimmy and Kwame and Jeremiah, Naomi and Lucy, anyone who will come and join and watch as the tide disappears the beach, will come and make camp with us, will pass the disposable cameras from person to person, making images, forging memories from joy.

My parents head up north, to Manchester, to visit some relatives. On a call, I tell Mum we're going to the beach and she tells me, again, this is what she used to do at my age, with Pops and her friends, her brothers and sisters too. On summer days, they would hop in a *tro-tro* and make the short drive to Labadi beach, where they'd let a boombox send sound across the sand, would stand by the edge of the ocean and be astounded. In this way, we're drawing a line towards our parents, our lives coming together, letting a loop form and close, letting it start again.

We smoke joints in the broadness of daylight, we drink spirits and blend them with mixers and song, letting four-minute cuts stretch time until it is unrecognizable, each second its own forever. We don't want this thing to end, this freedom, and it doesn't feel like it will, these moments looping, round and round, until—

15.

'We always knew this was a possibility,' Del says. We're standing in slight seclusion, round the corner of the main building of school. Near us, we hear excited chatter, the laughter, the whoops of glee on finding out someone else will be attending your chosen university, on finding out you won't feel so alone. Back home, my parents are waiting for my results. But right now, nothing else matters. I hold my envelope in a shaking hand, the results listed down the page. I'm not even close to the grades I need. It feels arbitrary to rely on a sequence of letters and numbers to decide we are good enough, when, up to this point, much of our judgement relied on *feeling*. And yet, even this cannot console in this moment.

'These things don't mean anything,' Del continues, trying to close the space widening between us. It's not disappointment I feel, but shame. I want to scrunch up the papers until they are small enough to be hidden away, out of sight. I want to do the same to myself, to fold away, hide. Del puts a hand on my forearm, to console, but I don't soften under her palm. I don't harden either. I don't feel anything, except shame, knowing that our song, our rhythm has had its progression disrupted. Even if the beach hasn't changed, or her doorstep, or her bedroom, or the way she holds her face when joyous, or the way we laugh when stoned, even if these things haven't changed, *we* have changed, moment to moment.

I sigh and fold the papers into my pocket.

'I gotta get to work,' I lie.

'Ask Auntie for the day off. I'll come with you.'

'Nah, it's OK. Stick around, celebrate. I'll text you, find out where you man are.'

She opens her mouth to protest further, but she doesn't push. Instead, a quick kiss, a squeeze of both hands. She rests her forehead against mine. I can feel her warmth, her kindness. I can feel her love as we rest here, two Black crowns in daylight. I want to stay here. I don't want this thing to end. But I know I must go. After a few moments, I squeeze her hands once more, and turn, walking away. I don't look back.

*

Even though I don't have to be at work, I make a detour via Auntie Yaa's shop on the way home, knowing I might find some solace in that space. When I turn the corner on Peckham High Street, the shutters are closed. A thick, heavy padlock pins the metal to the ground. I've never seen it before. There is a silence about it which feels final. I phone Auntie Yaa. There is no answer. I try her again. The phone rings out. I wait for a few more minutes, hoping she or Uncle will appear, and when no one comes, make my way home, hoping my parents might have some answers.

As I'm coming through my front door, I hear someone crying through a crack in the living-room doorway. I want to go in, but something stops me. I don't think this is a scene I'm meant to see. I stand, in limbo, as snippets of conversation reach me.

'*Kaa fo,*' I hear Mum say. Don't cry. Yet, the crying continues. I hear a soft palm rubbing a back which convulses with hurt. 'Yaa, *kaa fo.*'

'They can't do this,' I hear my father say. The crying escalates. The murmurs from Mum, trying to reassure, are having no effect.

'Yo.' Ray has appeared quietly at the top of the stairs. He gestures for me to come up and I join him.

'What's going on?' I ask, in the safety of our room.

Ray flops on to the bed, his hands laced behind his head. 'Auntie's shop is done out here, bro.'

'What do you mean, "It's done"?'

'Done,' he says simply, as if summing up a football match. 'Rent raised. Doubled. Tripled. She didn't say anything.' He sighs. 'What was she even meant to say?'

'But,' taking a seat beside Ray, 'it's so sudden.'

'I know.' Ray has seen this more than I have, but he doesn't need to explain. Over the past few years, we've both watched youth centres and hair shops and other cafes close. We all knew that this might happen. This phenomenon spreading like a virus, like contagion, that asks us to stop considering our people and community, and only think of value; value that can be rendered in words and numbers, can be exchanged with a signature. It asks us not to think of people but property. But what of the people? What of those, away from home, trying to build something here; what of their wants and needs? What of Uncle and his aviators and his Guinness, where will he make a home, where will he find a space? And Auntie Yaa, who looks after us all, who will look after her?

It's too much. My face contorts and I know I'm about to cry. Ray stands, sliding both arms across my back, holding me. I mourn the safety. I mourn our rhythms. I mourn the loop. I mourn the *space*. I cry until there's nothing left. We separate and I wipe at my face with the back of my hand.

'Everything's changing, bro,' I say to him.

16.

Since the one thing that can solve most of our problems is dancing, it only makes sense that here, two weeks after I've moved to the Midlands for university, after freshers' week has become freshers' fortnight and I've left my halls for the club for the seventh night in a row, looking for something, perhaps for closeness, for safety in numbers and bodies, for the freedom a dance floor provides, it only makes sense that here, surrounded by strangers, all of us anonymous in our desires, while the DJ spins garage cuts, music from the nineties, music our fathers swear by, I try not to remember what has brought me to this moment, I try my best to forget. I try my best to let this five-minute cut stretch time until it is unrecognizable, until the same breakdown has been playing forever. I try to lean into the unknown but soon it's four a.m. Soon the lights come up and illuminate my loneliness. I feel too raw, too open, and I dart out of the door, taking leave. I don't know if I can let anyone see my shame. I take a shortcut back to my halls, as the light begins to insist on breaking through the night.

After that night, I stop going out, only leaving the flat for lectures and the shops. This feels safe enough; Nottingham itself feels sprawling, a scrum of villages leading to a dense city centre, like it could swallow me whole. The campus is like a tiny city within the city – at orientation, I'll find out the mostly green plot of land spreads over three hundred acres – complete with cafes and woodlands, a lake too. Whenever darkness falls, I get the sense that I'll take a wrong turn, and forever be trying to find a way out, like a snake eating its own tail.

The ease in which I lived my life in London, knowing there

was always the potential to gather, to plot, the potential for *space*, disappears. I've leaned on the same group of friends for so long that here, so far from home, I struggle with the openness it takes to grow close to anyone new. I've never been surrounded by so many strangers. Back home, there was always the feeling we all knew each other, everyone a friend of a friend. And even in the presence of strangers I knew who I was because of the people around me. I was Ray's younger brother, or Nam's best friend; I was the guy who would happily kick a ball around for a day, or who might gather in someone's kitchen or garage for a jam session; I was me, I knew myself and how to present that to others.

People on my course are nice enough (in the end, it was a business degree I went for; Pops suggested I go for something safe when the chance of a music degree fell through, and I didn't have the strength to argue), and there are a few, like Michael and Temi and Luke, who I find myself huddled together with before lectures, or moaning when a lecturer refuses to let us out of a tutorial early. But when we're placed in a group for a presentation, and, after the work is delivered, a pub celebration is suggested, I make some excuse but don't follow up. I'm unable to find a way to say that since arriving, I don't feel like myself, or rather, I don't like this version of me, who's insecure and rarely at ease, who doesn't know how to dismantle his loneliness.

The same goes for my two flatmates in halls, Bryan and Mason, who are both from Birmingham, have known each other for years, always planned to come to Nottingham together. Despite their best intentions, each moment spent in their presence feels like I'm intruding upon something. After a couple of weeks, perhaps out of kindness, seeing how each invitation must flash tension across my features, they stop asking whether I'll join them for a kickabout, or whether I'll come along to the weekly pub crawl across the campus, the bar at each hall of residence thrumming with a drunken crowd on Saturday nights.

I stop checking in with my friends, unable to wrangle with the jealousy of their different clusters of comfort: Jeremiah and Nam taking some time away from education, figuring things out for themselves in London; Tony and Kwame studying further north, in Hull. Each update I see online, of nights out and kickabouts and just people hanging out, only reinforces this feeling of being on the sidelines of my own life. I cocoon, retreat, and the solitude I first take comfort in becomes oppressive.

A few weeks into my first term, I spend a chunk of my student loan on a set of speakers, and in the name of loneliness, listen to albums front to back. I'm happiest listening to *Kind of Blue*, because I know the record so well, the beautifully odd notes, the flourish of an extended solo, the mastery of it all. In the sections of the record when it's quietest and Paul Chambers plays his bass solos, I'm reminded of Del, of our own quiet, my head against the warmth of her shoulder. I'm reminded of my ambition, not long distant, of wanting to make music of my own. And then it's shame which visits, that I even thought it possible; the doubts my father had now feel justified. I feel tired inside, my spirit worn out by the effort it took to hope and dream, to believe, to imagine myself a future in which I could choose something for me. When, one evening, Ray calls, and I tell him about the shame and the tiredness, he reminds me what I once told him: how arbitrary to put your fate into the hands of a small group, when so much of the music relies on *feeling*. He tells me to go towards this, the feeling, to let it lead me towards my instrument, towards the desire to render these emotions in sound and rhythm. But I don't have it in me. My trumpet lies untouched. Instead, I smoke through my days, willing them away. I stay on the sidelines, let the edges of my days round off in my own haze, keeping to my room, keeping to myself.

Whatever I'm listening to, when the record is done, I let it loop. I've only known myself in song, in the space between the sounds we make to capture our quiet. The music conjures a time when

I was more open, a time when I had more faith. I only want to remember. I don't want to forget.

*

Del and I begin to speak most days. We tried to say goodbye in London, and it didn't work, so she drove with my family to the Midlands, where, after we had moved all my possessions into halls, after Ray had slapped my back with a grin, after Pops first shook my hand, then pulled me in for a hug, after Mum had held me close and, on separation, I saw the shimmer of tears threatening to fall, after she turned away, not wanting me to hold this burden, after all this, Del and I stood in my room, alone.

'This is me,' I said.

'That's my line,' she said, grinning. We came together, her head finding refuge against my shirt, my fingers splayed across the warmth of her back. There's so much I wanted to say, but any goodbye would have been insufficient in the face of how I felt. She took my head in both hands, kissed both cheeks. Our lips met, soft and momentary. We took each other's hands. Sat on my bed. Del shuffled closer. I slid my arm across her shoulder. We stayed like this, close. Minutes went by. Time fell away. Eventually, there was a knock at the door. Whoever it was – Mum, Pops or Raymond – didn't come in but it was the signal that our time was up. We didn't say goodbye – neither of us could bear it – but another kiss, *in a bit*, a promise to see each other soon.

One night, we try to render our closeness in language. I let the phone rest on my chest as we try to tap back into the rhythm of summer just gone. But we forgot that our closeness made language useless. That here, only sounds might suffice: an *ah*, a *hum*, a *gasp*.

'I don't know if this is working,' Del says across the line.

'Oh. Yeah,' I say. 'It's not really.'

'It's just not the same over the phone.'

We talk a little more but both tire quickly. When we sign off,

76

I feel our desire multiply with the distance. This thing between us, which I thought might be manageable, becomes monstrous and consuming. In the dark, I let *Kind of Blue* play again. I try to fill myself, even though I know I cannot be filled. I writhe and hum and gasp, until I spill and slip towards slumber. As Miles begins to croon a solo into the silence, I blink twice, trying to hold off sleep a little while longer, longing filling me, the room, this space. In this moment, I wish I could be closer to Del. Wish I could be more open.

17.

Another night, I call Ray, intending to ask if he can visit soon.

I intend to tell him it's been a couple of months now, but I'm struggling to see further than that. Winter will be here soon, the days are already shorter. I'll say, *there's something pressing at the inside of my chest, trying to break free.* And as I say this, maybe I'll realize it's me. Perhaps it's that I'm trying to make space for the version of myself who is secure, often at ease, who might fill summer days with trips to the beach and house parties, who might slide inside a moshpit until I'm pressed up against a sound, who might cradle my trumpet in hand, send a low hum out in the world, make a note a home for feeling. Perhaps it's that I'm trying to make space for the person who might feel something, rather than, several times a day, rolling a joint and smoking slowly, constructing walls from my own haze with which to lock myself inside.

I want to ask Ray how long do I have to stick this out for? Will I settle in here, or is this just not for me?

Dialling Ray's number, I press the phone to my ear, taking a seat at the desk in my room, pushing aside some of the food wrappers and course material strewn about for my elbow to rest on the surface, my head against my palm, waiting. When the line rings out, I go to call again, but Ray beats me to it. His voice is jubilant when I answer; in the background, I can hear commotion and clatter.

'Are you out?' I ask.

'Bro! We're out here! Everyone's here.' There's movement, and in the distance I hear Ray say, 'It's Stephen,' followed by voices I know: Tej, Koby, Nam, Jeremiah. I press the phone closer to my ear.

'Where are you guys?'

'Out! Celebrating. Your boy got a job!'

'Oh,' I say. 'Congrats.' The feeling of being left behind intensifies, and now I recognize it is longing pushing at my chest, a desire to be close.

'Yeah, man. Relief! Working for Nike, doing marketing; it's ideal, man. You good, though?'

'Yeah, yeah—'

'It's loud in here, I can't really hear you still, one second, lemme go outside.'

'Nah, it's calm,' I say. 'Let's chat tomorrow.'

'Huh?'

'Let's chat tomorrow.'

'You sure, yeah?'

'Yeah, man.'

We ring off and the courage abandons me. I probably won't call Ray tomorrow, and if I do, I'll hide my desire away. I'll hide away my solitude, how its enormity has turned it into something I don't know how to wrangle with, something thick and heavy and suffocating. Rather than tell him of the loneliness, I'll tell him it's all OK, everything is OK.

Instead, now, I push the window open as far as it'll go. The night is still, cool, quiet. I perch on the ledge, illuminated only by the blue of the moon. A joint I rolled earlier in hand. A light, a spark, a brief brightness, a soft glow. Down below, the music of excitement, a Saturday night, everyone eager, anything possible. I smoke the joint, slowly, down to the roach, and retreat inside.

18.

It's not long before Del visits for the first time. By now, I've settled into my own rhythm, have several pillars in my life: lectures on Mondays, Tuesdays and Thursdays; a daily phone call to Mum, to whom I insist I'm doing OK; afternoons at the library, coursework before the deadline so there's not something else looming over me; dinner at a Caribbean restaurant in the city centre, or passing by one of the shops which stocks spices I need to make food from home; in the evenings, walking the half hour from campus over to the Savoy Cinema, where it will usually be me and a handful of others, and for a few hours I might stay still and present.

It feels like a quiet life, but it's mine. I've tried to build my own small world in the vastness, and it's helping: I'm feeling more and more like the person I was, or the person I might become. But as Del's train pulls into the platform at Nottingham, I'm on unfamiliar ground again. It's just Del, I tell myself, but I worry the distance might have caused a drift. My shyness returns. Even from a distance, I can tell Del is anything but. She runs towards me, holding my face in both hands when she reaches me. Her eyes glint, bright in the late-October sunlight. I'm worried mine are dim from all the time spent alone in a darkened room, but she doesn't seem to notice, excitedly filling me in on her first few weeks at music school, the rehearsals, the jam sessions, the characters, the rigour, the *space*, all that space in which to say, *this is me*. She was worried about going to a London university, that there wouldn't be enough room for her to breathe and grow, but she's found she's leaning into the unknown, leaning into what she believes might be possible for herself, which, right now, seems infinite.

As she speaks, I think of my trumpet, wedged in the gap underneath my bed. I only really know myself in song, in the quiet, in the freedom, in the surrender, but I cannot remember the last time I did so, the last time I held my horn, the last time I leaned into the unknown. I don't feel like I have the space, not any more, not now the faith has left me. I think of what's missing, what I've lost: the jam sessions, the improvisation, the spirit. I miss the church I built to know myself, in the music of my days, the sureness of the rhythm, the ability to make a mistake beautiful.

Taking my hand, she asks, 'And how are you? Fill me in. Also, food. I'm starving.'

We head straight to the Caribbean restaurant I've been frequenting. They greet me warmly, as I thread together fragments of this strange haze I've been living in since I arrived here, telling Del of freshers' week turning into freshers' fortnight, of my flatmates and lectures, of music and spending time with myself, bending language and shifting parts so it's not a story of solitude I'm telling. She takes my hand again, grinning, glad I'm enjoying myself too. It's only when she asks when she'll meet my friends, and I make up an excuse – they're busy with work, I say – rather than tell the truth, that's when I feel something shift, something change between us. I've never lied to Del before.

'What's it like here?' she asks.

'The food is good.'

'No,' she laughs, 'I mean, in Nottingham. You know, how London has a vibe? What's it like here?'

I let out a heavy sigh, which pulls her towards concern, leaning forward in her seat to hear what might come.

'It's OK. The campus is quiet. There's a lot of trees, at least around me. I don't really—' I pause. 'I guess – it's not home, but . . . it's all right. Hard at first but . . . I'm getting there.' None of which is a lie.

She frowns. Studies my features. We know each other too well to be hiding. 'You sure you're good?'

'Yeah,' I say, perhaps a little too quickly. Her gaze is questioning; I meet it with a small nod, to which she shrugs, her hand on mine once more, saying, 'I'm glad I'm here.'

'Me too.'

As we eat, we order one drink, then another, one more for good measure. It could be summertime again. From her bag, she takes out a plastic pouch of photos, developed from the disposables she always carries around. It's a selection of me or her, or us: at prom, a portrait of me, moving my arms as I dance; at Del's birthday, the shimmer of sparklers lighting her face; there we are, on the beach, water lapping at our thighs, gripping each other in a joyful embrace.

'We should start a little collection,' she says, smiling.

Memory, image and possibility slide across one another. I imagine we might return to my halls, that I'll introduce her to my flatmates before we take refuge in my room. There I might put on an album, one we both know, the D'Angelo one. We'd let the music play, until one of us made a move, until we're back in rhythm, fingers splayed across a back, bunched fists on bedsheets, a head against the warmth of a shoulder. Until the quiet comes, until some small world, some brief infinity.

As we're walking home, shyness abandons me. I pull her short, and she turns towards me. My heart races, my chest tight, but I still bend slightly towards her, and—

'Wait,' she says. Her hand on my chest. We separate. Her shyness is back.

'What's up?'

'Something happened.'

'Are you OK?'

'Yeah, yeah, I'm fine. Look, erm . . . I got together with someone. In freshers'.'

'Oh. OK, right.'

'It wasn't like . . . it just happened.' She looks at me, trying to gauge a reaction. I gaze out into the passing traffic, the sound of rushing cars bringing me peace in this moment of strange grief.

'I just thought . . .' she continues, 'we kind of—' She sighs and starts again. 'You went this way and I went that way, and . . . you didn't say anything.'

'Why didn't *you* say something?'

The question quietens her. A bite of her lip, her gaze widens. I push at the point the way the world feels like it's pushing at my chest.

'What's the deal with you and . . .?'

'I don't know.'

'Why are you here, Del?'

'What do you mean? It's me, it's you, it's us. I'm here for us.'

'And what is *us*?'

'I don't know,' she says.

Another car passes by, the headlights leaning light across our faces, before darkness returns.

'Stephen?'

What is there to say? The silence is heavy. Somewhere in my depths, a deep ache. I stare at the ground, not daring to steal a glance. It's not shyness, but shame. I can feel her waiting. But what is there to say? And because I don't have the language, I do what comes easiest. I return to my solitude. I turn to her, my gaze sure and direct.

'I think you should go.'

'Stephen—'

'Bye, Del.'

Her whole spirit sags, dim in the darkness.

'Don't be like that,' she says quietly.

I try to dampen my rising frustration with reason. There was no conversation about the shape of the thing between us, whether it would continue, whether it *could* continue. I said nothing because I didn't know what would happen if I were to give us words, or rather, I knew what might happen, and didn't want to entertain the possibility that we, Del and I, could end our song in its current form. I also wonder if too much has shifted; if the life she's leading now appeals more than the one we shared. If, while I've been static and stagnant in Nottingham, she has blossomed and bloomed amongst new musicians and music and doesn't have the same interest or attraction. And yes, these are all maybes, but the feelings remain. And yes, all it might take to clear this up is for me to speak, but right now, I don't have the words.

'Stephen,' she says again. She upturns her palm in my direction, reaching towards me. My frustration multiplies, thickens, and because anger is so close to love, I go there. I can feel the heat swelling in my chest, red and beyond reason. Shame, betrayal, rejection – I try to pin down the growing emotion but all I can recognize is my own fury.

I say again, stronger and sharper, 'I think you should go.'

Her hand falls away. I let this space grow between us. I don't close it. She waits for me to say something more. She waits until too much time has passed, the silence too heavy for either of us to carry. I let her pick up her bag and turn away, and when she does, I do too. I don't look back.

I don't sleep that night because to sleep with grief is not to sleep at all. When I get back to my halls, after Del has left, I call Mum. She asks how I am, have I eaten? I say no, but *homo ye mi*. I'm hungry. What I do not say is that I am hungry for something I have lost. In response, her laugh is joyous and kind. She asks if I have any jollof left, and I say yes. When I sign off and have heated up a bowl, I have no real appetite but the scent of onion and garlic and tomato, the miracle which is a home-cooked meal encourages memory, image and possibility to fold in on one another. I am in the eye of a moshpit. I am in my mother's kitchen. I am the ebb and flow of the ocean. I am the beach disappeared by the tide. I am the breath between notes. I am the silence. I don't know myself any more. I am floating, floating. I am closed off, a total eclipse. I am on the pavement when Del leaves me. I am on the pavement when my father tells me, *I don't need you either*. I am unwanted. I cry so much that not even two hands can dry the tears. I cry until there's nothing left. I climb into bed and cradle my soft body, willing myself to sleep. But I don't sleep that night because to sleep with grief is not to sleep at all.

When morning announces itself with a whisper of light across the sky, I get out of bed, pulling my trumpet case from underneath. I haven't played since I arrived. I only know myself in music, but I wasn't – am still not – ready to share that in this new space. I can feel myself closing off, the light dim, near total eclipse. I pull out the case and leave my halls. I make my way out of the main town, where the roads begin to narrow but the space opens up. Towards the country park, where a pretty mist quietly kisses every surface. It's autumn now, green verging on brown. The grounds seem to sprawl endlessly. I keep walking until I am in the open. I make a base in the middle of everything. I take my horn from its case and, with no real cue, begin to play. I echo notes into the world, to see if anyone else knows this feeling. And when the notes begin to fail me, I place down my horn. I begin to beat at my chest. I know that grief makes language useless, and that only sounds might suffice, so I let out a dull hum, a shattered gasp. I shout and scream, tearing myself apart, making myself undone, pulling it out, all of it, these feelings which rest in my depths. I make my own rhythm.

PART TWO

A Brief Intimacy
2011

19

Since the one thing which might solve our problems is dancing, it only makes sense that here – following the part of the service where Ife, arm in arm with her father, walks towards the altar, towards Koby, whose features are slack with gentle awe, who, like all of us, does not know how to hold himself in such moments, one hand thrust into his pocket, the other held out like an invitation, her hand in his, a smile, a grin – they turn to face each other, we but witnesses to the quiet which falls, to this moment of surrender, to the moments which follow, in which the pastor asks us to pray for the pair, to make space, to encourage Koby and Ife to explore the depths and heights of their being, to say things which are honest and true, Godlike even, to encourage them to speak to both the people they are and the people they want to be, to lean into this quiet, into this unknown. It's then I want to turn to Ray, to nudge him and ask, when was the last time you were that open? But before I can ask for an answer, Koby's voice falters to a halt when he tries to say just what it means to love, tries to say everything in a few sentences, and the weight of it undoes him, like the way love might unspool our tightly wound selves, the way love might encourage looseness, might encourage us to be free, and since the one thing which might solve our problems is dancing, it only makes sense that here, long after Ife has reached a gentle hand to Koby's face and they have spoken aloud what they already knew, long after we've had to wipe the tears streaking our faces for photos, long after confetti showers and restless children racing up and down a patch of concrete, one of them falling, a scrape of a knee, tears, a sharp word from his mother followed by a warm embrace, long after the food has been served, the buffet piled on to plates, me and Ray marvelling at the miracle of party jollof – *It's just better, bro, don't ask me how* – long after the speeches, during which Koby describes the day he met Ife, in those first few weeks of college when they were awkward and aimless, not knowing the days they were spending – long, gentle days full of laughter and arguments and *closeness* – were the days they might grow to know what love might be, where they might grow to feel beautiful, to feel free, Ife and Koby take to the floor for their first dance, D'Angelo's 'The Root' moving them across the space.

It's not long after this that the DJ starts up in earnest. I join Ray in teasing the relative who doesn't know how to do the electric slide, but we still show her all the same. When an uncle beckons us towards the bar, we don't hesitate, taking one shot for the newlyweds, another for courage. And when the music begins to slow, and couples and lovers and strangers pull each other closer, making their bodies familiar, I catch the gaze of one of Ife's friends, her features slack with a kind smile. Her eyes won't let go of mine, a slight tilt of her head, her eyebrows raised, waiting for me to fill the space. And maybe it's the alcohol dizzying around my body, or the freedom I feel in this moment, but I'm bold and audacious, one hand thrust into my pocket, the other held out like an invitation, a smile, a grin, and then I'm making my way towards her, and she's meeting me halfway, her hand now in mine, and then—

20.

'So that's where you disappeared to last night,' Nam says. 'This guy is always on adventures.'

'I didn't disappear.'

'You were standing by the bar, and then you weren't. I call that disappearing.'

'Whatever.'

We're outside, in the tiny accidental courtyard behind the restaurant we both work in, both of us training to be chefs. There's a few hours left of our shift, our shirts soaked through with sweat, the only shade a memory. Nam struggles to light his cigarette as the sun glistens his fingers. I take it from him, one flick, another, and it's like I'm in a memory of last night, at the wedding: hiding round the corner of the venue, trying to protect the battered joint which had been taking refuge in my pocket from the stiff, hot wind, London succumbing to a brief heatwave in June. I was about to stub it out when there were footsteps. The woman I had danced with earlier in the night making her way towards me, rooting through a bag slung over her shoulder. She fished out a crumpled box of cigarettes before she spotted me, a quiet, tired smile on her face, a tight, neat afro atop her head, several hoops swinging from both ears, each slight movement of her head making soft clinks and clangs, making her own music.

'It's my dancing partner,' she said.

'It is.'

'You ran away.'

'Sorry. I'm not so good at . . .' I signalled at the space between us. She shrugged but it wasn't unkind. Took a cigarette from the packet, struggled to make fire stay in the breeze. I don't know what pulled me but after her fifth or sixth try, I reached across, taking and pressing her cigarette between my lips, using my own lighter, one flick, another, a slight crackle as it came to light, holding it out for her to press between her own lips, our eyes locked. She nodded her thanks and I waved it away.

'I'm Annie,' she said, between tokes.

'Stephen,' I said. From inside, I heard the DJ find some fresh energy, encouraged by the whoops and cheers of a group of people who didn't want the party to end. Above, the moon gave us a gentle half-smile, which I passed on to Annie.

'Stephen?'

Nam's offering me another toke. I shake my head.

'Trying to quit. Cigarettes, at least.' Nam raises his eyebrows. We've done this dance before; his hand doesn't waver until I, begrudgingly, take it.

'You gonna see her again?'

I shrug. We exchanged numbers but I'm hesitant. The prospect of opening myself up to Annie, a stranger, scares me.

'I don't know. She said she just got out of something long term.'

'I wasn't asking if you're gonna marry her. Although, she's definitely your type.'

'My type?'

'There was just something about her . . . she had a vibe.'

I laugh, without protest, running my forearm across my forehead, silently asking for a reprieve from the heat. Nam takes a hairband from his pocket, stretching it over a bunch of his dreads, trying to pull some of the hair out of his face. It's seconds before the band snaps with a slight twang. He reaches into his pocket for another, and after a quick search, gives up, several strands framing his features.

I'm thinking about heading back inside, seeking shade, when the back door to the restaurant pops open; out comes Femi, head chef and owner, his shaved head catching the light, bringing with him clarity: I hear the call and response of Fela's sax and voice, the drums somewhere between slow and sultry, or both. Born in Lagos, to a Ghanaian mother and a Nigerian father, Femi's allegiances are split: this restaurant he opened near Queens Road, Peckham only serves Ghanaian fare (he, like me, grew up beside his mother in the kitchen) but our daily playlist is filled with Nigerian musicians. Fela, of course, and Tony Allen, Ebenezer Obey and Babatunde Olatunji; music full of percussive heartbeats, lifelike rhythm.

Sometimes, when Nam and I are on a late shift, he'll tell us not to rush off, waiting until all customers and workers have departed, before bringing us through to the kitchen to prepare his mother's favourite meal: grilled fish, atop a bed of sweet peppers and rice. He'll set us to work while Ebenezer Obey's *Greatest Hits* play, slicing the peppers so they're uniform, paying close attention to the grill, so the skin becomes crisp but the fish is so soft it falls apart; prepping a sauce for the fish, as sharp as it is sweet.

As the night goes on and the second bottle of wine is opened, Femi will tell us the same story: of Lagos in the early eighties, his mother running a successful catering business, the long evenings spent watching her prepare waakye and fufu and light soup, meals for the Ghanaians away from home. He'll tell us of mandate, of expulsion from Nigeria, of *Ghana Must Go*, of having to choose which parts of your life to keep, which to let fall away. He'll tell us, though his father had been MIA for some time, he wanted to keep a part of him, wanted to keep his rhythm, his music, so Femi stuffed cassettes into the bags, into his pockets. They were fortunate to board a flight back to Accra, and back in Ghana, staying with his grandmother while his mother made her way to London, he would wait until night fell, sneaking down to his late grandfather's hi-fi system, playing the cassettes until they spilled out their contents. When his mother eventually sent for him, nearly a decade later, Femi would spend his spare days in record shops in Brixton, looking for second-hand copies of those albums of his childhood. Now, he can't let the music go, or rather, the music is part of him, the life he chose to keep.

'Air con's back on,' he says proudly. Then, theatrically, checks his watch. I laugh in anticipation of what's to come.

'Nam.'

'Yes, Femi.'

'I swear down your break was over five minutes ago?'

'Ah, my watch is messing around you know, Femz,' Nam says, pointing at the clock face. 'Look, it's a few hours behind.'

'I had a feeling you might say that. But I got something which will solve your time problems.'

Femi dangles a plastic black Casio in Nam's eyeline. I struggle to contain my laughter, as does Nam.

'Ah, Femi, you didn't have to do this!'

'Ah, but I did. Come on.' Femi hands him the watch, holds out the door for Nam.

'Catch you inside,' Nam says to me.

'Nah, I'm coming too. This heat.'

Back in the break room, Nam asks, 'You coming out tonight?'

Out means touching the yard only to shower and change, only to leave again. Tonight, out means being convinced to cross the river for a motive, riding the orange line to Shoreditch or further: Dalston or Hackney or London Fields. Tonight, out means skipping the cloakroom because they're playing oldies, music our parents might have danced to. Tonight, out means acknowledging that, for a sound to resonate, for us to hear it, it has to make physical contact with us, which is perhaps why the deep rumble of a bassline moves us so. Tonight, I might slap an open palm against the wall, might let my body bend to the bassline, like prostrating to something Godlike, something honest. Tonight, I might find my faith again, I might believe. And if it's going to happen, it will be where I know myself best: in the moments just before a beat drops, having been teased slowly for what feels like hours, beautiful chords sneaking through the mud of percussion, anticipation at its height, my eyes closed in reverence of this moment, gratitude that I could be taken that high, that I might scrape heaven with my outstretched hands. And it's not just me; catching another in the same motion, we might be drawn together, drawing so close our heads might touch, two Black crowns in the dim light of this ecstasy. Tonight, out means I'm content to stay in that space, just before the drums drop, in that moment where anything might be possible.

So when Nam asks me if I'm coming out tonight, the answer can only be, 'Of course.'

21.

There's rhythm happening, everywhere. The day breaks round four a.m., swaying into focus; we go from a Dalston basement, to the living room of a friend of a friend, to a party, the gathering stuck in those moments when you're willing the night to go on, when you're exhausted but your heart is still in it, your heart the reason you're clutching a plastic cup in a stranger's living room while bass beats at your chest, while melody makes you a place of comfort, the movement limited to a little two-step, a small beautiful motion from the hips, a small beautiful smile on your lips, the party tipping towards its close, the tiredness finally settling in your bones, the gentle nod of a sleeping head on the last train, or maybe the first, from east to south-east, everyone teasing as we gently separate, the sun less gracing my skin, more of a quiet embrace.

Back in Peckham, it's here too, this rhythm happening everywhere, as I take my time to wander home: in the dash of four boys dressed in black, trying to beat the bus round the curve, soft socks in sliders slapping the ground. The song of a passing car, distant bass finding a home in my ears, the low, slow rumble calling attention the way thunder might ask you to check the sky for rain. The haggling taking place at butcher's and grocer's, the disbelief that it's now three plantain for a pound, not four. In the sadness as I pass the spot where Auntie Yaa's shop used to be, where she would make sure everyone was looked after. In the joyful surprise, after I run into Uncle T, his mouth full of gold like its own sunshine. The couple I pass in the park, holding each other close, her head turned away from his, a smile on his face even as he pleads with her, *babe, I didn't mean it*. In the distance she holds him, to see if he'll come closer, because sometimes it's not enough just to say it, you have to show it too. In the conviction I share with many that this stretch, from Rye Lane to Commercial Way, is where our small world begins and ends. There's rhythm happening, everywhere; all of us like instruments, making our own music.

22.

The heat breaks the following day, and, after the night out, I take full advantage of the coolness, sleeping well into the afternoon, only waking when the sound of Mum singing drifts towards me, along with the melody of jollof being prepared: the way tomatoes are cooked so low and slow they hover somewhere between sweet and savoury, rice ready to miracle itself from pebble to pillow, the patience required its own process. I check the time before letting my stomach lead me out of bed: three p.m.

When I make my way downstairs, she's in full swing, spinning about the kitchen while gospel plays from the portable speaker I bought her for Christmas last year. The music is full and warm. I'm immediately reminded not just of the joy of praise and worship, but the theatrics, the performance, the need to express faith in that moment. From the speaker, the choir leader asks, *who has the final say?* and Mum joins the choir in responding, *Jehovah has the final say*. They go back and forth, Mum and this preacher, until the chorus arrives and all the voices join: *he makes a way, when there is no way, Jehovah has the final say*. I hover in the doorway, not wanting to disturb this moment, this magic, this freedom.

I step in as the song ends, and she pulls me into her arms, holds me close.

'You're just in time,' she says, lifting the lid from the rice. 'Shall we sit outside for a bit? It's almost ready.'

As Ray and I have grown older and spent more time away, the garden has begun to flourish, Mum's instinct to nurture finding a new home. A lemon tree droops with fruit, roses in red and white and yellow bloom, the thorns winking in the sunshine like a warning, a tomato plant leaning to the left, struggling with its own weight. We make our way to the small wooden table in the corner, and I spot strawberries and peppers, apples and apricots. We sit and I place a hand on top of Mum's, in admiration, with pride. She smiles, producing a bottle of cold Supermalt from nowhere, a soft hiss as she cracks open the lid. She places it in front of me and as I take a sip, she asks, 'How was the party?'

'How'd you know I was at a party?'

'It's in your eyes. You have the same look I had after your Auntie Gloria would drag me out, *after* a full day of work.'

'Auntie Gloria wasn't dragging you anywhere. I heard *you* were the instigator.'

'Me? Would I ever?' We both laugh at the guilt in this response. I continue to drink and I know that in the quiet which follows, Mum is thinking about her friend.

'How did you and Auntie Gloria meet?' I ask.

Mum says, when she arrived in winter she was so sure that in London, everything would be possible for her. What Mum didn't realize was that she was moving to a city in the wake of the Brixton riots and New Cross fires, a London living in the wake of explicit violence, a London in which there were people who might explicitly wish death upon her. Still, her older brother was already living here, so she quickly found accommodation halfway between New Cross and Lewisham, and work as a cleaner in Brixton. To get to work, she would walk to Lewisham bus station, riding the P4 until the last stop, her hands thrust deep in her pockets to protect from the cold. She met Auntie Gloria on the reverse of one of these journeys, on the way home at the end of a double shift. There was something familiar about the woman: Mum guessed they were around the same age, and they shared the same slow and measured rhythm. The woman sat in the seat adjacent to her, letting out an almighty sigh as she did, and they shared a smile, recognizing something in each other: two eighteen-year-olds, far from home, exhausted beyond their years. *Fei miiye mi, etomi pa*, the woman had said, perhaps without realizing. *I'm cold and so tired.* Mum understood she wasn't just saying, *I'm cold and so tired* but that *no one warned us about this cold. No one warned us it would be this hard.*

It turned out they were neighbours in more ways than one: they got off at the same stop, but were also from neighbouring suburbs in Accra, Mum's family living in West Legon, Auntie Gloria's in Achimota. Soon, the neighbours would become friends, taking the bus together when their shifts overlapped, cooking for each other when their shifts alternated. Soon, friends would become room-mates – they were spending so much time together, and why not do so and save money? And soon, room-mates would become sisters, when in March 1986, winter refusing to shift into spring, Mum having worked an eight-hour shift only to go on to another, her spirit bent, almost broken, missing my father, *miitao maya shia, I just want to go home*, Auntie Gloria presented Mum with a small gift-wrapped package: a portable cassette player she had purchased from a stall in Deptford Market the weekend before. Inside, dubbed on to the clear cassette, an hour's worth of highlife, that beautiful music with its loose, clattering production, the low hum of a bassline, a sweet and melancholic melody, music which speaks not just to the hardships of our lives, but the joys too. That beautiful music which can be a balm to the spirit, can transport us home.

They were inseparable. On Saturday nights, Mum's older brother Victor would swing by in the battered Ford he'd picked up for cheap, driving them over to wherever the party was. They would dance off the week into the early hours of the morning, coming home to sleep briefly, before heading to church, which wasn't anything but a small group of people, people who, like them, had come from Ghana and Nigeria and Senegal to London to make a new home for themselves, to make a life. On Sundays, they would gather together in someone's living room, and pray. Stood amongst the plush carpet, furniture with plastic covers, the thermostat turned up high, a customary hi-fi playing gospel in the corner, the volume low as they prayed, their prayers littered with phrases like, *where two or three are gathered, there you are in their midst*, this group of people reached towards their innermost desires, in a space they felt safe asking for anything.

From there, Auntie Gloria and Mum would make their way home, arm in arm, feeling ready for whatever the week might aim their way. And this is how they would often be, like sisters, until, many years later, Auntie Gloria passed away, suddenly, not knowing cancer was burrowing through her body. The last time we saw her, it was my eleventh birthday, a few weeks before Christmas. She brought over the trumpet Mum had bought for me but had not had time to pick up, and sang Stevie Wonder's 'Happy Birthday' until she grew hoarse. Later that day, she leaned on the kitchen counter, a little breathless. She spoke of the ache in her bones, the tiredness, the cold, but insisted all she needed was rest, just a little rest. This last part Mum doesn't mention, but she doesn't need to. Grief never ends, but we find a way to walk in the light someone has left behind, rather than living in pain's shadow.

'On that note,' Mum says, 'pastor missed you at church this week. You should come with me sometime.'

'You know I work on Sundays, Mum.'

A half-truth. Mum knows that for years, my faith has wavered, and the past few months have pushed me further away from believing. She opens her mouth to reply, to make her case, when a car pulls up out front. The slam of a door, the jingle of keys, the tuneless whistle Pops makes when he's done for the day. I gather myself and sigh. Since I dropped out of university and moved back home, Pops has done little to disguise his disappointment. He does not speak to me unless it's necessary, unless he has no choice. I know that at my age, Pops was already making enough money to save for a home of his own. I know that, because of how quickly he had to grow up, because he didn't know that period between childhood and adulthood, every move he made had to have survival in mind. There was no opportunity for him to slowly make his way towards what he might want his life to be, no opportunity to wander, to figure things out. And because of this, he expects the same of me. He expects direction, expects tangible measures of progress. Expects me to be engaged in survival, not discovery.

I stand and tell Mum I'll be in my room. I ask her to give me a shout when the rice is ready. She opens her mouth to reply, to make her case, but decides against it, letting me walk past my approaching father in silence, letting me walk away.

Later, after a subdued meal, I'm laid out in bed, watching what remains of the sun paint the ceiling gold, when Raymond appears in the doorway. I pull off my headphones as he sprawls on to his old bed, and it's like he never moved out. I struggle to reconcile the people we were and the people we are now; even as he shows me the latest photos of his son, Malachi, and describes his new sleeping pattern – non-existent – I still can't quite believe that, several months ago, around the new year, Ray had sat us all down in the living room, and told us that his girlfriend Tej was having a child, that he would be a father. I had gone towards him then, and held him, held him close, some love from the deepest place emerging. Mum had only smiled, already knowing, I suspect, in that way that mothers do. Pops grasped his eldest son's hand, proud; after landing that job at Nike, Ray becoming a father was another step in the blueprint Pops expected us to follow.

As we stood, I hugged Ray once more. I knew, as I did, that everything was changing and it would not stop: in December, I dropped out of uni and moved back into the family home; by the end of January, Raymond had moved out, to a spot in Nunhead with Tej; by the end of April, he was a father. Malachi arrived and slid straight into our lives, winning us all over, our parents included, with a wide-eyed trust, a little gurgle when he laughed, the way he could fall asleep in seconds in somebody's arms. Mum says he's more like me than Ray as a child: quiet, measured, contemplative. When I hold Malachi, we're both blood and kindred spirits, content to watch the world go by, to be immersed in its quiet beauty.

I understand there is a new life Ray is leading now, I've seen it, touched it even, but still, there is a gentle disbelief, and I wonder if this is because here, in front of me, he is unchanged. Same old Ray. When I say this to him now, he bellows with laughter.

'What did you expect? I'd become a dad and start levitating or something? This guy.'

Then we talk as we always do, always at a point of digression, conversations sprawling away and folding into one another, before finding a through line. Today, he's just come from a screening of a new Tribe Called Quest documentary, and we get to talking about films in which we can see versions of ourselves, or people we know, or our histories: *Babylon*, *Bullet Boy*, *Kidulthood*. I'm making the case for one he hasn't seen, *Burning an Illusion*, an intimate, personal glimpse of a young Black woman in London, when from downstairs, my name is called.

'I know that tone, bro,' Raymond says. 'That's sounding like an ambush.'

Sure enough, when I reach the living room, Mum sat in one chair, Pops in the other, a strained silence in the air.

'Have a seat,' Pops says. 'Have there been any updates to your . . . situation?'

I look from Mum, to Pops, and begin to explain I've been considering options, wondering what it is I want to do, where my heart is. Since Auntie Yaa's shop closed, I say, there's been something missing, and I want to fill it. I'm thinking of training to be a chef, and have managed to find some permanent work in a kitchen—

'How is that going?' Mum asks. 'How is Femi?'

Mum and Femi's mum, Dorothy, attend church together. It was her quiet word which led to Femi giving me a trial and, a month later, hiring me permanently, and on my suggestion, hiring Nam too. I tell Mum Femi has taken to both of us, walking us through the essential skills he received at culinary school: how to wield a knife, rendering sauces and stocks across the palate, how to turn dough to bread and pastries.

'That's good news—' Mum starts, before Pops cuts across her.

'How long can you stay working nothing jobs for someone else? Hm? You're shaming me.'

I want to say to him there's no shame in what I want to do – asking someone what they need, making space for them to be taken care of – but he continues before I can.

'So that's your plan? You dropped out of university to wash dishes?'

This isn't particularly sharp, but something crumples and folds in me. I want to hide. It isn't just that he doesn't believe in the possibilities I see for myself; it feels like he doesn't believe in me. I needed more from him. I wanted the space to say why I left university: I didn't feel like myself there. I didn't like the version of me, studying something I didn't have any interest in; who, after one setback, had given up on his dreams. I didn't like this me, who was insecure, and rarely at ease; who felt like he was living in a city with no community to lean on, no one to just spend some time with; who, not knowing how to dismantle his loneliness, cocooned, retreated. In that time, with only myself for company, certain memories would not leave me. The memory of Del leaving me on the pavement would not leave me. The memory of him, my father, leaving me on the pavement, would not leave me. I became even more closed off, a total eclipse. The light in me dimmed. And at that point, I felt so unwanted that I didn't even want to be with myself. I want to tell him, now, these feelings and memories pushed me up and over the brink, into a place I couldn't see any possibilities for myself. I want to tell him of Mum coming to visit, having to pull me up from the bed where I had lain for days, sadness pressing down like two hands on my shoulders. I wanted to tell him how I had cried, how I couldn't stop crying. How the only thing I could say to her was, *how come nobody wants me?* As I sit here, those hands on my shoulders return, and I want him to be more open, to allow me the space to say, *I feel broken*, and I'm slowly taking myself apart, so I might build myself up once more. And as part of this undoing, I want to ask him, why? Why, all those years ago, would you say, to your own son, *I don't need you*? I want the freedom to walk over to him, to pull him into an embrace, to be held; I want to feel the heat of his love against mine, to know if he really did love me. But more, I *need* more. I want to know my father because, facing this man, I don't know who he is, or who he was. I want him to tell me who he was at my age. I want him to tell me of movement, migration, burden, of having to choose which parts of your life to keep, which to let fall away. I want to ask him what he dreamed of, where he went to find freedom, do you know this feeling, this sadness on my shoulders?

I go to speak but he beats me to it, repeating, 'You're shaming me. I sacrificed so much for you to have a good life. Gave up on things I wanted. And you couldn't even finish your education? I didn't come to this country so my children could waste time.' He shakes his head. 'You're shaming me.'

And then, I am no longer hurt. That part of me which crumpled and folded, unfolds, stretches itself up, out, until taut, until it snaps.

'I guess we're even then,' I say.

And then, he is on his feet, because if I remember those times, on the pavement, in the car, then I know he hasn't forgotten, know he carries this shame around with him. And because anger is a necessary emotion, I choose it here. I take a step closer, letting my words linger in the space between us. Closer, still, until we're almost chest to chest, almost embracing. He's asking me to repeat what I said, and I do, again, and again, his voice beginning to rise, too, *oh, you think you're a big man, eh? You think you can talk to me anyhow?* And Raymond, hearing the commotion, appears in the doorway, and asks what's going on, but this only incenses my father further, his body bumping against mine, Ray trying to come between us, Mum saying his name, *Eric*, in that tone meant to calm, but he's so enraged he's out of our reach, shouting incoherencies until two words ring clear:

'Get out.'

'What?' I say.

'Eric—'

'I said,' his voice cracks, hoarse and brittle, like it's taking all his strength. 'I said, *get out*.'

This stills all of us. I wait for him to say something else, to say he's gone too far, but there is only silence. He retreats to his seat, brushing me with his shoulder as he does so. I gaze from Mum, to Raymond, before making up my mind.

'OK.'

'Stephen,' Mum says, 'you're not leaving until we sort this out, as a family.'

'Yeah, everyone just chill.' Ray turns to me. 'You don't need to go anywhere.'

'Ray,' I say. I pause for a moment to still the sadness threatening to overcome. 'I don't want to stay where I'm not wanted.'

This quietens them once more. My father's gaze bores into the wall. He won't look at me. With a sigh, I leave the room. I pack a bag of what I think I might need, ignoring Raymond's protests, ignoring the hurt making a home somewhere in the left side of my chest. I pick up my trumpet and put on my coat. I don't say goodbye to my father, nor can I bring myself to face my mother. I leave, walking out into the late afternoon of an early summer, when everything should be blossoming, everything should feel new and beautiful. I pray then, like I've never prayed before, asking not for money, or a job, but that this new world I'm walking out into, this new world I'm building for myself, I ask that it be constructed from peace.

23

June veers towards July, hot rain cascading down glass and brick and any person unprepared for the turn of British weather. Before he leaves for work, Nam and I have our daily argument about my contributing to the household – *at least let me cover the food*, I say – but he won't have any of it. His mum returned to Jamaica not long after Nam turned eighteen, for a short trip which became indefinite, leaving Nam alone in their house; when I left home, I didn't know what to do or where to go, or who to tell, until I bumped into Nam on Rye Lane and, hearing the sadness in the tone of my voice, the wobble in my words as they left my mouth, he encouraged me towards his place, asked me to sit at the dining table while he prepared a meal, searing chicken in a pan, just as his mum did for us, the kitchen fragrant with lemongrass. He didn't push or prod but gave me room, made space. When I was done, he insisted I crash on the sofa, and a few days later I returned from work to find my bags moved into the spare room. I've been living here ever since.

'Probably gonna head to Vanessa's after work,' he says, trying to run a comb through a dense beard. 'Back tomorrow. Maybe.'

'All right, but you're gonna miss the party.' Nam raises his eyebrows and I count out on my fingers. 'Me, Dilla, some chicken and that bottle of wine Femi gave me.'

'You are an old man.'

'I think the correct phrasing is *old soul*.'

'Sure,' he says, laughing. 'What about Annie, you don't want to invite her over?'

'Nah, nah, I just need some time to myself.' What I don't tell him is today might be the first in a long time I play my horn. There are certain moments which demand solitude, and I believe this might be one of them. Nam shrugs, coming over to embrace me, making his way towards the door, and, hesitating briefly at the sight of rain falling in sheets, heads out into the world. I run up to my room and bring the instrument downstairs before I can change my mind.

I haven't felt the same pull towards playing, and I wonder if I'm scared of what I might hear when I do; that when I lift the trumpet to my lips, I won't be able to hide. Sure enough, opening the case, sliding the mouthpiece into place, trying to make a sound, the horn shrieks, reflecting my tentative approach. I smile, remembering that, when playing, it's not just sound you're expressing, but spirit; not just music, but feeling. I try again. The tone is steadier but still low, still quiet. I close my eyes and try to remember those times I would play with Del and the guys, try to remember the space we would make for each other, try to remember the feeling of freedom, amongst the glitter of hands running across keys, the steady rhythm of percussion, the deep thrum of bass which might reach towards the depths, might build a space from an innermost desire, a space which might house us all. I play to these memories, feeling something shift a little in my spirit. I play towards that summer of 2010, when we smoked joints in the broadness of daylight, asking time to become soft-bodied, to stretch and pull and fold, when the days were endless, when we made images of our joy, letting the moments loop round and round and round. I play to those moments of shame, of turning my back on my best friend and the small worlds we used to make together. I play towards each moment of vague possibility, across the years, in various instances: at train stations, or in the dimness of a house party, or, leaning across the bar at a club, where light takes on a certain quality, falls at a particular angle, and I write into the story that this is the moment I see Del, so sure it's her by the way light clasps on to her neck, by the rhythm I recognize, even when still. I play towards the disappointment, when, looking closer, I realize it's not her, that the time for me to explain myself is not now.

I play until I am spent, until the lines dividing who I am and the sound I'm making blur and thin. I play until the feelings are causing me to wobble and shake, until it doesn't feel like I'm playing but taking part in something *spiritual*, something I didn't know I needed.

And then, placing my horn down, I do what I do at least once a week: in the name of solitude, I let a record play front to back. I've taken to relistening, because, like the moments of our lives, it's impossible to take everything in the first time. In addition to Coltrane and Davis and Sanders, I've become a disciple of Madlib and Knxwledge and Flying Lotus, artists who repurpose snippets and sounds to communicate what is urgent, those who will stretch a sound so far, just before that place where it might break.

But, regardless of where these listening sessions start, I always end up back at Dilla, back to *Donuts*. Looping back to those memories of that summer, Del and I playing the record, only to play it again, falling into that music, beautiful and warm and full, falling into that *thing* which had sat between us for so long, a closeness which was beautiful and warm and full. By the time 'The Last Donut of the Night' comes on, I'm moved from sound to spirit, from music to feeling. I always end up back at Dilla, back to the memories, because even then, surrounded by all that joy, it was impossible to take everything in the first time.

24.

In that time between lunch and dinner, when footfall has fallen, the restaurant quietens, until it's empty. There's a couple hours left of my shift when Annie texts me—

What time you finish work today? I'm in the area.

I shoot her a quick message back and the phone burns hot in my pocket while I wait for a reply. Before I can pull out my phone again, Femi beckons me over to our open grill, taking any opportunity to impart some culinary wisdom. Today, scallops. I follow his lead, patting the shellfish dry, treating with salt and pepper, letting a stick of butter sizzle in the pan. The trick, he says, is a few minutes each side, the scallops need to be charred on the outside, their centres semi-translucent. I nod as he speaks, not really hearing him, burning three scallops in a row.

'Where's your mind at today, bro? You have a date or something?' I can't make up an excuse quickly enough, and Femi pounces. 'You have a date!'

'I don't have a date. I mean, I don't really know what it is.'

'Come on, I need details, photos, what are her intentions for you, young man?' I wave him away, but he insists. 'I'm serious, bro. I think of you like my son.'

'Femi, there's ten years between us.'

'It's true, though. Plus, you're not coming to work if you're heartbroken, so I need to know.'

'It's a first date, Femz.'

We try again with the scallops, while Femi entertains me with stories of his worst first dates, including a cinema trip to Peckhamplex. It was in the weeks after he finished culinary school and he was so broke, he pre-booked the tickets because they were cheaper. They ended up having a drink beforehand in Brixton; his date suggested they skip the cinema and go back to hers, but Femi was insistent, not wanting to waste the little money he had. On arrival, the cinema was packed to capacity, and Femi had to sit separately from his date. A few minutes into the film, the stranger next to him fell asleep, and snored throughout. I laugh so hard I don't even notice my clocking-off time slide by. It's quarter past five when I burst outside to find Annie leaning against a wall, neck boughed over a book, her eyes wide behind her glasses, the light grazing across her face, a quiet on her features, a quiet I don't even want to disturb, but she senses the shift, turning, smiling as she makes her way towards me.

'What were you doing round here?'

'I had the day off work, so . . .' She shrugs.

'What do you do?'

'I work in a bar,' she says. 'Saving up to go travelling.'

'Nice,' I say. 'Where?'

'Ghana, where my family is from.'

'Mine too.'

'My parents moved back last summer, just after I was done with university. But I kinda want to see it on my own terms, you know?'

I nod. A quiet emerges as I follow her lead.

'So have you got friends round here?' I ask.

She stops us both where we walk. 'I came to see you.'

'Oh. Oh right.'

She smiles at my awkwardness. 'Shall we?'

'Where to?'

'It's a surprise.'

We make our way from south-east to east, chasing what's left of the day. On the train, trying to cram years into minutes, asking the questions we're supposed to of each other. She's the youngest of three sisters. December birthday. She's stuck in the nineties, from fashion to music. *The Miseducation of Lauryn Hill* is the only album anyone needs to own. She's not sure what she wants to do, but she's figuring it out.

As the overground slides into Canada Water, Annie tells me she was born in Ghana but moved to London when she was five. She spent most of her childhood moving across the city, across the country: Seven Sisters, Leyton, Wood Green, Barking, Milton Keynes, Telford, back to London, to where she is now, between Shoreditch and Old Street. Their family was constantly rehoused, split, separated, returned. Now she's in her twenties, she's found she wants to slow down, settle a little, rest her spirit. She would like to find a place to call home, to return to, or to a place, within herself, where home might be.

As we talk, I notice she has tattoos on the inside of both forearms. She follows my gaze and begins to explain: the thick black stalk with fronds on either side is an Adinkra symbol, *nyame nti*, meaning God's grace; the other, a Bible verse: *in my father's house, there are many mansions*. Her name means 'grace' and it was the closest thing to it, but she, like me, was brought up in the church, and even though that faith had wavered, dwindled, she wanted a reminder that it was possible to believe in something. The quote only reinforces this, meant to imply that God is everywhere, in all of us, in some way, in rhythm, in love. Everything is everything, she says, with a smile.

We hop off the train at Dalston Junction, making our way up Kingsland High Street. Around us, the evening is in limbo, that place in time where you're willing the night to begin, queues already winding across the streets for bars housed in basements, trying to magic a near-empty restaurant into existence, the checking of phones for a motive or a text message saying *come over*, each instance its own opportunity for that closeness we all value, that closeness we all need.

I continue to follow Annie's lead, until we're almost in Stoke Newington, turning off into a side road, towards a building which could be an office, or someone's home. There's a bouncer in a black bomber, and Annie greets her like kin, pulling her into her arms. She opens a heavy door and we go up a set of stairs, and another, a crowd growing closer, their sound and energy coming towards us, one more set of stairs, out into a bustling room, conversations spaced about the place. Annie makes towards the bar, squeezing into a corner and, one hand on the counter, pulls me close towards her, the warmth of her against my chest, leaning her head back so her little afro rests against my shoulder.

She takes me through to the next room, where a crowd has already begun to form around a set of instruments. There's a spare table and a single chair; she's bold and audacious, directing me to sit and making a home on my lap. We fit, like few might, like few will.

'So,' she says. 'Ife told me you were a jazz musician, so I thought . . .' She nods towards the instruments, then shrugs, a little embarrassed.

'Erm . . . yeah.' I pause, looking into my drink. 'I've kinda been away from it for a bit, so thank you.' We clink glasses, and both of us exhale with a smile, not realizing we had been holding our breath. After a few moments, she asks, 'Why jazz?'

I consider before leaning back in my chair, finding myself relaxed, finding that I don't feel the need to hide. I say, I've always felt something pushing from just under the surface of me, some instinct to express who I am, how I feel. To say, *I am here*. I grew up speaking English but being spoken to in Ga, my mother's language. Annie nods as I say this, a smile of understanding; so, emboldened, I carry on. I came to both languages through violence: the Ga I speak was warped and muted, many years ago, after British invasions, the same invasions which are the reason I speak English. Language, then, has always struck me as less tool than burden. It's always caught between somewhere, something always lost between expression and emotion. This is the reason I have always turned to sound; how a croon can signal heartbreak or a yell can speak to our elation, or a groan might speak our grief. Music, rhythm, undeniable. Sound helps us get closer to what we feel. Besides, language always has to be so exact and I never know *exactly* how I feel. Sound, and specifically, jazz and its improvisational spirit, not only allows room for error, but for this error to be something beautiful.

And then, before I can say anything more, or Annie can reply, the musicians appear on the makeshift stage, and Annie and I fold into the sound, into the moment. The sadness loosens its grip on my shoulders. I open up, unspool, surrender.

At the interval, we break outside, into the dim blue of dusk. I overhear someone else describing the music as *something spiritual*. I tell Annie, 'I didn't know I needed this.' She leans against a wall and I'm but a step away, as she takes out a joint, and hands it to me to light with a smile. After an inhale I pass it back, and we split the spliff in quiet, each slight crackle from the inhale its own comfort. Her face becomes gentle, becomes content. She looks towards the sky and says, 'There's nothing like it.'

25.

And, because it's summer and everything is possible, I'm making my way back from Annie's one morning, towards work, having fallen into an easy rhythm, where she'll pull up outside my workplace, or I outside hers, in that time where day tries to resist night's call but inevitably gives in, or when the bell marking last orders rings, and, after a shift, might head back towards mine, where I'll cook for us both while something from the nineties plays, maybe Mos Def's *Black on Both Sides*, or Jay-Z's *Reasonable Doubt*, if only for the Foxy Brown verse on 'Ain't No . . .', which never fails to get Annie moving across Nam's kitchen, while I make that fish the way Femi showed me, the way his mother showed him, and the smile on Annie's face after the first bite is worth it. Sometimes, we'll go to hers, an older block of council flats, into the lift which hums as it rises, hums like the quiet anticipation standing in the space between us, along the corridor, into her flat, through to the kitchen, through a stiff, slender door, into the coolness of the night, up a set of stairs, narrow and winding, emerging on to her roof, across it, and in a practised action, she hopping up on to the ledge and perched on the edge, one leg dangling, then two, her hands outstretched, trying to catch whatever breeze there might be with her hands, either feeling immortal, or, knowing death and believing in this moment, it can't touch her, knowing life and choosing to indulge. She'll hold out her hand, as if she is asking me to join her in a shallow of a body of water, like it is that easy. Her smile is easy and sure, so I'll take one step, then another, until my hand is in hers, until I'm approaching the ledge too, until I hook one leg over the edge of the world, until both are dangling. I'll want to say to her, *it's been a long time since I've trusted anyone like this, since I've been this open, since I've felt this kind of freedom*. But I don't know the words will suffice, so I will just smile into it all. She'll turn towards me, one leg back on the roof and I will mirror her. Between us, a selection of snacks, her pack of cigarettes, a tiny speaker. She'll play 'The World Is Yours' and, winking at me, spread her arm out across the view of the city and its blinking lights, the small worlds, the tiny pockets of infinity.

We've had one of those evenings, where we made the night familiar on her roof. Annie, in preparation for her travels, had pulled out her mum's old film camera, hoping to inherit some way of seeing the world, some way of being. She had snapped one image, two, three; it was so dark up there, I imagine when the photos come out, she and I will be but energetic blurs.

I'm making my way towards work, when a black BMW pulls up beside me on Rye Lane, a short blast of its horn, the window sliding down to reveal Uncle T. Because it's summer, he's joyous, his spirit threatening to spill out of his seat.

'I don't see you no more, you don't love me no more,' he says, his grin golden and full of mischief.

'Never that, Uncle T, never that.'

'You know I'm playing. Where to?'

I tell him I'm heading to work, and he curves towards Queens Road, telling me to wheel up the song playing. The dub shakes the body of the car, shakes our bodies as notes and voices play, delayed endlessly, destined to reverb about our ears forever. The bassline is thick and the hi-hats rattle clear but the middle of the music is bare, leaving space for us. I ask him what's playing, and he taps at a CD case tucked in the dashboard: *King Tubbys Meets Rockers Uptown*. I wheel it up again, letting the feeling of freedom loop for the short journey.

Before I get out of the car, Uncle T takes the joint from behind his ear, handing it to me.

'One for the road,' he says, 'I can't leave my nephew with nothing! But don't tell your mother.'

I smile quietly, ignoring that I haven't seen her for a couple of weeks, since I left. I try to push aside how much I miss her. She calls every night, around eleven. Unable to stick her head around my door and say goodnight, she calls instead, and when I don't pick up, will leave a voicemail, reminding me that I'm loved, that she's praying for me.

Today, Femi shows me how to make red-red. He has me wash black-eyed peas as if I'm washing rice, then fill the pot with the beans in with water, bringing to the boil, then letting them simmer until tender. We make a stew, blending onions, garlic, ginger and Scotch bonnets, frying the paste in oil, adding chopped tomatoes, letting it cut a sweet scent in the kitchen. After an hour, we combine the beans and stew, and while this mixture simmers, peel and slice plantain to be fried and served as an accompaniment. As we work, he asks what I'm up to tonight, and I say a party in Deptford, with Nam, Jeremiah and Annie.

'Annie, yeah?'

'Don't start.'

'I didn't say anything! But . . .' he says, splitting open another plantain, 'you have been spending a lot of time together.'

'I like her,' I say, shrugging. Femi smiles and continues to chop. Speaking this aloud encourages my mind's voice to echo, to wander: I like her. I like our closeness and everything in between. How quick she is to laughter, or the way she speaks with her hands when she's serious or excited. The way sometimes we'll catch each other smiling, perhaps both of us aware of the feeling of falling for one another. I like that we already have our own language, our own rhythms: the sharp quips and softness of our exchanges, both spoken and wordless; the warmth of her body against mine when night falls, how her tiny afro will nuzzle against my cheek, or the gold chains swinging from her neck will tap against my chest. I like being able to be open, vulnerable. I like that nothing feels too serious right now; that I don't have to dwell too much on the heaviness of the recent past, but can make a new future for myself, with her. I like who I am with her: secure and at ease.

Most of all, I like that our time together always feels endless, easy. That it doesn't take much to convince her to let a night go on and on; that it doesn't take much to convince me to cross the river to link up with her, so we might join together in that place where I might find my faith again, somewhere in a basement with the drums about to drop.

26.

We're barely past the brink of August when, late into the evening, Nam calls, his voice quick in the rush of static. There's
commotion on the line too, and I ask him, what's going on, is he
OK? He's good, he says, he doesn't really know what's going on,
but he's good. Says he was with Vanessa, his girlfriend, visiting his
goddaughter, somewhere between Wood Green and Tottenham
Hale. Her parents aren't blood but treat him like kin, mixing him
wicked drinks, the red punch knocking at his spirit in the heat.
As if this wasn't enough, several tightly rolled joints being passed
around the garden, he and Vanessa like stone islands. The afternoon passed by in a haze of laughter and smoke, until the edges
began to fade, until they realized how late it was and said they
needed to make a way. *We were faded like, bro, I thought I might drift
away, but made our way outside all the same.* And outside, the streets
were ablaze. Nam says, the crowd was as thick as carnival, sirens
an unwanted melody, blue lights leaning across police on horse-
back. There was a burst of fireworks, a crackle as they were lit
in the seclusion of broad darkness. Anger happening, everywhere, in the launch of a brick disappearing a glass window, in
the black plumes of smoke rising to the sky, in the fire, there's
so much fire. *Thought I was dreaming, you know. Turn on the TV,
see for yourself. We still don't really know what's going on, but we're
inside now, we're good.*

I ring off from Nam, and Mum calls as I turn on the TV. She
asks if I'm OK, if I'm at home. I let her know I'm indoors and I
can hear the heaviness in her sigh. *That poor boy*, she says, *I'm praying for his mother.* I ask her what she's talking about. She tells me
to turn on the news, so I turn up the sound.

The details are selective but, from what I can make out, a few days ago a man named Mark Duggan, who was a Black man, a husband, a father, was killed by the police. He was subjected to what is known as a hard stop: where three police cars surround and engulf with the intention to subsume those whom they suspect. This is how Mark's demise was forced upon him: enveloped and subsumed by violence. His family were not informed, and so they, along with a few hundred others, marched to Tottenham police station, looking for answers. Little to no effort was made by the police. The story his family needed was going untold. They were being erased. The crowd grew desperate, and after still being ignored, desperation morphed to necessity. I tell Mum, as another fire erupts on-screen, we're watching a group of people who are tired of being erased, tired of being forced into where they do not fit, tired of inhabiting a restless spirit, tired of crying, tired of being, tired of being murdered in the seclusion of daylight. I tell Mum, we're watching what happens when a community feel they have nothing to lose: how they turn to protest to make their voices heard. Otherwise, what else is there to do but sit in the silence? What else is there to do but wait until next time? What else is there to do but wait until it is your mother, or brother, or you?

*

I take the long way to work the next morning, cutting through the estate. Bleary-eyed, because last night I felt the anger, I felt the loss, and to sleep with anger, to sleep with grief, is not to sleep at all. I pass Uncle T's and he's by the window, beckoning towards me. He meets me on the patch of grass outside his ground-floor flat, holding a steaming mug of tea, the honey and lemon and ginger drifting from the cup. Lowers himself on to the bench Ray and I helped him assemble several summers ago. I join him and we both sigh into the quiet.

'You OK?' he asks. I shake my head. A few moments pass before he asks, 'You angry?' I nod. 'Good,' he says. 'Anger is just love in another body.'

He takes a sip of his tea before continuing. 'Looting! They're saying looting. Nobody steals rice unless they are hungry.' Another sip, he savours this one. 'History is haunting them boys, so they're out on the street, haunting the city. We're all haunted in some way. All my dance moves are my father's. I know every time you play the horn, each note is thick with all that's come before. You see what's happening, we're seeing what happens when a solo is silenced. The chorus swells and rises. I've been here before.' He counts on his fingers. 'Brixton, in '81 and '85 *and* '95, when your father and I were running around.' I'm surprised to hear this, then guilty, having not told Uncle T I left home. 'I heard. No judgement here. Sometimes you gotta make your own way.' A sad smile on his face.

'Usually, after something like this, they try to disappear us, like magic. They'll lock us up with doors which only open one way. But you see what you're feeling right now? You have to hold on to it, you hear?'

I nod and close my eyes, the sunshine resting on my eyelids. Around us, there's quiet, as if there are many of these conversations taking place, and they've all reached their collective break. To the world I'm calm like a river, but inside there's a tide shifting and sweeping, thundering against my edges. I feel like I'm on the brink, somewhere on that narrow line between anger and sadness. I want to get up from where we sit, to knock on the doors of the estate, to ask whoever I meet if they feel this too, if they've suddenly found their language to be useless, if they too don't know what to do with this extraordinary grief.

Uncle T is asking me to remember this time, to remember this anger, to remember this loss, remember the days in which the city burns with the anger complacency and deceit make. How will I ever forget?

27

Perhaps a week later, I try to turn into Raymond's road, but the road is blocked off by a handful of police cars. Approaching the boundary, I lie to avoid any back and forth, telling them I live at number 37, and they let me walk on. I pass two girls, in their late teens, who are holding each other up, mumbling words to each other to make sense out of none. I hear one say, *I can't believe it.* I hear another say, *this is gonna kill his mum.* I know how this goes: I probably won't ever know his name, or how it happened, or why it happened, but from reports, I might find out his age, find out his parents have been notified.

Since Mark Duggan's death sparked protests across London everything has changed. Not with us, in our world, because we always understood what it might mean to occupy these bodies, to be these people. No, there has been a raising of public consciousness, a shift in perception so that now every instance of violence feels like spectacle. Not least because we're reminded of Mark Duggan several times a day, on TV, or plastered across the newspapers or during one of the escalating number of stop and searches on the streets, knowing this was the path Mark was forced down, until he was brought to a halt with one last hard stop, designed to engulf and subsume. There's fear amongst us; it could've been any number of us whose parents had to be informed of their child's demise by way of the news cycle. There's anger amongst us because a witness, watching the commotion from his ninth-floor flat, described the event as an execution. And while anger is a necessary emotion, it feels more frequently misdirected; this misdirection how the death we know in multitudes multiplies further, and much of this misdirection emerges from not having *space*, from feeling like this city is closing in, trying to magic us away, encouraging our disappearance.

I noticed, in the days and weeks after the protests, each time I picked up my trumpet, my hands shook. Each note I played became wobble and shriek, the tone produced by some place deep within me, filled with ache. But at least I had this space. What happens to those who don't have the room to express their ache, are unable to tell their stories? What happens to these histories which might only be spoken?

Reaching Ray's, I knock once, twice. The door swings open. Ray has his phone tucked between neck and ear. Malachi, his baby, in his arms.

'Here,' he says, holding out his son. When he's sure of my grip, he turns back into the house.

'What—'

'Just don't drop him.' Ray disappears into the kitchen and closes the door. I kick off my shoes, careful not to shake the sleeping baby in my arms, and take a perch on the edge of the sofa in the living room. Evening approaches and soft light slides into the room through the slots in the blinds. That Wu-Tang album, *36 Chambers*, plays softly in the background. Malachi lets out a little snore. I take in the parts of his face not buried in my chest; it's like a baby Raymond is in my arms, the earnest features, the slight frown in his forehead. Now, I mirror him – Malachi – sliding into the corner of the sofa, closing my eyes, the fatigue from playing football making me sink.

When I stir awake, Ray is looming over me, his son back in his arms.

'Wake up, man,' Raymond whispers. 'This guy can't stay awake for two minutes.'

I try to stretch away the sleep. 'Didn't know Wu-Tang would have me napping.'

'It's the only thing he listens to.'

'This is the only thing your kid listens to?'

Ray shrugs. 'At least he has good taste.'

The front door goes, closing in what sounds like a practised quiet. After a few moments, Tej sticks her head into the living room, surveying the situation. She grins in my direction, but goes towards her son and Raymond first, pulling Malachi into her arms, letting her forehead rest against Ray's. They stay here for a moment, no need to speak; I know, in this way, they can feel the love they have for each other.

'Lemme take little man,' she says, 'you guys can have a conversation that isn't whispered. But don't leave without telling me how you are.' I nod and she leaves me and Ray, who signals to their front garden, which is really some misshapen concrete, a few flower beds I know Mum planted. But it's theirs.

Outside, the police cars have disappeared, the whole instance magicked away. Ray leans on the bonnet of his car, tobacco on rolling paper, a sprinkle of something extra. He takes care, considering each part of the joint, before he moves on. A ritual in praise of slower times.

'Tej know you're smoking that?'

'I'm a father, not a monk,' he says, licking the arrangement, pressing to seal.

We watch as the world moves around us, ignoring the requests for it to slow down. Everyone on their way from one motive, heading to another, or going to check in on family, trying to find food, something which might feed them, might bring some joy, some peace. A car passes us and beeps twice, three times – the acknowledgement of recognition – and we both raise a hand in greeting, despite not knowing who it is.

'How's life? Heard you got a new lady friend.'

'Nam told you?' I ask. Ray nods and holds out his hand.

'What?'

'Show me a photo then?'

'Actually—'

I pull out a pack of photos I had developed earlier, from one of the disposable cameras, and rifle through until I find one I took of Annie last week: we were at her place and she offered to cook us dinner. I asked if she needed any help and she waved me away, saying I needed to be off my feet after a shift at work. I took the opportunity to take a shower, but when I returned, Annie was stood in the middle of the kitchen, both hands laced atop her hair like a crown, shaking her head. *Truth is*, she said, *I wanted to cook and impress you but I'm so tired. We must get a takeaway*, she said, laughing, and that's when I took the photo and there she is: her brown eyes round and wide behind her pair of thick-framed glasses; the laughter moving from her mouth to her chest, through her body; that smile of hers, toothy and endearing, always putting one on my face.

Raymond inspects the image and nods.

'She's nice. You just carrying this round, yeah?'

'I just got them developed, bro.'

'Sure. So when's the wedding?'

'We're just hanging out, man. I don't really know where it's going.'

'It's all right. You don't have to know. You're young.' Ray shakes his head. 'Sounds like she's your type anyway.'

'What type? Why does everyone keep saying this?'

He shrugs, grinning. He passes me the joint, which I take between forefinger and thumb, letting the smoke trail into the dying light.

'So . . .'

'So?'

I raise my eyebrows as I inhale, feeling an ambush on the way.

'Dad's having a barbecue tomorrow and Mum told me to tell you to come.'

'Mum said that?'

'Yeah.' I hold Ray's gaze. 'OK, she asked me to convince you to come. Same thing.' I continue to smoke, but feeling my chest tighten, pass it back to Ray, who stubs it out.

'Look, I spoke to Pops.'

'And?'

'And, he's saying if you apologize—'

'If *I* apologize?'

'Nah, I told him that wasn't happening. But look, bro, how long is this gonna go on for? Something has to give.'

'Well, you let me know what that is when you work it out.'

Ray folds his arms, annoyed. 'Why are you being so difficult?'

'Why are you siding with him?'

'There's no sides here—'

'Really? Because it doesn't feel like that. Ray, you don't get it. You've always been able to do whatever. And when you've messed up or been in trouble, I've always covered for you. I've always had your back. Why won't you just have mine?'

'Bro, I've *always* got your back. Always. But I just want some peace, man. For me, for you. For Malachi.' His gaze is direct, disarming. 'You don't want that? You don't want those good times again?'

He's asking if I remember those years, when we'd spend those long summer days, Pops letting music blare from his sound system, only turning it down at the request of Mum, *Eric, my ears, it's too loud*, after which he would entertain with stories of his days as a DJ, the time he played a gig at Stratford Rex, the time he moved an entire crowd, mixing 'A Little Bit of Luck' into 'Gabriel'. He's asking if I remember when he would send us out of the house, crumpling a five-pound note into our closed fists, so he could have a few quiet hours with Mum, and, on return, he'd embrace us with so much love, we were moved to grin, moved to laugh. He's asking if I remember the good times, and this is why all this trouble with Pops hurts so much; it's not that I don't remember, but that I cannot forget.

I sigh. 'I'll try and come through. No promises.'

Ray relights the joint with an easy flick of the lighter. 'I'll see you there.'

28.

When we were teenagers, once a year, before my parents' annual trip to Ghana, Pops would suggest we have a barbecue. This was always a family affair. Together, we would try to work out how many people the garden might hold, knowing Mum and Pops would always add an extra ten on top. Ray and I would rock, paper, scissors, to see who would be woken at four a.m. to accompany Pops to Billingsgate Market, where there were rows of vendors selling fish wholesale. Raymond never lost, so he'd go to the butcher's with Mum.

I grew to love the brief quiet moments with Pops, the anticipation as we drove through the pink dawn of a London summer. We'd always detour back via McDonald's for breakfast, and once we'd reached home, Pops would set to work immediately, cutting, chopping, blending for seasoning. He'd ask me to fetch the case housing all his CDs, all his feeling rendered in sound. At this time of the day, it was always the CD with *oldies* scribbled across it in permanent marker. Mum used to tease Pops about his supposed DJing days but he knew how to arrange songs, how to conjure a mood, with Marvin Gaye, Minnie Riperton, Otis Redding. By the time Bill Withers came on, Mum in his arms, I knew what love was, what it might be.

The next day, after the meat and fish had been seasoned, veg cleaned and chopped, the barbecue itself dusted and scrubbed – an enormity of a grill, which could easily have three people manning at one time (Mum joked it was one of his midlife-crisis purchases) – after Pops had chosen what music would play, and when, the party would start. The days were often glorious, those sorts of days where the sun won't leave, and when it does, only with real reluctance, splashing trails of coloured light across the sky. Every few hours, I would return to the grill, an empty plate in hand, content already on my face. Heaps of jollof, meats grilled so perfectly they tasted sweet. By sunset, the children had run themselves ragged, and had to be run home by whichever parent volunteered, or was begrudgingly sent for, leaving a group of adults, drunk, or well on their way, and us, those who felt grown, to continue the party. And this we did, finding ways to sneak alcohol, ways to take on the looseness we were witnessing. By this time, the soul of the sixties and seventies had become the sound of the nineties, those joyful garage cuts which encouraged movement. By the time 'Rewind' came on, we were already calling for the reload, asking that we might be the people we were moments before, that we might stretch our joy towards infinity, towards forever. Before the song could start up again, we were already shouting our favourite lyrics, me facing Ray, Pops embracing us both, Mum watching on, amused, moved by the part she'd had to play in all our lives.

Those days I was sure I wanted this small world we had made to stay in this shape forever.

Instead, the world looks like this: I arrive early, knowing there might be a scene and not wanting one. I feel like a stranger in the only place I've called home, but I try to push away the apprehension, the feeling of being unwanted. I try to be open. Ray is already there, Malachi wriggling in his arms, being cooed over by my parents. There's a moment, when I'm about ten metres away and no one has seen me yet, when Malachi climbs into my father's arms and Pops cradles him close, the warmth of his grandson resting against his cheek, hand on the back of his head, Ray's hands on the small of our father's back, Mum holding her face, moved by the part she's had to play in this. That's when I take out the disposable in my pocket, snap an image. I just want this moment to stretch, pull, hold. But the flash goes, and I am an interruption. Something shifts. It's on Pops's face as he hands Malachi back to Ray and walks towards the house. He passes me but looks past me, as if I have been disappeared from his mind. I call after him, but there's no reply. He leaves me to carry the shame of a man who doesn't know how to say how he feels, or rather, doesn't know how to bridge the gap between feeling and expression, and fears trying, fears what he might find out about himself. He leaves me standing there, holding the shame of a son whose father won't speak to him. It's a beautiful day, I think, as I notice the dismay on Ray's features, Mum's struck by sadness, their faces framed by the kind of warm light which will go on and on. I can feel myself closing off, trying to protect a reopened wound. Mum comes past me now, a tender hand on my forearm, telling me, *don't go anywhere*. But I can think of nowhere I want to be less, in a space where my father doesn't have to say he doesn't want me around, since he's showing it. Elsewhere in the garden, children shriek and squeal with delight. The barbecue sends smoke to the sky, like a beacon. Bill Withers is playing, 'Can We Pretend?' The world goes on. I shrug my shoulders in Ray's direction and turn. He doesn't chase, which I'm grateful for. I don't want to make a scene. I leave my family home, quickly, through the side door in the garden. I try to leave behind this ache, which has long made a home in the left side of my chest, but I fear this is the shape of the world now. I fear it might be forever.

29.

After the barbecue, I stop going out, only leaving the house for work and the shops. I take on extra shifts and take solace in the rhythm of the work. Someone profiles Femi and the restaurant in a newspaper; he begins to open earlier and close later. At its peak, the space begins to heave, but every time I glance across the floor, I'm sure it's still mostly Peckham locals booking and dining, still those who have come from Ghana and Nigeria and Senegal, come from elsewhere to London, to make a new home for themselves, to make a life. I take solace in knowing for those drifting through the doors, the food is not just sustenance but memory, nostalgia, evidenced by snippets of conversation which carry towards us: *just like Mum used to make it* or *this tastes like home*.

One night, after closing, while Femi and I prep a vat of vegetable stock for the next day's meals, letting the mixture simmer until it cuts a warm scent across the kitchen, I tell him I'm proud of him. That what he's doing is special. I tell him, there's freedom between these walls, that he's made a place for people to eat and drink, to plot and breathe. To be. I tell him, this is what I've always wanted: a place for us, a place we could call home. He turns away from me then, but not before I see the glimmer in his eye.

I keep intending to link up with Annie, but whatever she and I are engaged in comes to a halt when, a week after the barbecue, she meets me after work and tells me she's leaving.

'Leaving where?' I ask.

'London. I'm heading to Brazil.'

'Didn't realize you would go so soon.'

She shrugs, saying, 'I feel ready now. And,' she says, smiling, 'I've been trying to convince my sisters to come, they've finally given in. All our schedules work out, so it has to be now.' She's hoping to find out more about her family history, knowing that, like mine, they arrived in London by way of Ghana, but there was a journey before that, a round trip to Brazil by way of force; this history only spoken and, if not spoken, in danger of being lost. She's hoping to hear the stories that nobody got to tell, hoping to find out more about the making of her.

'Wow. When are you back?'

'I bought a one-way ticket.'

I gaze at the ground. Annie shuffles on the spot. I don't think either of us know what to say. In a way, we're already mourning the looseness we felt in each other's presence, the freedom. I tell her she's inspired me: I've been trying to hear my own song again, picking up my trumpet almost every day, sending sounds into the world. She kisses me and the world quietens. This closeness, this brief intimacy, feels final, feels like goodbye.

*

A few days into August, Nam takes a week away with Vanessa, so it's just me. A familiar rhythm emerges, my solitude becoming loneliness. And in the name of loneliness, I continue to listen to albums front to back. I'm happiest listening to The Roots's *Things Fall Apart*, not just because I know the record well, but the energy, the beautiful melancholy, the precision of the production, the ease of its rhythm, the playful mastery of the MCs. Listening to The Roots, I'm reminded of the group efforts of those jam sessions, back in schooldays. In the sections of the record at their fullest, I'm reminded of the energy we would make in those spaces, engaging in that strange expression of improvisation where we enter those spaces and lean into the unknown. I'm reminded of the small and beautiful world we would make together at our closest, to house our energy, joy and chaos and all. When the record is done, I let it loop.

*

I'm getting ready for work when Theo calls. I hesitate for a moment, before picking up.

'Long time, bro, I—' The rest of his sentence lost in a wash of static.

'One sec, bro,' I say, knowing Nam's house is filled with dead zones. I step outside and it's still gorgeous. I perch on the front steps as Theo says he'll just get to it: 'There's a performance going on today, at Bussey Building, you know that spot? Just off Rye Lane. Doing a little jam session, improv stuff, hoping to get a weekly session, with a core and a little audience, and whoever's in the crowd can jump in. But look, I'm missing a trumpet player. I've got a mix of old crew, new crew, and I just need you. Today. Four p.m. You in?'

Theo stops talking, letting the proposition dangle in the quiet. I gaze out into the world. There's rhythm happening everywhere. Another patch of heat approaching, and in the middle of the street, a family already seeking reprieve, grabbing water balloons from a bucket, giggling as they dash, laughing as they dodge. A group of teenagers drive past, crammed into a silver Peugeot – two upfront, four in the back – one sprawled across the legs of three, trying to escape the heat, I imagine, heading towards the beach. I spot Marlon walking by, drenched in the midsummer sun, the light sliding across his face at intervals, a languorous swing in his arms. He's in his own small world, attention elsewhere – he's slowly getting back to himself, or a version of himself who might live with his father's passing, because while the grief is never over, we find a way to walk in the light someone has left behind – but when he does spot me, he crosses the road, running into the glorious space the sunlight is making. I tell Theo to hold on, as Marlon envelops me in a quick, warm embrace – 'Can't stay, on the way to work' – but taking a tender grip to my arm, he insists we link up soon.

As he walks away, I bring the phone back to my ear, and consider. I consider what it would take, after so long, since those days Theo and Del and I would gather in school rehearsal rooms and kitchens and gardens. I wonder what it would take to lift my trumpet to my lips in the presence of others, to fall into that space where I might meet myself, to lean into the unknown. I'm considering, and then I hear myself say yes. I ring off, and text Femi, asking if there's any chance I can swap for a later shift. There's something I have to do.

30

Climbing the last set of stairs, the music which had been creeping towards me, soft and muffled, spills, now whole and full, like sunlight finally rising high enough to breach the shield of the horizon; not just the music of instruments, but excitement, the music anticipation makes when left to build and gather. I feel this strange hunger, this tension in the hand holding my trumpet case, brought on by my longing. I didn't realize how much I wanted to be here again: amongst musicians, amongst those willing to play a few errant notes on the keys, or drum out a quick rhythm, to see if anyone might follow, if anyone else was willing to lean into that unknown, where anything might be possible. When I enter the room, I let out a long exhale, not realizing I had been holding my breath, not knowing how long I had been holding this feeling in. I haven't been this person in a long time, I think, as I raise my arms in greeting, quick introductions, embracing friends I haven't seen for a year, everyone back in the city for the summer. There's an impromptu jam session already happening: Amma, warming up her vocals; Robin, on the keys, following, beside her, behind her, playing chords everywhere Amma's notes are not. We're all appreciating in our own way: a quiet nod, the snaps of fingers, the raising of hands in admiration, in awe.

When I've chatted a little, I tap Theo, the drummer, asking for the toilet. He gestures in the general direction of the hallway with his drumstick. The corridor is blank. Tucked in the corner, there's a sign which I follow with confidence but somehow I'm sent in a loop, in the same corridor I started. I turn back round, looking for the set of stairs I came up, maybe there's something on the floor below—

'Stephen?'

I turn again and Del is in front of me, outside the door of the rehearsal room. I try to play it cool but the words tumble over themselves, twisting my tongue into a knot which spools into silence. In the next room, I hear Theo darting after Robin's melody. I don't need to be in the room to know her fingers are dancing over the keys, while he gives chase with a skittish, skipping beat. For a moment, the sounds take us: the pluck of guitar strings, the insistence of a kick drum, laughter from the playful pair. Del tilts her head slightly, as if to acknowledge this break in proceedings, before turning back to me. I don't know how to hold myself in these moments, where the magic of language fails to manifest itself, but she has always made it easier. I look at her, and she looks at me, her eyes roving what she can see and what she cannot. It's just us in the slender corridor. No one comes, no one goes.

It's been forever since I've seen Del. Let the space grow between us and made no attempt to close it. When I came back to London for Christmas, I had intentions of knocking for her, of trying to talk, but I could never make it all the way. Once I stood on her doorstep, fist poised in the air, ready to knock, my hand fell to my side. My shame rendered me mute, any courage deserting me.

It's been forever since I've seen Del, but here she is. Close enough that I can see the conflict of emotions on her face. Close enough that I could reach towards her and touch. After a moment, she does just this, reaching up for my shirt collar, and, where it had been crooked, plucks it straight, pulls it down, tugs it into place. Flattens with a tender palm. She's close to me, as close as can be, her hand sliding from my shoulder to rest on my chest. It's just us in the corridor. I open my mouth to speak, not knowing what I will say. She leans even closer as if to better hear what is not being said.

'Del, I need you in here real quick!'

We separate. There's a tiny wry smile on her face, as if to

acknowledge the break in proceedings. Her hand falls further, her fingers briefly grazing mine; a squeeze, she goes, and I follow.

The space we've been given to perform is on the ninth floor of a converted car park in Peckham. I climb the remaining level, to the roof, and when I emerge it's grey and heavy. London's skyline hiding behind a curtain of fog. Del is pressed against a railing at the edge of the roof, and I join her.

'Still smoking?' I say.

She laughs out some smoke. 'I'm in the process of quitting.'

'Same,' I say, pulling out a pack. We both laugh at this. 'What's the reason this time?'

'Auntie put her nose in my afro and said it smelled like a chimney.'

'How is she?'

'She's good.'

She watches me, intently. It's not quite a smile on her face. She leans against the edge, looking down. I take a short step in her direction. This closeness is familiar. Our bodies often used to do this, like two plants bending towards the light. She continues to smoke, as do I. I close my eyes. The nicotine tickles something in me.

'Remember . . .' She closes one eye, focusing, pointing in the vague direction of south-east London. 'Deptford? When was it, 2009?'

When she asks this, I know she's asking whether I remember that summer, two years ago. When it was bright and clear and warm, and we were having daily jam sessions in someone's spare box room in Deptford. She's asking if I remember when it felt like jazz was surging through London, and our own music was so clear, so sure, and we were happy and free to improvise, going from venue to venue every night, letting small performances erupt into wicked parties. She's asking if I remember the time before Michael's bar closed, and then Prince's, and then Joy's. Before we two began our own tug and pull, our own closures and ruptures.

143

She's asking if I remember us.

'I think we were happy then,' she says.

'We were. Something like that.'

Downstairs, the room we're playing in is bright and clear. There's something about live performances, specifically jazz, where players trust themselves, and take off, grazing whatever place houses their heaven. Here, the small audience eggs us on, as I curve notes from my horn into the space between each piano chord, the drums laid over and under and around, Amma, our vocalist, not saying words but her choral notes a language we have christened ourselves.

I don't know how to hold myself in these moments, but Del always makes it easier. I look at her and she looks at me. It feels like it's just us in the room.

After a moment, she reaches for one string, a second, a pluck, a pull, a tug. The rest of the music falls away and I hear something which has always been playing. I don't have to feel notes, just the rumble beneath our feet. The thrum of fingers saying, *I am your spine*. The bass is as much about the quiet as it is about the sound; in the same way a heartbeat contracts and relaxes, filling with life, a single note needs stillness to breathe. My trumpet swings loose by my side as she closes her eyes and draws inside herself, playing from something like a memory of a different time, a memory of something honest and true. She draws inside, until she is a house from which sound spills. So clear, so sure, jazz surging within her walls. She goes and I follow. She's asking if I remember, and I want to say, *how could I forget?* But I don't say anything. Not here, not now. Del opens her eyes and it's a familiar grin on her face.

I raise my trumpet to my lips and we turn this small gathering into a party.

31.

A few hours after our performance, my whole being still vibrates with something large and unknown, something which shimmers and shines, something which excites and terrifies. I snuck away shortly after the session, rushing straight to work, knowing that everything in me wanted to stay, wanted to be amongst those I had just played with, saying things like, *I didn't know I needed that* or *that was something spiritual*.

I snuck away knowing that everything in me wanted to stay, to be close to Del. I'm wondering if she noticed me sneak away, if she asked after me, or whether, from that mix of emotions I saw earlier on her face, anger took over, or disappointment. I'm wondering whether she has the same number, if I should message; what I could message her, after all this time, that could possibly suffice. That's when she comes in, flush from the heat and the excitement of our performance. She gazes around the room as if she's lost something, and spots me in a booth at the far side of the restaurant. She comes my way, balancing her double bass, and, squeezing into the booth, sits opposite. The chain with the tiny pendant still swings from her neck, with another – a tiny infinity loop – beside it. The light has made her eyes wide and open, something of a smile on her features. She's still so beautiful.

'You ran away,' she says.

'I had to get to work.'

She looks at the half-eaten meal in front of me, raising her eyebrows, as if to say, after all this time, *I know you, there's no hiding here.*

'I'm on my break,' I say. 'Besides, I didn't wanna—'

'Make things awkward? Like they are now?'

She sighs, pulling my meal towards her, and takes a slice of plantain.

'So, you work here. Theo told me where to find you.'

'Yes. Trying to get experience, work my way up to being a chef.'

'You want to be a chef? Since when?' I shrug and she continues, 'I knew you wanted to run a place but didn't realize you wanted to be a chef too. I thought you always wanted to make music.'

'I can't do both?'

She raises her hands in surrender and takes another cut of plantain, chewing, considering. Over the speakers, D'Angelo's 'Devil's Pie'. Del taps along to the bassline on the table. The sound triggers something in both of us, taking us back to last summer.

'You ran away, Stephen,' Del says quietly. She looks into her lap, the sadness pulling her features down, pulling her into herself.

'I'm sorry,' I say, knowing it won't suffice. I want to reach over to her, to take my hand in hers. I want to ask her what she's doing tonight, if she has any free time. But it's been so long, I don't know that I can. I don't know I have the courage to. But Del, knowing me, knowing what I might be feeling, fills this space.

'I'm DJing in Deptford tonight. You should come. Gonna play some stuff I've been working on.'

'You've been working on?'

'Don't sound so surprised,' she says. 'Here, move up.' She gets up and squeezes in next to me in the booth. Plugs her earphones into her phone and offers me an earbud. I slide it in, and she has to slide closer, to avoid the earphones slipping out, close enough for our knees to knock as the music starts. Close enough that I might feel her warmth, her love. In my ear, the thick pluck of her bass; atop this, a set of quiet, powerful piano chords. I tap the beat on the table: two, three, four, break, two, three, four, break, the one always silent because beginnings are hard to pin. A voice breaks through this all, and I'm about to ask whose it is when—

'Stephen.' Femi approaches our table, stress etched on his forehead. 'Sorry to pull you from your break, but I've just had to send Leonie home. Do you mind helping me in the kitchen while I find cover?'

'All good, bro.'

Femi turns to Del. 'You must be Annie.'

'I'm Del.'

'Oh.' He looks from Del to me, then back. 'Erm—'

'Femi, I'll meet you in the kitchen,' I say pointedly. Femi nods and turns away, not before mouthing *sorry* in my direction. Del and I separate, the moment broken. She slides out of the booth and I stand to face her. I open my mouth to explain but she cuts across me.

'I'll text you the details for tonight,' she says. 'You on the same number?'

'Yeah. Yeah, I am.' I go to explain once more but think better of it. 'I should get back to work.'

'OK, well . . .' She looks down, before meeting my gaze. 'Maybe I'll see you later?'

'Yeah,' I nod. 'Yeah. In a bit, Del.'

'In a bit, Stephen,' she says, some trace of a smile in her eyes. She extends a fist for me to bump, and when I do, she turns away from me, taking her double bass, turning to give a wave on her way out. I stand, rooted in the same spot, feeling a change, feeling a shift. I stand, in the wake of the space Del has left, my whole being vibrating with something unknown, something which shimmers and shines. I stand, thinking about seeing Del again tonight, feeling excited, feeling terrified.

32.

In the second half of my shift, something pulls me towards Mum. Armed with some red-red and plantain I made at the restaurant, I plan to do a doorstep drop-off – it's Friday, so I know Pops will be at the Gold Coast bar. I want to head home before I go out, but when she opens the door, Mum, on the phone, a broad smile, mouths, *don't go anywhere*, pulling me into the house. Over the speaker, I hear Auntie Yaa, who, after the heartbreak of losing her shop, after the heartbreak of being made to feel like she wasn't at home in a place she had tried to make a home, moved back to Ghana. Back home, she's thriving in the sunshine; she opened one shop, then another, and is considering more. I send over a greeting in Ga and they both laugh at me. Mum always says my Ga has come in a suitcase, like I'm a visitor in my own language. My ear can hear it all, can hear the music of my mother tongue, but my mouth won't allow for certain things, since my Ga is one that travelled, coming in Mum's suitcase.

I make for the kitchen, placing the food on the counter. Listen as Mum and Auntie Yaa go back and forth, their quick snippets like two MCs going back to back. I'm reminded of times Mum would send Ray or me out to the newsagent's, to buy a phone card, and on return, she'd scratch the strip on the back for the pin, carefully dialling in the numbers, opening a portal back home, an hour's worth of conversation, ninety minutes if she was lucky. Sometimes, when the conversation was more serious, or longing had struck and she couldn't bear to let go yet, she'd send us out again, and we'd race there and back, hoping to arrive before the call cut out, Mum not wanting the rhythm to be broken.

I take out some plates, in case Mum wants to eat. I notice, next to a small pile of letters with my name on it, a pile of photos. The one on top is a Polaroid of Mum and Pops, worn away slightly by time and distance travelled; I'd guess they are around the same age I am now. Their hands crossed over each other's laps, eyes only for one another. The next image is my father, leaning against the boot of an old Merc, in that time of day where dusk arrives, the light heavy and blue and everywhere, his hands in his pockets, one leg crossed over the other where he stands. Another of Pops cradling his hi-fi player, looking away, caught between here and there, some gold swinging from his neck, LPs scattered in stacks around him, a poster of Stevie Wonder plastered on the wall. In the next image, he's more pensive, cross-legged, poring over a newspaper. Pops and Uncle T in matching denim and blown-out jheri curls; Pops alone once more, half-lazed across his bed, gazing at two photos of Mum on his dresser; one of him against a red curtain, his shoulders relaxed, a smile not dissimilar from my own on his face. The last is outside of a church or a hall of some sort, a guitar in a loose yet sure grip swinging by his side. I stare at this one, trying to listen for his music, his rhythm. There are a few in Ghana, but most of the photos look like they were taken in London, in the late eighties, when he was beginning to build a life for himself. It's beautiful, this part of him I've never known.

From the living room, I hear Mum say to Auntie Yaa, 'I'll call you back,' and ring off. She comes into the kitchen and pulls me into a hug.

'Who is this man and why is he holding this guitar?' I say, pointing at the photos.

Mum laughs and takes the one of him clutching a guitar round its neck.

'This was when your father was in a band. With his brother, Kweku, and my brother, David. They called themselves No Wahala. Don't look so shocked. They were good! I've got some cassettes somewhere.'

'I cannot believe I've never heard about this.'

'Where do you think you got the music from? You should ask him about it.'

I raise my eyebrows, my lips pressed together, as if to say, *we both know that's not happening right now*. She doesn't push and I change the subject.

'How's Auntie Yaa?'

'She's good. I can't wait to see her.'

'When are you guys flying out?'

'The end of August, a bit later this time. But your father will come after me, sometime in September.' She opens the fridge, pulling out a pair of Supermalts for us both.

'Why?'

'He couldn't get all the time off work. There's been redundancies, and so there's a lot on him.'

'Hm,' I say, considering. 'Can I come with you?'

Mum almost drops the bottle opener in surprise. Ghana is always with me, as a way of thinking and feeling and seeing the world, but it's been years since I last touched down on its soil. Perhaps when I was eleven or twelve, when it was my grandma's – Mum's mum – ninetieth birthday. The trip often comes to me in fragments: the languorous pace the heat encourages, the way we celebrated with food and drink and music that played long into the night, the way Mum had relaxed, letting out a long exhale, not knowing she had been holding her breath.

'You want to come?'

'Yeah.'

'I always thought you didn't want anything to do with the place.'

'Nah, it's just . . . complex.' Mum nods, understanding. For Mum, every trip back home is an endeavour, in which she finds herself wrangling with who she is against who those back home think she should be. Every trip serves to close the ever-widening gap, the place she used to call home unaccepting of her in her current form. In order for her to make her way from Accra to London, she had to choose which parts of her to keep, which to let fall away. Who she was warped and shifted, as she made an attempt to settle and make a home here. With every year which passes, her roots deepen in this city, and her roots in Accra weaken, and in some cases, like when her mother or sister passed, sever. I'm even more removed from this place, it's never really been home, not really, but it is a part of me, informs how I move through the world. Besides, Ghana could never really leave me; it's in my rhythm, in my blood.

'Let's make a plan,' I say. 'I'll check ticket prices.'

'OK,' she says, nodding, smiling now. 'I can help you with the ticket.'

'You don't have to do that.'

'I want to. That way, you just have to bring yourself. Let me help, please.'

I consider Mum, the smile on her face, and I'm moved by her love. By the ability of someone to love, without question. I wonder if there was a moment when she looked at Raymond or me and understood there was something she felt for us, something in her depths, that could not be ignored.

'All right,' I say, checking the time. 'I have to cut. But I'll call you tomorrow, we can figure this out.' I kiss her on the cheek, feeling the excitement thrumming in me. My whole body vibrating, alive, I take my leave, waving goodbye over my shoulder as I do so.

33

Tonight, I touch my yard only to leave again. Tonight, I don't need to be convinced to cross the river for a motive, instead taking the 177 bus to Deptford. Tonight, there's no cloakroom but a short queue to get into the bar. Tonight, by the time I squeeze my way in, the party heaves and sways with excitement. Tonight, I acknowledge once more that, for sound to resonate, it has to make physical contact, which is perhaps why the deep rumble of the bassline moves us so. Tonight, there's rhythm happening, everywhere. I don't really know how to hold myself when I dance, but I do know how to surrender, how to let my body bend to the melody, like prostrating to something Godlike, something honest. Tonight, I might find my faith again; I might believe in my own ability to love. And if it's going to happen, it will be where I know myself best: in the moments just before the beat drops, Del mixing one of her own songs into Kyla's 'Do You Mind', the version remixed by Crazy Cousinz, her face contorted in concentration, the melody looping and looping, anticipation at its height, my eyes closed in reverence of this moment, gratitude that I could be taken that high, gratitude that, in a way, I could be close to her.

Tonight, when Del's set is done, I intend to ask if I can buy her a drink. I intend to explain myself. I intend to ask if, in the quiet which falls in a lull of conversation, she would like to make her way to the dance floor, where we might catch each other in the same motion. We might be drawn together, so close our heads might touch, two Black crowns in the dim light of this ecstasy. And in that moment, we might be eighteen again. We might be overcome.

But when she climbs out of the booth, to applause, the first person she meets, a man I don't recognize, pulls her into his arms, kisses her cheek. It feels like they might be more than friends, that there might be *something* between them, in the way their heads bend towards each other in the darkness of this moment, his hands taking tender grip of her elbow. And I know I don't have any right, since it's been so long. I know I'm being unfair, but I freeze with hurt, with shame. I might be eighteen again, in that limbo where I know how I feel about Del but don't know how she feels about me. I'm wondering what it meant, after all this time, for Del to ask me here tonight, whether she felt what I did earlier, my whole being vibrating, thrumming, light, like I might fly away. I'm thinking about asking her, but all my courage deserts me. I watch on for a few more moments, before I weave my way through the crowd, out on to the street. I walk to the bus stop, taking the 177 back to Peckham. I make the journey without any music, and when I get home, I roll a joint. I smoke until my senses leave me, until the day's edges round, until I'm in a cloud of my own haze. Right now, I don't want to remember. I only want to forget.

34.

Raymond convinces Mum to look after Malachi, so the next morning he swings by to pick me up. When he asks why I'm so quiet, I tell half a lie: I was out late last night, so I'm just gathering myself. By the time we hit Peckham Rye Park, my mood has already shifted. It's the kind of day where we'll kick a ball across one of the flatter patches of grass, with a group made of Raymond's friends and mine. We'll play and compete and watch as Jeremiah, the real player amongst us, runs his defender ragged. We'll play until Raymond has his hands on his knees, complaining about his premature old age, until my vision swims in the heat. We'll play until a lanky teenager, urged on by his friends, asks for touch of the ball in this lull between games, and one of us, more trusting, will roll it his way. The boy will take one touch, two, flicking it up – and that's when I know, in the space of time the ball hangs in the air – before booting it into the distance. He and his group will scarper. Ray will give chase, briefly, before pulling up. *Nah*, he'll say, *am I fourteen for a man to be toe punting my ball like that?* All of us will fall about laughing and even Ray will see the absurdity of what just happened. I'll volunteer to get the ball and, on the way back, close my eyes for a moment, the sun overhead a burning comfort, the little breeze a short reprieve.

When we decide there will be no more games played, we lie sprawled in the grass, considering our options, on this Saturday afternoon in August. Someone will tell a story about an escapade from last night, winding a tale until it falls apart under the weight of its own absurdity. Someone will ask what the next motive is. Someone will ask, *have you seen my phone?* Someone will express their hunger. Someone will ask, *where's Kwame today? Where's*

Tony? Where's Koby? And because our world is so small, it doesn't take long to answer these questions: Kwame says he's hungover. Tony hadn't seen his mum in a few weeks, so took her out to lunch. Koby is a question mark, which arouses suspicion because he organizes these kickabouts. Theories are posited, more questions asked. I decide to call, and I'm surprised when his wife, Ife, picks up. I hear it in the wobble of her voice. She says, she doesn't know what to do, but I should come over.

*

Koby says, he was on the way home from the pub, and they were on there, on the bus, the number 3. They were sitting at the back, on the left side, four of them. One was using the open window as an ashtray. They were playing music from their phone. They were loud in a way that wasn't joyous. Koby says, he jumped off early, because it was late, and his body could feel trouble. As he stood to get off, the bus swerved and he landed in the lap of one, his arm swinging to steady himself and knocking another, the man's joint leaving his hand, out of the window. They launched a flurry of words at him, the usual suspects, *dickhead, wasteman*. Koby says, he apologized and rushed off the bus. He didn't hear the footsteps behind him because he had his headphones on, the ones which seal out the sound to create a small world of your own. He took a shortcut, one that would cut his walk home in half, and this is when he was struck. The base of his neck. The small of his back. Target areas. Bullseye. Koby says, there were four of them and one of him, which wasn't fair. Two, maybe, because you know, he has a swing on him, remember, he used to go to Damilola Taylor Centre for that boxing session on a Tuesday? You remember, right? Please, tell me you remember. Koby says, they circled round him, making a space in which he had no space at all, the way hunters trap prey. They hit him and kicked him with might, with hate he didn't know could be held in the body, let alone expressed on his body. It lasted seconds but stretched on forever. He doesn't know if, or what, he believes, but he prayed then, harder than he ever had, that they might disappear, magic themselves away into the violence of the night. He says, he was scared then, not just of dying, but of the shadow he might leave behind. That's when they left him there, and he crawled home, clutching his ribs. He says, he made it home, into the shower. He winced as he towelled himself off. He took a bunch of painkillers and poured a measure of spirit for the ache. He says when Ife called him from her night shift, he lied and told her he was OK when he was anything but. He says, he thought about calling each of us in turn and asking whether we could drive around all night, looking for the four who were probably posted up in a park, playing music from a phone and laughing about how they could've killed him if they wanted, his life in their hands. But he said it was easier to stop resisting, to fall into sleep. Koby says, it was easier to try not to hold on, to try not to remember something he would never forget.

We stand in silence, the air heavy with things we don't like to say to each other but can never forget: to forge these worlds for each other means to collectively dream of our freedom. In the wake of violence, acute or prolonged, we ask what we might need, how we might weather this time, how we might care for each other, how we might cultivate the space which encourages honesty, which encourages surrender. How we might build a small world, where we might feel beautiful, might feel free.

We all fear the phone calls or text messages, which remind us that outside of these spaces, we are rarely safe. Remind us that dreaming is difficult when we feel like we're so close to death. Remind us that the world was not built with us in mind, and that someone, at any time, might intrude upon our homes, crumbling our walls, making dust of our foundations. It's days like these which remind us that we don't have *space*, that the city feels like it's closing in, trying to magic us away, encouraging our disappearance. Days like these remind me of Auntie Yaa's tears the day she lost her shop. Remind me of the nightmares I've had since Mark Duggan was engulfed and subsumed. Days like these remind me why my faith wavers.

But in the wake of it all, we gather. We come together and build towards our freedom. Nam asks Koby, *when was the last time you ate?* When he says, *I can't remember*, the operation begins swiftly. Nam does a shop run and, on return, I set everyone tasks, like I've seen the head chef at work do. Jimmy chops onions and vegetables, someone soaks and washes the rice, I season and flour the chicken. Raymond mixes drinks. Delilah stands beside me and quietly asks for tips on how to fry chicken. We all cheer when Tej arrives. Raymond and Jeremiah posit theories about the football – Ghana crashed out of the African Cup of Nations this year, and there were rumours of arguments in the camp, the need for payments and bonuses, special treatment. A shame, the chorus agrees. Nam plays 'The World Is Yours'; we nod our heads, rapping along. We all take pleasure in these small, brief intimacies, even if they arrived by way of disaster.

While we cook, Jeremiah tells the story of the lanky teenager at the park, and we all remember a time, not so long ago, when we were that brazen, that carefree. We invent a whole backstory for the young man, the tale spinning itself into something larger, until it falls apart of its own volition, the absurdity proving too much, all of us unable to contain our laughter. A quiet falls, interrupted only by the sputtering of chicken in oil. Someone asks if Koby wants another drink. Ife holds Koby's head close to her chest when he begins to cry. In the quiet, Jimmy makes a joke. We all laugh through our own tears, but don't rush them away. We allow each other to feel through the motion of our hurt, allow each other the space to break.

By the time the light has begun to dim in the room, the food is ready. We eat, hungrily, messily, until our hunger is sated, fingers and lips glistening. That's when Koby's voice, small and strong, says, 'I'd like to go out tonight. I'd like to dance.' No one argues with him. We ask him, once, if he's sure, and when he nods, carefully, with a smile, we do not press, knowing at the end of the night, he might say something like, *I needed that*, or *that was something spiritual*. So we gather ourselves. We make a plan to separate and regroup here, at Koby's house, in a couple of hours. We ask where, tonight, we might surrender, where we might feel beautiful, might feel free.

★

Since the one thing that can solve most of our problems is dancing, it only makes sense that here, having crossed the river to reach the bar where Vanessa, Nam's girlfriend, works, where we'd order one drink and she'd give us four, after the bell was rung for last orders, we all looked at each other, searching for another motive, searching for another place to house our motion. Jeremiah suggested a bar in New Cross, but when we arrived, taking the orange line back into south-east London, the lights were already up, the night dwindling to a close. But we had not danced, not really. Sound had not made contact, a bassline had not shaken our beings, which is to say we had not felt anything yet. We're posted up on the street, when Jeremiah, receiving a text message, waves his phone in the air like a beacon. There's something close by, he says: a pair of DJs going back to back, playing garage and grime, music we grew up with, music which might get us moving. And since the one thing that can solve most of our problems is dancing, the consideration is short. We make our way through the back streets of New Cross, towards Deptford, where we end up at the same spot I was yesterday, where my courage deserted me. But, several drinks in, shoulder to shoulder with my older brother, all of us surrendering to the possibilities of the night, all of us so open, I can only feel courage. We breach the borders of the bar, making our way into the area in front of the decks, making our way into that space, and that's when I see Del behind the decks once more, her face contorted in concentration as she slides one track into another. Raymond magics himself next to

159

me, arm around my shoulder, the disbelief in his voice, 'Is that Del?' We call her name and she recognizes us all, recognizes what we need to get us going. She doesn't miss a beat as she runs through the classics: 'Next Hype', 'Wot Do U Call It?', 'Oi'. By the time 'P's and Q's' plays, we're already calling for the track to start again, asking that we might be who we were before, we might be eighteen again, we might be open, we might be free. Later, Ray will tell me there's twenty-eight seconds before the beat drops, which means there's enough time for us to form a circle, to clear the floor, to push the edges as far as they will go. I don't even have to signal to Koby to join us; he's here, beside us, saying last night there was no space, but tonight, tonight he will indulge in the freedom found in the eye of a moshpit, the brief intimacy of being pushed up against a stranger. Soon, after the fifth or sixth reload, we begin to tire. Soon, Del's set is over, and she comes down from the booth, into the arms of friends, old and new. Soon, we're disappearing into the warmth of the summer night, dashing after the bus as it bends round the curve of the road. Soon, it's Del and I sat together on the bus, so close our knees touch. Soon, it's Rye Lane, where our small world begins and ends. Soon, we're splitting off into the night, and I'm walking away from where I live, in the direction of Del's place, until we're on her road, until we're on her doorstep, shrouded in the soft light.

She turns towards me, something of a smile on her face. I take a step closer. It's just us here. It's the quietest it's been all day, all night.

I want our heads to meet, two Black crowns in this delicate light. I want to murmur, into the endlessness of this night, *I missed you.* When we separate, I want to be open with her, I want to explain. I want—

'I'm exhausted,' she says.

The courage deserts me once more. 'I guess I'll leave you to it,' I say.

'You don't have to go.' I hesitate and she must see this flicker.

'My auntie's not home,' she adds. She takes a step closer now, and touches under my arm, tender yet firm.

'OK,' I say. She looks down at the ground, before meeting my gaze. It's so quiet. Just us. The jangle of keys, and her door is open. I exhale, and follow her inside.

35.

When I wake, the heat is still lapping at my skin. We slept atop the covers, Del drowning in a big T-shirt, me down to my boxers. We were almost on opposite sides of her bed, our only point of contact Del's long arm stretched to graze my thigh. It was too hot to be as close as we had been before. Besides, there was something growing between us, or perhaps the chasm was growing more apparent.

On our return, Del poured us each a glass of water. Not much had changed since I had been there last, except her auntie's leather sofas were a bit more heat-beaten. Otherwise, we slid into a familiar rhythm, Del putting on a record, something easy for the evening, that Coltrane and Hartman LP, the one which makes me think of two lovers, making long, meandering journeys towards each other, the one in which Hartman sings and Coltrane plays with so much faith. She made her way towards her bedroom, and I followed. Over to the far side of her room, by her window, and drew the curtains shut. She cracked the window open a little and a tiny breeze blew through. We faced each other, barely outlines in the dimness of her room.

'I'm gonna get ready for bed,' she said.

'OK.'

She turned away from me then, pulling off the big shirt she was wearing. Some light caught her skin and I caught a glimpse of those two scars, zigzagging down her back, before I turned away, to give her some privacy. My hands shook as I stripped down to my boxers, and waited. When I heard her get on to the bed, I did the same.

'So, how you been?' she asked, her voice already trailing off into sleep. I remember us both laughing at this, at how much needed to be said, at how little could be said in that moment. From the living room, Hartman and Coltrane played lush, comforting music. I wanted to stay here a little longer, to commit this moment to memory, but sleep pulled me down.

'Are you working today?' Del looks at me now, through one eye, the other scrunched shut.

I shake my head. 'I've been working overtime, so I've got a few days off.'

Her breathing deepens and I think she might be asleep, when she says, 'Food.'

I suggest a Persian cafe, on Peckham High Street. She says she's gonna shower and that if I want to, everything is where it used to be. If I need clothes, check the bottom drawer.

I pull the drawer open, and I spot several T-shirts, a short-sleeved shirt, some underwear, a couple of pairs of shorts. Clothing for the summer. I press a T-shirt to my nose and I'm surprised it doesn't have the stale smell of unworn garments.

'You've been wearing these?' I ask.

'It's not like you were,' she says, heading towards the shower.

At the cafe, I'm clumsy and shy, knocking over the sugar container with a casual sweep to the floor. Del, by contrast, appears even and calm, even in the face of this large unknown between us. I try to take her in: the rings on her hands, the tattoo I notice clasping the back of her calf, of a Black hand, clutching on to a rising balloon. She's pulled her hair back into a tight, neat bun and her eyes are still wide and open, a soft sheen like they are giving out light rather than catching it. There's still a little smile on her face, as if she knows something I don't but would be willing to share. As we order tea and some paklava, I'm still trying to notice what might have changed, hoping to close the gap between us. She watches me watching her, and blinks at me. She's never been able to wink, and her attempts always make me smile, have always reassured me.

My phone vibrates across the table. I ignore it.

'Do you want to get that?'

'It's Ray. He's probably calling to ask about you. Oh, and—' On cue, Ray messages me: *Have you lipsed her yet?* I show it to Del and she laughs. Our tea arrives and I take a deep inhale.

'So, how you been?'

She opens her mouth to reply and thinks otherwise of what she was about to say, instead taking a sip of her tea.

'I wouldn't know where to begin.'

'Anywhere,' I say.

'Well, hm. Lemme think.' She taps on the table, impatient with herself. 'I dropped out of uni, like, halfway through my first year. Wasn't for me. After the first few weeks, I was already being booked for gigs, doing studio bits. Then after a few months, I felt like I was paying to study what I was already doing.' She shrugs. 'I guess, I thought it would give me something more, something I couldn't learn onstage, but it was too rigid; I thought there would be more space, you know?'

I nod. Hearing her say this, I'm glad I didn't get in. It feels counter-intuitive to rely on a small group to decide what's good enough, to teach us how to express ourselves, when our chosen modes of expression rely on improvisation in the moment, rely on feeling. The hours I have spent alone with my instrument have been more useful; a space where I can improvise, experiment, play what's on my spirit, make music from error. A place I can be free.

'I didn't last long at uni either,' I say, 'we dropped out around the same time.'

'Copycat,' she says. 'Why did you drop out?'

I want to say, I left university because solitude became loneliness; this loneliness became oppressive, the sadness of it pressing down like two hands on my shoulders. I want to say, I felt so unwanted, I didn't want to be with myself. I want to tell her of the tears, of feeling broken. Auntie Yaa's shop had gone; she, Del, and I were not talking; I was so far from home and the community it held; my small world was crumbling, being made dust, and rather than reaching out, gathering what I could, trying to build myself anew, I let my grip loosen, let the world go on without me.

'I was really, really sad.' Del's features soften. I take a sip of my drink and turn the attention back towards her. 'What did you do afterwards?'

'Came home and listened to records for a few months. My auntie was spending more and more time in Milton Keynes and Ghana, so she wasn't bothering me, really. I think she got a new man.'

'No!'

'Yes!' She leans forward. 'His name is Robert, but I know *nothing* else about him. He's like a ghost. Anyway, that gave me some freedom to just spend some time with myself, you know. Spent some time with the instrument, really immersed in the craft. I'd head to jam sessions with the guys I'd met at uni and I dunno . . .' She pauses, considering. 'I always knew I wanted to do this, to play music, but around that time I realized, I *needed* to. I realized I only really knew myself when I was holding the bass.'

'I hear that,' I say.

'It was weird. I spent so much time alone. I wasn't really hanging out. I saw Lucy a couple weeks ago, and she was like, *you just disappeared!* It felt like that. I dunno. I just started going wherever the music would take me. Played with a lot of people, a lot of studio sessions, backing bands. Travelled *a lot*. But now, I'm back. I'm ready to do my own thing for a bit, you know. Ready to put my head down and try and,' she shrugs, 'make something. Or start to. I'm still trying to work things out. Nah, I'm trying to accept I'll always be trying to work things out.' She sits back in her chair. 'And you? How's things?'

Our food arrives. Del looks at her pastry in disdain, as I take the moment to consider what to say. Wordlessly, I ask her, what's wrong? She narrows the space between her forefinger and thumb, to signal it being smaller than she imagined, and we both try to stifle a laugh.

'So?'

'Nothing as exciting. Dropped out of uni. Came back home.'

'How are your parents?'

'Mum's good. Dad and I don't really talk.'

'You stopped talking to everyone, huh?'

'I deserve that,' I say, smiling.

'Lemme guess? *I've sacrificed all this for you and you can't even complete your education.*'

'Wow, it's like you were there.'

'That generation. It was hard for them and they don't know how to deal with that. He'll come round.'

'We'll see. I dunno. Been bouncing around jobs, working in kitchens, trying to build experience. I was so sure of this chef thing, until recently. I picked up my trumpet again and I just can't let it go. Honestly? I feel like I'm just kinda . . . floating right now.'

'Nah, you're good. You're just trying to work things out.' She smiles with her teeth, her eyes, and I can't help but do so too. I wish I had her faith.

'Your . . . erm – your music sounds so good.' When she looks puzzled, I add, 'I came to your gig, when you were DJing.'

'I know. I saw you.'

'You didn't say anything.'

'Last time I tried to say something to you . . .'

'Yeah.'

She looks into her lap, takes a deep breath.

'What happened back then?'

So I tell her, on the pavement, memory, image and possibility folded into one. I tell her the story of my father, of the ease of being discarded by someone you loved, by your own blood. I tell her, despite knowing that's not what was happening, that's what it felt like. I tell her, I knew in that moment I was being unfair – not only in that moment, but in the time after, when I let the space grow so far I couldn't see her in my life any more. I tell her I'm sorry. I let the tears fall into my food. She begins to cry too. I want to tell her, *I'm always wishing we could be more open*, and since we're here, I want to tell her the truth: that I love her. That

I've loved her since we were young. I loved her when we'd head up to central and the laughter was the spine of our days. I loved her every time I walked her home. I loved her when she was in motion, when she was still. I loved her when I recognized the way light held her neck and, in that moment, just after I called her name but before she'd turn and smile, I loved her then because the brief anticipation made me believe.

I want to tell Del that I've loved her and probably always will, but when I open my mouth, no words emerge which could suffice.

She sighs into the space I've made, the quiet heavy and tender.

'I could've done more. I kept thinking, I'll pick up the phone, I'll call this guy. One time, around Christmas, I found some of the photos of us from summer, you know on the beach. And I don't even know what came over me, I just got up and walked straight to your house, and I was ready to bang down your door. But I got there and I couldn't. I stood outside for a time. And then I just left.'

'What stopped you?'

'I thought you'd still be mad. I definitely was.' She shakes her head, and is quiet for a moment, like she's struggling for the words, like her anger is returning, which is just love in another body.

'I've never missed someone the way I missed you,' Del says.

We both look down here, our wounds still fresh. I understand that when we split away that day, we both had to mourn what we had lost.

'I do love you, Stephen,' she says. I meet her gaze, direct and sure. 'I always have, and I always will. You're my best friend. Even when you're being a bit rubbish.' She gives my hand a squeeze now and goes towards the remainder of her pastry. 'This is the part when you say it back, by the way.'

'I love you too, Del,' I say. I look into my lap and when I look up again, she's mirroring my smile.

'What now?' I ask.

She checks the time. Afternoon light leans through the glass of the cafe.

'I've got something on later. A studio session,' she adds.

'Same – well, not the studio, I gotta help Ray with some cooking and a little DIY.'

'You doing DIY?'

'I've always been good with my hands.'

Del lets out a quick laugh and even I'm surprised at my own boldness.

'I'm free this evening,' she says, coy, a palm to her face. 'You can cook me dinner. See these skills in action. But I have to warn you – I'm up early tomorrow. Heading out of London.'

'Where?'

'Brighton,' she says. 'For a gig, I'm DJing. I like it there.'

'I've never been,' I say.

'You should come. It's only forty minutes on the train.'

'I'd love to.'

'But?'

'I dunno,' I say, suddenly nervous, the feeling making my language useless. She waits for me to gather myself and I try again. 'It's been so long since we hung out.'

'So? It's just me. And you. Like we've always been.' The memories come back in a rush: our tiny histories, our brief intimacies, this small world.

'*And*,' she continues, 'you're my plus one. They'll cover travel, we can stay the night.' I open my mouth to protest, to say I'll pay my way, but knowing me so well, she beats me to it. 'You're gonna refuse a free trip, because of what?' And now she is her father, or a version of him. '*Ego? My friend, ego will be the death of you.*'

I don't need too much convincing. Already, I'm wondering how this might happen: in the morning, we might take a train from Peckham Rye to London Bridge, London Bridge to Brighton, Del magicking a set of cards to pass the time, until we first glimpse the ocean, vast and endless. We won't smooth over our closures and ruptures, but ask each other to be open, to lean towards each other, to be close. Ask that love might grow in the space between us, where we might feel beautiful, where we might feel free.

'You trust me, right?' she asks, interrupting my dream of possibilities. I nod. 'Well, then.'

'All right,' I say, grinning. 'Let's go to Brighton.'

36.

'Why are you playing this *old-man* music?' Ray asks, as we drive. 'They Say It's Wonderful', John Coltrane and Johnny Hartman, the radio tuned to Jazz FM, me tapping along to the thick bassline as we slide down several residential streets, hoping to beat the pockets of Sunday traffic. We're heading towards Nunhead, to Sonny's little storefront, which, since Auntie Yaa's shop closed, is the only place to get food from back home at decent prices.

Ray had grand plans for this Sunday afternoon: seeing how hard a time Tej had been having at work, the long days teaching at a primary school beginning to take their toll, he had arranged to have Malachi stay at our grandparents' for the weekend. In the morning, as soon as Tej had left to see her grandparents, he'd gone from room to room, cleaning and rearranging their house, which since Malachi arrived had become less their place of pride and more like their son's playground. The final piece would be a home-cooked meal of Tej's favourite, red-red. Ray had asked for the recipe a few days before; I hadn't even made it past the stage of washing the black-eyed peas before he was shaking his head, both of us laughing.

'I will owe you *forever* if you come over and cook for me,' he had said.

'For you, no; for Tej, always.'

We turn on to the street and park in front of the shop. Ray pulls up the handbrake but keeps the engine running. 'All right, you stay here, I'll be right back.'

'You're leaving me in the car?'

'Yeah, to keep watch,' he says, pointing to the traffic warden posted up on the corner of the road.

'Why don't I just go in?'

'Because you're too friendly and have no sense of time. He'll have written me fifteen tickets by the time you come back. Chill in here and listen to your old-man music.'

Ray leaves the car. I slide down both passenger and driver windows, willing a breeze to blow through the vehicle. As I do, a pair of teenagers wobble by on a bicycle, he pedalling hard, trying to keep the bike from toppling over, she perched on the handlebars, both letting out squeals of delight. Five minutes pass, then ten. Jazz FM seems to be playing most songs from the John Coltrane and Johnny Hartman album, and I have no complaints. I let my mind drift, thinking about taking this trip to Brighton with Del tomorrow, let my mind wander back to the last trips we took to the beach, that endless summer.

All the while, I watch the traffic warden pace up and down this short strip. After his fourth or fifth time passing Ray's car, a little frown appears on his face. Not wanting to risk a ticket, I beep the horn, once, twice, willing Ray to emerge from the shop. No movement. I beep again, and Ray emerges, but he's not alone. Pops is beside him, his hand on Ray's shoulder. They turn to face each other and move like mirrors – the same music to their movements, the way they might tap at your arm or chest to push at a point or exaggerate their shock with both hands to their head, how laughter might twitch on the edge of their lips before it surfaces or the way their gaze can convey their care and concern. They continue to talk for a minute or so more before Ray pulls Pops into an embrace. Pops turns towards his car and doesn't glance my way, or maybe he didn't even clock I was there. Maybe Ray didn't mention my presence. Whatever the reason, the hurt is the same. That ache in my left side returns, or maybe it didn't leave. I wrangle with the jealousy I feel here, seeing how Pops and Ray embraced, knowing my father hasn't held me like that for some time. Knowing he probably won't for the foreseeable. And it's not Ray's fault – sure, in the past, whenever there were disagreements with our parents, especially when it came to Pops,

Ray and I were always allies. But I can't blame him for not changing his relationship with our father.

I steady my breathing with a deep sigh as Ray gets back into the car and releases the handbrake, saying, 'I didn't realize—'

'You don't have to explain, bro. Not your fault.'

Ray shrugs and reaches into one of the bags, bringing out two bottles of Fanta – not the canned version, but the sweet, syrupy stuff which comes in a glass bottle, which we've always known as Ghana Fanta. A peace offering.

'Didn't know they sold that here,' I say.

'Sonny just got some in,' Ray says. I pop off the caps with the bottle opener attached to my keys and hand him one. We clink bottles and both take a swig. He twists the dial on the radio, turning Ahmad Jamal's 'I Love Music' up.

'This old-man music isn't bad,' Ray jokes. I offer him a quiet smile. My breathing steadies as we pull out, but even as we make our way back to Ray's, the ache remains.

37

Peckham Rye to London Bridge, London Bridge to Brighton, each stop announced over the tannoy bringing us closer to our own excitement. We play cards to pass the time which is rushing past us anyway, the glimpse of the ocean appearing as if we blinked and it's there, like magic.

'Your phone is ringing,' Del says.

'It's Mum,' I say, without checking. 'She calls around this time.'

'Every day?'

'Every day. Morning and evening. She'll leave a voicemail, saying she loves me, she's praying for me.'

'I miss your mum.'

'I'm sure she misses you.'

'What's it been like since you left home?'

'Hard. Lonely. I miss Mum a lot. But we're going to Ghana together, in a couple of weeks.'

'I went to Ghana,' Del says. 'In February. Saved up what I had made from gigging and just went. I got there and asked my cousin to drive me straight from Accra to Cape Coast, where my mum was from. Pulled up to the house, it was midday, felt like the sun was beating me up. It's like this big compound, and every building is yellow. And we're standing there, wondering if we should go in, and an older woman, maybe in her fifties, appears from nowhere, almost like magic. And she's moving through the walkway dividing up the buildings, coming towards us, but before she reaches, she turns into another corridor and disappears.'

'Just like that?'

'Just like that. When we got back to Accra, I asked one of my aunties who it could've been, and she said no one's lived there for years.'

'Who'd you think it was?'

She shrugs, smiling. 'A ghost. A kind spirit. I dunno.'

'How d'you feel when you got back?'

'Different. I've always known who I was but I didn't really know where I came from. Got to hear all these stories about Mum and Dad, things I've never known. Got to walk the streets they grew up on, see where they hung out. And the photos! You know how we like to take photos – I was looking over albums from the forties and fifties. It was a way for me to remember a time I wasn't part of but, in a way, is part of me. I came back here and the grief didn't feel like a shadow any more, it felt like light.' Del sighs, draws a little closer to me. 'We're here.'

We check into the hotel, and Del tells me a friend will meet us here, to help her out with her hair. The humidity, she says, is having its way. When Fatima arrives, she greets Del like they are sisters, takes a hand to Del's scalp, a heavy sigh from her, as if to say, *I understand.*

'You don't have to stay,' Del says. 'This won't be long.'

We're not far from the water, and I follow its call, sliding down the stones towards where shore meets sea. I stand here for a moment, letting the water lap at my feet, taken by the rhythm of something unquestionable. The ebb and flow, the steady crash of wave on land, slow drift of the tide, the strong pull of the tow. It's been so long since I was this still, since I was this close to quiet. I let it wash over me, like music might; and like music does, I let it take me elsewhere, inward, towards myself. The summer has rushed past, and I try to grab at these new memories: Koby and Ife's wedding, Femi's restaurant, Nam's generosity, Annie's rooftop, Dilla's loops, my father's anger, my mother's love, solitude and loneliness, the city haunted, anger and protest and violence and grief, a sense of loss, light and shadow, sound and spirit, jazz as a way of being, Del's return. I'm overcome by all that's sitting under the surface, but I don't push it away. It's been so long since I was this open and I take a moment, wanting to commit this feeling to memory.

When I return, they're still going, Fatima on the edge of a straight-backed chair, Del settled between her legs, her head tilted back, just a little. Fatima moves quickly, making the process look effortless. It's fiddly work and I watch as her fingers dance a nimble number across Del's scalp, the rhythm steady, pull and twist, pull and twist. I want to commit this to memory, to be able to hold this moment, forever. I take out my disposable and make an image, a smile on Del's face as I lower the camera from my eye. A smile on mine too, moved I could witness this brief intimacy.

We head to lunch down by the beachfront, keeping an eye out for seagulls, which we're told might swoop and steal any food not protected by a lid. As we eat, I ask Del what she plays in her DJ sets.

'It depends,' she says, mouth half-full. 'People usually want something specific: oldies, or garage, or disco – getting a lot of disco requests of late. So I feel like I have to always be digging, always getting new stuff in. We should go to a record shop while we're here too.'

'Let's do it.'

'Tonight, it's a private function but I've got free rein. The guy running the party goes uni here but he's from ends, he lives in New Cross. He said keep it mostly hip-hop, so I wanna play some of this new Jay-Z and Kanye.' When she doesn't get the reaction she wants, she prods further. 'The *Watch the Throne* record.' I shake my head.

'Man. Used to be you putting me on to new music! How times have changed.' She sets her fork down. 'I'm so glad you're here. It's cool to do what you love but it can be a bit lonely sometimes.'

'Me too,' I say. 'Me too.'

'Stephen?' I give her my attention. 'Are you seeing anyone?' She must notice my face shift, because she laughs, saying, 'This isn't a trap.'

'No. Well, I was, sort of.'

'Annie?'

'Yeah. Annie.' I hold her gaze, daring her to ask more.

'And?'

'She left. Went travelling. We cut it off. You?'

She shakes her head. 'Same boat. I was, but we cut it off.'

After a few moments of trying to play it cool, I can't help myself. 'Why? Why d'you ask?'

'I'm trying to figure out what this thing is,' she says, I think referring to the shape of the thing growing between us, growing us closer.

'And you waited until after you invited me to another city to ask this?'

She doesn't reply, only smiling, her face wide open, like an invitation.

Back at the hotel, sitting on the bed, Del grazes my forearm and it's like a soft scratch of a needle on a record at the beginning, at the end, looping, endlessly, and then there's rhythm happening, everywhere, in the slowness of our first kiss in a year, neither of us wanting to pull away, until we do, and then we're undressing at pace, nearing frenzy, ecstasy waiting somewhere for us both. We go to that place, where only sounds might suffice, that place where desire makes a home for our longing. Del and I fall back on to the bed, our foreheads meeting, two Black crowns in the haze of our own joy. I kiss her, as we grow closer and closer, her fingers splayed against the broadness of my back, bunched fists against the bedsheets. A familiar rhythm. Wherever I am, Del's right there, her head tucked into the warmth of my shoulder, muffling her *ah*, her *hum*, her *gasp*. We approach the brink and go over the edge, where the outcome is unknown. It's so quiet here. It's just us. It's like someone has turned down the volume, so we might better hear what's being said. That's when she says, *I'm close*, and I know I am too. I take a knot of her fresh braids in fist and she gasps, eyes ablaze, the graze of her finger on skin becoming a scratch, our whole beings overcome, closer, still, rhythm, happening, everywhere, until for a few moments, we let everything else cease to exist. It's just us, in our small world.

By the time we leave the hotel, giggly and giddy, we walk along the streets at dusk, singing the chorus from the Nas song; we point to each other, in response singing *the world is yours*.

Around us, the city comes into focus. Wine spins in glasses, people spill from bars, cigarettes tucked between fore and middle fingers, whispered conversations in small crowds. Around us, the people are beautiful and loving and tired and joyous. People are living. The energy of the city fizzes, reflecting ours.

Del and I split at the venue: while she does a soundcheck, she sends me towards the shops, for tobacco and a pack of Haribo. I detour on the way back, making my way to the quiet of the beachfront once more. The energy is different now – blue of moonlight, the murmur and buzz of those on their way to dance, a summer night in full swing – but no less vast, no less beautiful. As I'm thinking about heading back, my phone buzzes in my pocket. It's Ray. I pick up, pressing his voice to my ear.

'Yo, bro,' I say. 'What you saying?'

'Where are you?'

'In Brighton. With Del. Remember I told you we were heading down?'

He doesn't say anything but I can hear his breathing, quiet and heavy.

'Ray, you good?'

'You need to come home, bro. It's Mum.'

The world quietens around me. I feel like my head is being held underwater, which is to say, I'm drowning. The city becomes a blur. I lose my faith where I stand. Raymond is still talking. He's saying the right things, he's using his logic. He's saying, *we will have to make decisions, quickly*. He's saying, *we'll have to work out if we can afford a funeral*. He's saying, *you need to come home, bro*. I'm thinking about the ache making a house in the left side of my chest, which is to say, I'm thinking of heartbreak. Ray's voice continues to echo: *heart attack, bro. She didn't make it.* He keeps talking but I don't hear another word. Around me, the city blurs. The mourning is immediate. I open my mouth to call for someone, but there's no voice, no rhythm, no music. I open my mouth to call for someone, but there's no one here to tend to my grief. I open my mouth to call for someone, but the world is so quiet now. I'm all alone.

PART THREE

Free

2012

38.

Since the one thing which might solve our problems is dancing, it only makes sense that here, long after my mother's body and spirit separate, long after we lower her into the ground and we're invited to take some crumbling earth in a closed fist, letting it scatter on the casket like light rain, each fistful of soil like a soft hand against a door, knocking, knocking, knocking – knowing there can be no answer – long after I've stopped saying *thank you* to those who say, *I'm sorry for your loss*, long after the grief has made my language useless, only ahs and gasps and mournful hums slipping from my lips; long after I lose my language and my faith in one quick motion, long after a Christmas in which I cry more than I smile; long after spring arrives, Auntie Yaa calls and, hearing the wobble in my voice, convinces me to fly to Ghana, to take the trip I was meant to take with my mother.

I ask Femi and he gives me half of June and all of July off work, knowing the trip won't rid me of my grief, but might begin to shift something. I arrive several hours early to the airport, out of nerves. The last time I left the country was almost a decade before, a trip to Ghana when I was eleven or twelve, and as the world rushes around me where I stand, that trip comes back to me in fragments: the round of applause which broke out as the plane landed. The joy of my grandma, being able to feel my face in her hands, rather than pressing the shadow of my voice over a dusty phone line to her ear. The fight my father found himself in the eye of, that trip being the first since both his parents passed in quick succession, and unable to contain this grief, he let it find another home in anger, and he let this anger manifest, multiply, misdirect—

But before I can dwell, before I can try to remember what I've forgotten, pushed away, they announce the gate. And, long after the swoop in my stomach at take-off, the slight bump on landing, followed by pockets of applause and *praise God, we've made it*, the immediate heat, each sly bribe to an official, notes clasped in the folds of documents, the roulette of the baggage carousel, the folded arms of customs officers, who, on seeing the glint of my trumpet when they ask me to open my case, tell me to close it quickly, in case another officer makes his or her slow lope towards us, eyes gleaming with greed, asking, *what have you brought for me?* Long after this, I burst out of the airport, into the arms of Auntie Yaa, who greets me like her own, her smile still a warm glint in the darkness, still the smooth scent of shea butter on her skin. We make the journey to her place in Kaneshie, the streets vague and familiar, like the way a memory hovers at the edge of our consciousness, just out of reach, with no real form, just feeling.

I've been in Accra a few days, slipping into an easy routine, waking early, sleeping late, eating more than I've done in months: kontomire and plantain, fufu and soup, second and third servings of waakye. One evening, Auntie Yaa taps me on the shoulder, telling me to get dressed, to wear shoes I can move in. We drive over to North Ridge, where we meet a couple of my older cousins, Nii and Kwabena, both all limbs and attentive eyes, both quick to smile. It's been a decade, but they treat me like it's been a week, a short embrace, that handshake which ends with a click of fingers. They gesture for us to head into the bar, Club +223, where there's a band onstage already, playing funk covers: I hear the sultry growl of James Brown, the alluring glitter of Rick James. We settle on a table near the front, just as the music is beginning to speed up, the rhythms looping on themselves. I see something shift in Nii, some hunger in his eyes, the same smile on his lips. He gestures for us to rise and since the one thing which might solve our problems is dancing, I don't hesitate, both of us making our way into the area in front of the band. I breach the borders of my sadness, letting myself spill into the space we share, our motion tender and vivid, the rhythm taking us higher, elsewhere, past the selves we recognize to those parts we don't always get to confront, those honest parts of ourselves, and with the drummer playing faster still, we go higher, further, faster. I let myself be split open like fruit, ripe and ready, everything which had been hovering below my surface rising, flowing, spilling, deluge, the sadness, the grief, the mourning. I want to say, *I have lost, I have hurt, I have ached.* For so long, this pain I've carried has made me feel ugly, like I have no place in this world, but right now, as I take a step for each one Nii does, in this church we've built for each other, both of us flinging our arms about as if caught in rapture, in prayer, I feel so beautiful, so free. Later, he'll tell me the rhythm the drummer makes comes from a technique known as *sikyi*, an Ashanti drumline meant to reflect the flirtation between men and women, the way desire might spill into space, but the only thing which matters to me in these moments is how long this song might last, how long I can stretch this freedom.

Soon, by the third encore, I've sweated through my shirt and I'm all joy, all belief. Soon, we're breaking out of this small world and into another, piling into Auntie Yaa's car, heading towards a *kyinkyinga*, an outdoor kebab joint on the corner, where sliced yam fries in a pot of oil, kebab skewers sputter on the grill. Soon, my cousins are teasing me, an arm around my shoulder, a tap on my chest, *You showed us you were a true Ghana boy tonight! Those moves!* Soon, too soon, it's time to split, Auntie Yaa speeding through the mostly deserted streets of Accra's suburbs. And since it's Friday night, as we drop my cousins off, we bump fists and say, *soon*, which isn't goodbye, but a promise that we'll link up again, tomorrow if we can wrangle it, and we'll feel just as alive.

39.

I wake to the call to prayer competing with a crowing rooster, the rooster quickly giving in. I start the day as I always do: listening to the last voicemail Mum left me. I put my phone on speaker and it's like her spirit is in the room, telling me how excited she is for our trip, listing our potential itinerary: Labadi beach, where she met my father; the botanical gardens at Aburi, which she describes as the only place she's known true quiet; and Cape Coast, not only to see the castle, but the house she was born in before she moved to Accra. Today, Auntie Yaa and Nii have agreed to take me to the latter, which means an early start if we are to beat the traffic. Nii arrives not long after I've showered, and after I cook them both eggs, we set off into that strange hour before day arrives.

Already, Accra is alive: the heat hums like a low drone. Men pack into the trailers of trucks, heading towards work. Motorbikes swerve through the traffic – taxis, Auntie Yaa says. I notice most people hold on to two handles jutting out of the sides of the vehicle, but some will allow the intimacy of placing their lives in the grasp of another. I notice a tight grip around the waist as another swerves by, barely missing a young woman selling from a bowl of boiled eggs, the rider turning back to smile an apology. Those selling goods are planted at intervals on the street, or will swarm vehicles at traffic lights, with bofrot or koko, handkerchiefs or iced water. At police barricades, some cars are told to pull over for a brief stop, their real interest the lining of their pockets as opposed to crime.

Soon, day breaks without incident, as if it had never been night. Nii drives quickly, leaning forward, almost out of his seat; I think it's because he's willing the car on, but later, Auntie Yaa tells me it's because he's supposed to be wearing glasses, and in a certain light the road is a slight blur. As we drive, Nii plays the music he remembers from the few years he lived in Milton Keynes, between 2003 and 2006, for university. He runs through Nelly and Mary J. Blige and Jadakiss, while we talk about MTV Base, how those music videos on loops were like small movies, worlds built on-screen which reflected our own. We laugh about how Sean Paul briefly had the world in a joyous headlock, his music spilling from every open window, and his videos, how they were like the parties our fathers organized.

I drift off as we hit the motorway and, when I wake, Nii has slowed and the roads have narrowed. It's a little quieter than Accra, but there's a presence I can feel, even being inside the car, some quiet hum, something drawing me in. We drive for a few more minutes before Auntie signals he should park. We cross the road, heading towards a towering compound which casts us in shade.

'This is it,' she says.

It's enormous, but without any life, like the cavern of a heart after it's stopped beating.

'Can we go in?' I ask.

'I don't know who lives here any more. If there's anyone, it will be some distant family . . .' She exchanges a glance with Nii, who nods her way, looking around for any observers. Auntie Yaa reaches over and undoes the lock, the gate swinging open with a low creak. Auntie enters and I follow.

We could be in another world. There are several houses in the compound and they each loom in silence. The hush is its own sort of strange beauty, a strange and painful beauty, knowing if no one is here, they have said goodbye to this house, through circumstance or death. There are still signs of life scattered about: a washing line, boughed, a little slack in the middle; a traditional broom propped up against a wall; a couple of plastic buckets disfigured by the sunshine. But no voices, no music, no rhythm.

I follow Auntie Yaa, as she leads me from memory, each footstep echoing about the place, until we come to what appears to be the largest house. We take the back door, through what was the kitchen, up the stairs, and then we're in a space painted the same colour as the house, a pale ivory.

'This was your mum's room. Mine is just down the hall. We came back here to stay a few times when school was out.'

The room is bare, aside from the wardrobe built into the wall. I open each door but each cabinet is empty. I take a seat on the floor and gaze about the space, trying to imagine my mother as a child, piecing this vision together from what I've seen in photos, what I've heard from her older sisters: a strong, defiant gaze; often stubborn but always kind; the kind of person you're drawn towards, a presence, a light. I think about what she left behind, and how I'm trying desperately to avoid the shadow of grief, wanting to walk in the brightness of her spirit.

'You hear that?' Soft, faint, unmistakable: footsteps.

'Hello!' Auntie Yaa calls out, loud as she can.

'Auntie Yaa!' I hiss.

'What?' We wait a few more seconds. There's silence. I expect several people to come running in, demanding our reason for the intrusion, or without words, their anger speaking for them. But there's nothing.

'Your mother must've come to visit. Come,' Auntie Yaa says with a smile, extending a hand to help me up. 'Let's go see the castle.'

40.

Our guide at Cape Coast castle, Thomas, is sweating. He's standing in the shade the Door of No Return makes. He has already led Auntie Yaa, Nii and me into the darkness of a space labelled *Male Slave Dungeon*, explained that we're standing in the aftermath of disaster. His face crumpled when describing the proximity of a pit, giving view to said dungeon, the entrance of which was next to the classroom. He implied our language is a burden, switching to Twi, then Ga, for my benefit, while trying to explain the cruelty the slave owners wanted their children to inherit. He took us to the master's quarters, several floors above, where high ceilings let wind billow through the space, a welcome reprieve from the already blistering heat. From the window, we can see another castle in the distance, Elmina, which he told us was constructed by the Portuguese, taken by the Dutch, then the British. He told us, these castles are but two of many dotted across Ghana, across West Africa, which were first used to trade goods, before being used to trade humans and lives. He sighed then, and opened his mouth to say something, but could not. He tried again, I imagine, thinking in Twi, then in Ga, but there was no voice, no music, no rhythm. Thomas was trying to express what cannot be expressed. He was trying to say, *this is our pain, this is the making of us*. He was trying to say, *we are standing in the aftermath of disaster*. He was trying to fight the inability to speak with his desire to. I think this happens often to many of us, this language we have less tool than burden, caught between somewhere, something lost between expression and emotion. Sometimes, silence in the face of trauma is useful. It allows time for those grieving to mourn, to organize, for a feeling to lose its haze and ossify, and to try to give words to what has been done unto us. And if not words, then sound, music, rhythm, an ah, a gasp, a hum, a groan, spillage, deluge. But a continued silence, this might consume us.

Eventually, Thomas shook his head and led us deeper into the castle before we emerged back out into the open. Towards a door half my height, on the other side of which lay a tiny space, where rebels and revolts were squeezed into, where they rarely emerged from. We all, Thomas included, refused to enter, knowing that this is where restless, motionless spirits dwell. By this time, we're tired. It's midday, and the heat is unrelenting. The silence is consuming. Thomas can see this, can feel this, and takes us to the Door of No Return, where he now stands, sweating. He wipes his brow with a sodden handkerchief, explaining this was where Black people lost their names. This is where we lost ourselves, or rather, where we were taken. After walking through the doorway, you were not expected to make your way back. Thomas invites us now to break this notion, to come through the doorway and make our way back. He undoes the latch and a deluge of sunshine spills through the open door. Auntie Yaa goes first, followed by Nii. As I come through, I glimpse the ocean, hazy and slow-moving, each movement rising from a knowledge so deep it's like a secret. Down by the water, fishermen pull their boats in, or push them out, ready to cast their nets. Two boys, wearing old football shirts, sit on a ledge overlooking the water, sharing a lunch, in their own small world. I look from Auntie Yaa to Nii to Thomas, and wonder if they too are feeling what I cannot give name to, if they too are fighting the inability to cry with the desire to do so. I wonder if they too are struggling to comprehend such immense loss, such extraordinary grief. And I'm thinking, how does one begin to comprehend such loss when it does not stop? I'm thinking of fire and anger and violence. I'm thinking of Tottenham and Brixton and Peckham. I'm thinking of all the places we, as Black people, are made to disappear.

I go to speak but I cannot. I try again in Ga, but there is no voice, no music, no rhythm. I stay silent and walk back through the door, back to the world as we know it, ready to stand once more in the aftermath of disaster, in the wake of our pain.

It takes us hours to make our way back to Accra, traffic almost at a standstill. It's late afternoon by the time we're driving through Jamestown, where my father's family is from. Auntie Yaa points to the port, which has been bought up by foreign investment; and rather than investing in the existing community, asking what it is they need, the people have been sent away, the foundations of their lives made dust for the sake of capital. Where are my father's family? I ask, and Auntie Yaa says simply, scattered. When she tells me this, the grief of the day collapses in on itself, immense and extraordinary. An anger hums inside me, stoked by some knowledge so deep it's a secret. I remember what Uncle T said about anger, how it's just love in another body, but right now, it doesn't feel like that, it feels like something rotten rattling about my body, it feels like the thing which could consume me. If only I could speak, if only I could speak. But there is no voice, no music, no rhythm. I stay silent, even when we arrive home and Auntie Yaa suggests we go out to eat, go out to drink, I stay silent, even though all I want to do is sleep.

We arrive at the bar at seven p.m. By eight, my words are a blur; an hour later, vision a slur. That's when I fall for the first time, the barstool wobbling from underneath me. Hands snatch at my shoulders, and I brush them away with the same speed, insisting I'm fine, sure of it, everyone around me sure I'm not. I take my seat, my features dull and slack in the low light of the bar, a man stripped of his gleam, a man who does not believe. I just want to lie down, I think, but I'm always mourning so I don't sleep. If only I could speak, if only I could speak.

Nii hears a song which moves something in him and gestures for us to dance, and since the alcohol is dizzying around my body, I'm bold and audacious, flinging my limbs with what I mistake for freedom, all my dance moves my father's, and his father's before that, because the dead never leave. They're in the slink of our hips, the swing of our limbs, in our whispers, our screams, our ecstasy. I take out my phone to take a picture of us both, when someone knocks it out of my hand. I see it shatter. When I pick it up, I break, a flare of temperature; I look for the source and swing and miss, Nii's hands reaching out to me as I trip. Somewhere in the near distance, the music has stopped. I'm shaking my head and pointing at my phone. I can't stop shaking. I can't stop saying, *there are messages here I need. There's a voice on this phone I'll never hear again.*

41.

If only I could've spoken, then perhaps I wouldn't be lying here, my body pressed to the bed, my tongue thick with heat and thirst, light filtering through the slots in the blinds. I look for some indication of the time and find my phone on the bedside table, the cracked screen a souvenir of last night's madness. I press and hold the On button, hoping for some magic.

'I tried last night but I don't think it'll work.' Auntie Yaa stands in the doorway, her smile a little muted.

'I'm sorry,' I say.

She shakes her head. 'I think you needed to get it out.'

'I don't remember much.'

She comes in and perches on the edge of the bed, offering me a bottle of water. I drink, slowly, as she tells me, after I had fallen, I got up once more and I screamed, grunted, groaned, pleading with whoever would listen, asking who could fix my phone. And when I felt no one could help, I hummed and whimpered, collapsing where I stood. I wouldn't move. Nii had to hook his arms under my shoulders, another young man holding my legs, and together they took me to the car, driving me home.

'There was just so much . . . noise in me. And I couldn't get it out.'

Auntie Yaa takes my hand now, presses it between both of hers. In the seclusion of this soft light, I cry quietly, allowing myself to rupture and break in this space.

'I have to go to the shop,' she says after a while. 'Will you be OK for a few hours?' I nod, and she stands to go, turning back when she reaches the doorway. 'Rest today. Tomorrow, I'll take you somewhere quiet.'

*

Somewhere quiet means a long winding road from Accra towards Aburi, up into the mountains, where the botanical gardens lie. It means being greeted by towering royal palm trees, by a coolness of the air. It means wandering around the sprawling grounds with no reason but because we can. It means walking amongst the abundance of spices on the ground, picking up and pressing leaves and seeds to our noses: the crackle of pepper, the sweetness of cinnamon, the spice of a bay leaf. It means, after several hours of walking, several gourds of cold palm wine, the sweet fizz spinning in my body. Somewhere quiet means I begin to understand why Mum would've brought me here: the presence of serenity, the same quiet present amongst blossoming flowers and trees and plants, boughed with fruit, in Mum's garden in London.

From there, we glide back down to Accra, Auntie Yaa driving fast, my hand out of the window, trying to clasp the sunshine into my memory. Somewhere close to home I hear the loose echo of distant drums. I signal for us to turn off the main road, and Auntie follows the sound into an arts centre, where a six-piece drum outfit are in full swing. I remember what Nii told me about the *sikyi* rhythm, played with a flirtatious flourish, meant to simulate the linger of desire between young people, the slow start, the sense of time stretching and warping and speeding and slowing, the melodies of the drum and bell and shaker in a continuous loop, building and building, anticipation at its height. As they play, the drums speak not only to the desires between others but my own desires, those things in me which I don't confront every day. The drummers begin to chant in Ga, *we're coming, we're coming*, and I go into that space, where there are others dancing too, an elegant shake of the shoulder, an innocent strut, a flinging of limbs, some freedom in the deluge, a moment of peace.

When the performance is over, Auntie Yaa taps me to say we should go, but rather than heading home, we take a detour, past Osu, making for the water. The world quietens as we approach Labadi beach. There's a slight haze being pulled in by the tide. Young people thrash about in the ocean, racing the water in, knowing there can only be one winner. I try to imagine the excitement of my parents as teenagers, climbing out of vans and cars, boomboxes swinging from hands, infinity stretching out in front of them, everything possible.

'I'll be over there,' Auntie Yaa says, gesturing towards a bench in the shade of a canopy. I walk ahead, towards the shoreline, and the sand makes souvenirs of my motion. I pause where the water breaks. I don't have anything to offer but myself. Kick off my shoes, wade in, knee-deep. The surface is calm, but the undertow shifts and sweeps. I stay steady, placing my hand just below the surface, the motion of the ocean like a mother's caress. I look up and the haze has cleared, the sky the water's mirror. The sea swells and rises like a chorus; a small wave rises from the depths, slapping me in the chest. I speak back to the water: *Miiŋa bo*. I am greeting you. *Me shwe bo*. I miss you. *Kaa fo*. Don't cry. After a few minutes, I turn away but not before pausing once more at the break, where water meets land, where spirit meets earth, and there, as another small wave emerges, swelling, rising, just before the fall, the whisper of a spirit at rest, not saying goodbye or farewell, but *soon*.

42.

I've never known what it means to fill your suitcase with souvenirs from home, but here I am, in Auntie Yaa's living room,
trying to work out what I take with me and what I leave behind.
Auntie drifts in and out, filling a suitcase with food and drink I
cannot get in the UK: muscatella, a fizz somewhere between van-
illa and caramel; shito, dried fish and prawns, blended with chilli
and garlic and oil, to make a sauce which goes with everything.
From the kitchen, I can smell jollof on the stove, my last meal
before I leave, some of which she'll place in a plastic container
for me to take onboard the flight.

'You gonna miss me?' I ask.

'I already do.'

'You gonna come to London soon?'

'Maybe,' she says. 'I don't know. I don't miss it like I thought I
would. It was so endlessly *hard*. Don't get me wrong. Things are
hard here too, but I can take my time. There's sunshine.' She
shrugs. 'I miss you, that's all. And your father. And Uncle T!'

'Speaking of, Uncle T told me to tell you he's ready for your
love, whatever that means.'

'You tell him, I'm right here, if he wants to come.'

'You know what,' I say, standing upright. 'Whatever you man
have going on, you need to sort it out between yourselves. I won't
be your love mule.'

'I'll call him myself, see if he wants to join me in the sunshine.
That reminds me, I have something else for you to take home.'

She leaves the room once more, returning with a large, battered flight case, which she places in front of me, gestures to
open. I undo the locks and, inside, the case bursts with records,
all housed in their original plastic sleeves. I pull out the first and

it's the Delfonics' eponymous album, with that cover giving off *cool*, one band member reclining, looking skywards, another crouched with his hands clasped in front of him, the last with his hands on his hips, his gaze direct and disarming. I slide the record from its sleeve and head to Auntie's hi-fi system, placing it atop the turntable, watching the needle lower, the vinyl spinning, the crackle of the horns announcing the first song, 'Didn't I (Blow Your Mind This Time)'. The sound is warm and full and dusty, breaking a broad smile on my face.

'This one,' Auntie Yaa says, 'we were at one of your father's and Nick's parties one weekend, when this one came on, towards the end of the evening. There was a guy there I'd seen before but I didn't know. I had such a crush on him but I couldn't . . .' She gestures, as if trying to suggest emerging her desire. 'Anyway, this song came on and there was something so sensual, so beautiful about it. It made me brave. I walked straight up to him and asked if he wanted to dance. The smile on his face.' There's a smile on hers. 'I'll never forget.'

'What happened to him?'

'Fred? Oh, I never saw him again. But the dance was worth it!'

We laugh as the record makes its transition to 'Funny Feeling', and I ask, 'Are these yours?' Gesturing to the flight case.

She shakes her head. 'Your father's. He used to spend *all* his money on music. He always said he would take these back to London and start a venue where they only played records.'

'What happened?'

'Life got in the way,' and she says no more.

Last year, when Mum passed, grief broke the stubbornness in my father and me. We spoke to each other in spurts and bursts, before settling into a mostly cordial silence. Neither of us have the desire to revisit our argument and so, aside from checking how the other is, there's not much more to say.

Still, of late, I've felt the urge for *more*. I've always had a decent grasp on who I am, or where I might find myself, but I've never really known where I've come from. This trip has started a shift.

There are gaps which my father might fill, with his own story. I want him to tell me who he is, or who he was. I want to know who he was when he was twenty. I want to know what he dreams of, where he finds freedom.

'I'll take them back for him,' I say.

'Make sure you pick the ones you want first,' she says, with a wink. She crosses over to the record player and lifts the needle; from memory, finds where she wants it to drop. Another brief crackle, before a piano intro, leading towards a slow, measured instrumental number, dusty and warm, full of strings and keys and horns. She heads back towards the kitchen, and I sit cross-legged, pulling out each record one by one, holding in hand these parts of my father I've never known.

43

The journey home, from Accra to London. And by home, I mean south-east London, I mean Peckham, where my world begins and ends. Where there's still haggling taking place, where butchers and grocers take pleasure in the back and forth. Where an auntie might call to you, *my dear, please*, plastic bags of shopping cutting into her hands, only a short walk to her flat, she says, and you'll help her, despite knowing you'll complain to your friends later that auntie duped you, *her flat was miles away*. Where we might queue at a bus stop for the number 36, hoping it will take us to Marble Arch, towards Hyde Park, where we might light a spliff in the seclusion of daylight, hoping that time goes slow. Where, because it's summer, two young people might notice each other at that bus stop – you know, that way in which you see someone you don't know and there's the sudden desire to want to know, to go towards them, to ask them who they are, to see them smile, to see what their gaze looks like in the sunshine – and because it's summer, maybe you make the few steps to close the gap between you, introduce yourself, see what blooms in the space, what *closeness* might emerge, or maybe you don't, maybe he or she or they will be another person you describe to your friends, another person you'll wonder if you'll ever see again. Where I don't notice Marlon approaching me – I'm in my own small world, attention elsewhere – but he crosses into my path, into the space the sunlight is making, offers me a long, slow embrace, because he understands I'm slowly getting back to myself, or a version of myself who might live with my mother's passing, because while the grief is never over, we find a way to walk in the light someone has left behind. Where, after Marlon leaves, insisting we link up soon, Uncle T zooms by in his black BMW, all mouth full of gold, all joyous beeping of the horn. Where, from an open window, I hear someone belting 'Let the Sunshine In', ad libs and all. Where there's rhythm happening, everywhere, all of us like instruments, making our own music. Where I go down Rye Lane, along Peckham High Street, cut through Kelly Avenue and, instead of a left, make a right, round the bend of East Surrey Grove, where I raise the side of my fist to meet Del's door like a kick to a drum. Where she opens the door, and, expecting me a day later, begins to laugh in disbelief, the sound an instrument of joy, the music of happiness.

'You're early,' she says.

'I can go back, if you like.'

'Ha. Come in, I'll grab my bag and we can head out.'

'Where are we going?'

She points in the general direction of outside, as if the answer is obvious.

'Anywhere the sun is shining. It's so gorgeous.'

*

We take refuge on a flat patch of green in Burgess Park, lying across a patchwork picnic blanket. Del propped up on her elbow, my head turned towards her. Between us, a tiny speaker plays Frank Ocean's *Channel Orange*. We're somewhere between 'Sierra Leone' and 'Sweet Life' as Del fills me in on her recent trip to New York, where she played with a five-piece band opening for a set of smaller, intimate shows with Common. She tells me of the rehearsals, the jam sessions, the characters, the rigour, the *space*, all that space in which to say, *this is me*.

As she speaks, my surface is calm but inside I'm being thrown about by a tide of confusion, knowing the happiness I feel for Del, but also knowing I feel like I'm being left behind. This place she's speaking of, where she might breathe and grow, lean into infinite possibilities, I long for it too. I long to be amongst the energy improvisation generates, to be housed in the small, beautiful world a handful of people make to house their joy and chaos and all. Yes, I have the kitchen, I have my culinary dreams. But I long to be making music, I long to be in that *space*. And I don't want Del's space, I just want my own.

There's also a sense of guilt: when Mum passed last summer, Del was always there, interrupting her touring and recording to return home, to check on me, knowing intimately the grief tugging me apart. I worry that she'll continue to return because she worries; that I'll be like an anchor when all of her is primed to lift off, to fly away.

'What's on your mind?' she asks. I shake my head and as she reaches across to lay a hand on my chest, I catch a glimpse of black ink etched into her forearm.

'You got another one,' I say.

'I did,' she says, angling her arm towards me. Near the joint, near the elbow, etched into her skin: a three-piece drum set – kick drum, snare, hi-hat – a hand with the loose grip of a drumstick, in the moment before the snare is struck, in the moment where anything might be possible. I pull her arm towards me, let my lips meet her skin. She smiles and she arranges herself so that my chest is like a pillow, her head facing skywards.

'What you tryna do today?' I ask.

'Honestly, nothing. I just want time to slow down, so I can spend some more time with you.'

More time means we walk in circles around the park. I speak about Ghana, the serenity of Aburi, the unity of the drummers, the infinity of the ocean at Labadi beach. After our sixth loop, we leave the park for food, hitting the Caribbean takeaway for patties, eating them as we walk. Del suggests we hop on the 12, and we head into central, trawling through Soho, going from record shop to record shop, digging through old soul and funk records, music our parents would've moved to. She finds *The Delfonics* LP in good condition and is ready to buy when I tell her I've got one, describing the flight case full of my father's records, these parts of my father I've never known. We make a plan to head back to mine to collect them, then we'll head to hers, where we'll eat and drink and spin records into the night, but not before she's had a chance to shop for a new outfit for an upcoming gig, which ends up being a denim jumpsuit, the blue ocean-deep, her face playful as she asks me what I think. She undoes the zip a little, so I can see her chains – her father's pendant, the infinity loop – swinging from her neck. The light coming through the window in the shop has made her eyes wide and open, a slight smile on her features. I can only nod, smiling in disbelief at the part we have to play in each other's lives.

By the time we reach Del's, we're sun-drunk, giddy and slow. Hunger is beginning to grip at both of us, so, finding a pack of chicken in the fridge, I lean on what I know, combining in a bowl with coconut milk, garlic, ginger, thyme, salt and pepper. I season the flour with spices, and douse each piece in the flour mix, before letting it sputter in a pan full of oil. While it cooks, I raid the bottom of her fridge for veg, finding a pack of broccoli, sautéing in a frying pan with butter, garlic and chilli. Del follows the scent into the kitchen, leaning over my shoulder to gaze at the stove.

'What are those for?' She points at the broccoli.

'So we feel less guilty for eating a plateful of fried chicken.'

'No one should feel guilty about something which makes them feel so good.'

When we've eaten, tearing apart the chicken with glistening fingers, Del opens a bottle of wine and we drink until our bodies are dizzy with the sweetness. We're both silly, mournful drunks, already nostalgic for yesterdays and moments before, demanding wheel-ups like our lives depend on it. She brings out her decks and we go from singing Frank Ocean's 'Sierra Leone' to crooning Willie Hutch's 'I Choose You', to playing rapper, Del mixing Hutch's into the song it birthed, 'Int'l Players Anthem', the sample pitched up, the feeling spilling into the room, our spirits spilling from our bodies. We go and go until the energy deserts us, the alcohol collapsing us in a heap on her sofa.

'I could do this every day.'

'Let's do this tomorrow.'

'I can't, I'm away again, for that gig. I thought I was gonna miss you when you got back, to be honest.'

'Oh,' I say, looking into my lap.

'Don't look so sad, it'll only be a couple of days.'

'It's not that.' Del sits up, trying to tease apart my silence. 'I feel like I'm holding you back.'

'What do you mean?'

'Like, I'm weighing you down. If it wasn't for me you'd be travelling the world, you'd be putting out records, you'd be flying.'

'You're not holding me back. I am flying. And you're one of the reasons why. And anyway, this is my home.' She points to the cavern of my chest. 'I'll be back. I'll always come back.'

'Sure you'll remember me?' I mean to joke, but it comes out tender, wandering, raw.

Her features soft in the dimness of the room, she takes my hand, holding tight. 'How could I forget?'

44.

Sunday afternoon, deserted car park of a supermarket, daylight bright and breaking through the windscreen of Ray's car, my palms wrapped around the steering wheel, Ray telling me to try again. I put the car in gear once more, and go to pull out; there's a soft pop and the sound of the engine falls away, stalling. Ray pulls at the handbrake.

'Where's your head at today, bro?'

I'm elsewhere, in the memory of Del and me, last night, two Black crowns in a haze of our own joy, clasping curves and edges, closer and closer, her fingers splayed against the broadness of my back, bunched fists against the bedsheets—

'It's been an hour, might as well stop there,' Ray says.

'Sorry, bro.'

He flicks on the car's sound system and it's static on the radio. 'Beg you go get me an ice cream, please.'

'Shop's closed, man.'

'Petrol station's open.'

'Why don't you go get it?'

'Is that how you're gonna treat your brother for giving you *free* driving lessons?'

'Fine. What do you want?'

'The usual, please.'

When I return with Magnum ice creams, Common's 'The Corner' is blaring from the speakers. Ray has bust open the doors, willing a breeze to blow through the vehicle. I mirror him, sitting in the driver seat, my legs splayed out of the door. We're both quiet as bass shakes the frame of the car, nodding our heads along to the beat.

'So, what you saying? Back from Ghana a changed man, yeah?'

There's mischief in his eyes but kindness too, in the way they glitter and widen in the light.

'Something like that.' I sigh, tapping out the beat on my lap. 'Definitely feel a bit more at peace.'

Ray makes a knowing sound. I'm sure he's heard from Auntie Yaa about the trip, about my rupture, my deluge, but he doesn't push, doesn't pry.

'So, what you saying, Raymond?'

'Don't use my full name like that, it's weird. You sound like Pops.' His voice deepens and he plays our father again. '*What are your plans, Raymond? Are you saving, Raymond? Life is too short, Raymond.*' Ray shakes his head as I laugh.

'Actually, I'm going Jamaica,' he says.

'When?'

'In two weeks, for two weeks. Don't worry, I'll be back for Mum's one-year celebration. Tej's parents have been out there for a minute, so Malachi hasn't met them. Plus,' he exhales, 'I need a holiday.'

'I hear that.'

'But look, while I'm gone, I'm gonna need you to look out for Pops.'

'What do you mean?'

He raises his eyebrows and begins to count out on his fingers.

'Go over every day—'

'Every day?' I ask.

'Every day. Make sure there's food in the fridge *and* he's eating. Check the bills are going out. Check he's going work, sometimes he has bad days, it doesn't happen. Just look out for him, really.'

'This all seems a bit extra, he's a grown man.'

'What do you think I've been doing for the past year?'

'You haven't said anything about this.'

'You haven't asked.' Ray turns towards me. 'We lost Mum. He lost his everything. He's different now. Every so often you catch a little something of him before, a little of that energy, but otherwise . . .' He shrugs.

'But, Ray, every day? I might as well move back in with him.'

'Honestly, that would probably be best.'

I twist in my seat, softening. 'Is it that bad?'

'It's worse.'

He doesn't need to say much more than this. I imagine how, for Pops, solitude has become loneliness. How there's no spillage but an ache deluging inside him. A man stripped of his gleam, slack and dull, awash with sadness, the line between despair and anger a blur, no voice, no music, no rhythm.

'Two weeks,' Ray says. 'I need some peace too, Stephen.'

'I've got you, bro. I've got you.'

45.

Ray dropped off a duffel, my trumpet and the flight case full of records a few hours earlier, so walking over to my father's house, my arms swing free by my sides. It's early evening, high summer, everything exciting, full of anticipation. I let the sunshine graze my face as I try to will any anticipation away. The last time Pops and I lived together, the only thing I was anticipating was ruin and disaster. It's been a year and even though Ray insists our father is softer, I can't help but remember the years before, the times when he didn't believe in the possibilities I saw for myself, didn't believe in me.

The walk is short, Nam's place perhaps fifteen minutes away. When I arrive, Pops is in the front yard, washing his car, an extension cord stretching out from the house like an errant thought. Golden hour has begun to fall, the world doused in a glamorous haze. Pops spots me and draws himself to full height, wiping his hands on the back of his jeans.

'Stephen,' he says, holding out his hand. I take it and he pulls me in, not quite so we're embracing, but close enough that he can rest his palm under my elbow. His eyes have more lines around them than I remember, wide and honest in the light. The tenderness stops me where I stand.

'Pops.' I signal to his car. 'Do you need a hand?'

'Oh, I'm good, I'm good.' From his car, I hear the rhythm of gospel, all praise and worship and rapture.

'Have you eaten?' Pops shakes his head. 'All right, dinner in a few hours.'

I open the front door with my own key – a key I never lost or let go of, perhaps hoping that one day I would use it again – and enter the house for the first time since Mum passed, since the sittings and memorials and the funeral. Now my father's house has many rooms and I enter them all, going from space to space, trying to discern what might have changed. The living room is the same, two long sofas and a tiny armchair Mum often took to falling asleep in. The kitchen too, except it's devoid of the scent of oil and spices and comfort, of someone cooking, or having cooked. My and Ray's room is more lived in; I assume Ray has been sleeping over, his bed roughly made. I pause at my parents' room and, out of habit, knock. When there's no answer, I enter.

The room smells stale. I go over to the dresser and there's a fine layer of dust settled on the wood. The bed is made and is immaculate, but something tells me it has not been slept in for some time. Perching on the edge of the bed, I reach for the photo Mum always kept on her side table: Ray, Pops, Mum and me, on holiday in Spain when I was a teenager, the four of us huddled together, grinning. A reminder of a different time, one we won't see again.

With a sigh, I put the photo down and head back to the kitchen, opening the fridge to find it fully stocked – Raymond's doing, I guess. Nestled near the back of the bottom shelf, the red bag the butcher's just off Rye Lane uses; inside, some cuts of beef. I take out the heavy pot and fry the cubes of meat, letting them brown. As the food sputters in the pot, I pull out the blender, blasting onions, garlic, ginger and a few Scotch bonnet peppers, until the mixture is smooth, then fry this in a separate pot in some oil, adding several tins of chopped tomatoes and letting it simmer. I wash several cupfuls of rice, then, realizing I've been cooking in silence, find Mum's Bluetooth speaker tucked away in a cupboard, plug it in, select Pharoah Sanders's 'Love Is Everywhere' to drift into the space, the joyous clatter making good company, before adding the rice to the stew, then, when the rice has begun to miracle itself from hard pebble to soft pillow, I stir in the meat. Sliding the hob down to low, I wash and chop some leaves as well.

By the time Pops comes in, the sun is a recent memory. I hear him washing his hands as I serve us two plates, pour him a

Guinness too. He joins me at the table and, after a mumbled grace, digs a fork into the jollof. Chews slowly. His eyes wide again, surprised.

'Where'd you learn how to cook this?'

'Mum,' I say. He doesn't push any further, but nods, gazing at his food. We eat in quiet, the clatter of cutlery like percussion. Pops is soon scraping his plate, trying to gather the loose grains of rice. I try not to let any of my pride escape into the space but I can't help but smile.

'Thank you,' he says. 'I needed that.'

'Do you want dessert?'

He considers. 'What have we got?'

'I think I saw an apple crumble in the fridge. I'll pop it in the oven.'

We eat dessert with the TV casting shadows across the room, watching reruns of *My Wife and Kids*. Pops laughs until he's wheezing, which means I'm laughing too, laughing at his glee, laughing until I cast a glance at my father, this man who I clashed and fought with, who is now grinning in the darkness of the room, holding the bowl up to his chest, spooning mouthfuls of apple crumble and ice cream, and when I see this, the laughter becomes silent tears, mostly because my father's tenderness moves me, but also because I suspect that he cannot cry.

After a few hours, I'm exhausted, not realizing how much tension my body had been holding and, now I've stopped, finding myself sinking into my own fatigue. I suggest we turn in and Pops follows me up the stairs, towards my room.

'Where are you going?' I ask.

'I've been sleeping in here.' He throws a glance towards his own room and I see him stiffen. 'I can sleep on the sofa if need be.'

'No, no. There's two beds. Unless you're planning to sleep on them both.'

He shows me the first hint of a smile since I've arrived, and it's gone as soon as it came. I open the door for him and head back downstairs to grab a toothbrush and a T-shirt. He's already in

Ray's bed when I return, facing the wall, his hand held to his face in a lover's caress. After switching off the light, I get into my own, finding the way by memory.

I lie on the covers, facing my father's outline in the dimness of the room. I want to ask him what he thought of the jollof, to ask how he's doing, how he's been. I want to ask whether, these days, he dreams when he closes his eyes. I want to talk; I don't want this strange reunion between us to end. I whisper, 'Pops?' but his breathing has already deepened, a soft snore interrupting this otherwise quiet moment. I smile to myself, somewhere between content and melancholy, and as I lie on my back, trying to commit this moment to my mind, it's seconds before sleep pulls me down too.

46.

In the morning, I fry eggs for us both as Pops gets ready for work. Kanye and Jay-Z are going back and forth on the radio as he comes into the kitchen, sliding an envelope on to the worktop beside me. The confusion must show because he says, 'For the embassy.' I raise my eyebrows, sure I won't like what comes next. 'My visa for Ghana. I go in just over a month. Ray said he would go to the embassy for me. And since he's not here . . .'

'Ray said that?'

Pops nods. I check the clock on the radio. I should've left an hour ago if I wanted to make it in and out of the embassy.

'Can't I do this another time?'

'My appointment is today,' Pops says simply, shuffling away. I fight the urge to hurl some words at his back. Some old anger rises, and even though anger is a necessary emotion, I don't let it multiply or misdirect. For his sake, for mine, knowing our grief, wanting peace. A deep breath, a moment to steady myself, making quick calculations as to what this day might look like. I text Del to rearrange: *On Daddy duty – can we do tomorrow?* Her reply comes after a few moments: *Please. I'm so hungover.*

I'm showered and dressed, going from Peckham Rye to London Bridge, London Bridge to Archway, emerging from the depths of the Underground before realizing I've been moving in silence. Pulling out the tangle of my headphones, I let Nina Simone's 'Sinnerman' push me up Highgate Hill. By the time I arrive, slightly breathless, at the Ghanaian Embassy, there's already a haphazard queue of people pressing towards the entrance, most trying to make the yearly pilgrimage to the home they left long ago, some looking for an easier passage next time round in the form of dual nationality. There is a slight hum of anticipation, everyone hoping

217

their appointment is smooth, everyone hoping they've packed the necessary paperwork. This place feels like the last barrier between the desire to return home and the ability to do so; it is the last place of waiting and yet the wait is so long; knowing you could come so close, could wait hours and hours, and be denied a visa is a prospect no one wants to entertain.

Inside, stiff plastic chairs and floor-to-ceiling windows which produce as much heat as they let in light. As I sit, with one earphone in, the other dangling, I want to believe there's a system here, but the numbers are called at random: 355, 172, 501. A woman approaches a desk when no number is called, and after a short back and forth, a rustle of papers, is served immediately. Another woman watches me watching this interaction, watches my sigh and frustration and shuffles along a seat, a little bit closer to me, holding out a bag of plantain chips as a balm. I shake my head but she produces another one from her handbag, insists. I smile at her kindness and take it. We both try to settle into our seats, pop open the bags, crunch quietly. I finish mine quickly and she gives me another, asking if the visit to the embassy is for me. For my father, I say.

'I used to send my son too. I'm sure he's grateful,' she says.

'Where did he go? Your son.'

'He's gone. Long gone. America. My husband left me behind as well. I buried him last year.'

'I'm sorry,' I say, knowing how useless the words felt when people were saying this to me every day.

'It's OK. I knew one of us would have to go sometime.' She shakes her head, smiling, some distant memory coming into focus, but doesn't share, keeps whatever tiny intimacy in her head, close to her chest. 'It's just lonely. It begins to consume you, make you small and quiet. That's why I'm going back home. My sisters are there, the three of us will live together. I've been shuffling in small circles around my flat. I want to live big again.'

There's no meaningful reply which comes to mind, so instead I ask, 'When will you go?'

'In three weeks. When I get back, I'm going to try planting a garden. I'm taking seeds with me, and I'll buy some out there. I'll have a lemon tree and oranges, and mangoes, coconut, bananas. I want some flowers too, jasmine is my favourite. Any tree I plant, I hope it outlives me.' Another number is called. 'That's me.'

She shuffles over to the counter, pulling out a plastic wallet thick with paper. The interaction lasts a couple of minutes; I hear her being told to return tomorrow, to pick up her new Ghanaian passport. She waves my way as she leaves and I recognize something in her; her rhythm, her youth, her hope: she reminds me of Mum. Suddenly, I'm in my mother's garden, which, even now, nearly a year after her passing, is visible from our kitchen window, blossoming and blooming, her spirit still stretching upwards from the earth. I lean forward and put my head in hands, willing myself not to cry here because if I do, it will not be spillage but deluge. My heart thuds at the walls of my chest, threatening rupture. The grief as fresh as a new wound, I inhale, exhale, inhale, exhale, until I'm steady once more. I settle into my seat, and I'm wondering if, like the woman, Pops has thought about going back, when my number is called. The interaction is painless; the official at the desk barely glances over the forms before asking me if I would like to pay by card or cash. I'm told to return next week to pick up the visa. As I emerge, there's a fresh flood of Ghanaians making for the plastic seats of the embassy, the seemingly long and impossible wait. I check the time as I leave. It's barely been an hour. How strange time becomes in the face of uncertainty.

Later, after another evening of food and television, my father and I lying in the darkness of my childhood room, in that place just before slumber pulls me under, he asks me, 'How was the embassy?'

'It was OK, didn't have to wait too long.'

'Thank you for going. I haven't been there for years.' He pauses. 'It's strange to think of making the trip without her.'

For the second time today, I'm without reply. From outside,

the drift of cars, parties winding down or gearing up, a neighbourhood alive in the summertime.

'Pops? You ever thought about moving back?'

'To Ghana?'

'Yeah.'

He's quiet again, and I'm almost sure he's fallen asleep when he says, 'I've thought about it. But your mum and I were always meant to do it together. I don't think I could do it without her.'

'That makes sense.'

'Anyway, thanks again. Goodnight.'

'Goodnight, Pops.' I turn away from him, on to my side. I ask sleep to come quick but to sleep with grief is not to sleep at all. Around two a.m., rumbled by a hunger I cannot shake, I make my way downstairs, to the kitchen, where I heat up a small bowl of jollof, more for comfort than anything else. I eat where I stand, quick mouthfuls by the window.

My mother's garden beckons. Guided only by starlight and the faint hue of the moon, I wander amongst the plants, let my fingers graze the waxy skin of the lemons, each gentle flower petal. I pluck a few mint leaves and head back inside, brewing a tea with a spoonful of honey.

When I return to the room, my father is lying on his back, his eyes open. He looks at me and smiles. I kneel by his bed and take his hand. Moonlight casts our union in a faint blue. He gives me a squeeze, and quickly lets my hand go, turning towards the wall once more.

47

'I can't believe he has all these records.'

Del and I are in my living room, the flight case with my father's music popped open. One by one, we've been pulling out each vinyl, awed by his early collection, all this music and motion and feeling preserved in plastic sleeves: the Isley Brothers, Anita Baker, Eddie Kendricks. I'm about to ask Del what we should play first when I hear the front door. My father's heavy footsteps. A sigh as he lets the day fall off his shoulders. A smile on his face as he comes into the living room and sees us.

'You remember Del, Pops?'

He throws a look my way as if to say, *how could I forget?* Holds out his palms in greeting, beckons her towards him. They hold each other close, like kin. He asks after her wellbeing, after her aunt; she asks how he's doing, and he shrugs, says he's getting by.

'We're just checking out your records,' Del says, gesturing to the flight case.

Curiosity softens his face. He sits cross-legged on the floor and pulls the case towards him. Pulls out an Al Green record, then a 5th Dimension one. He points towards his chest, his brow furrowed a little, asking, *these are mine?* More assertion than question, but I nod regardless. He pulls the case even closer, his head boughed over the records like a branch heavy with fruit, rifling through the music, the sound of satisfaction when he pulls one out: *City Life* by the Blackbyrds. Heading for the turntable in the corner of the room, he places the vinyl on the player. A slow smile spreads across his face as he tells us a story, parts of which I've heard before: how he would party on Saturday nights, and he remembered, once, Nick breaking open the plastic on a new record, and this, he says, pointing to the sound drifting through the room, here, now, is what played. Nothing had ever stirred him that way before.

As he speaks, I see the light in him glow. I see the glimpse of the man he was, of how it might be possible for him to grow from his grief. He plays us more records, each accompanied by a story or tale: *Whatcha See Is Whatcha Get* was the first record he bought and he played until it would play no more; *+'Justments* by Bill Withers is what he played when he wanted some comfort; 'Waiting in Vain' was playing the day he pulled up to the beach and met Mum. Pops gleams with every twist and turn of his stories, and I encourage him, wishing he could always be this open.

As another song comes to a close, Del gets up, stretches towards the ceiling, gives me a small nod. I check the time: it's almost nine p.m.

'Pops, we're gonna go get some food.'

'Do you want to come with us?' Del asks.

'No, no,' he says, with a trace of a smile. 'You young people go and enjoy.'

'But you'll be on your own,' Del says.

'I'll be OK.'

As Del goes out into the hallway, I take a few steps towards him. 'Sure you don't want to come with us, Pops?'

He shakes his head. His voice a bassy whisper, he says, 'I know what it means to want to be close to someone. Go. Enjoy. I'll see you tomorrow.'

I open my mouth to protest once more, but he waves me away, saying, '*Go*,' already unsheathing the next record. I head towards the hallway, about to follow Del out of the front door, when I think to tell Pops there's food in the fridge. Leaning my head through the doorway, a glimpse of my father, caught in rapture: he's playing the record I played in Ghana, *The Delfonics* LP. The crackle of the horns, the sound full and dusty and warm. Pops sings to the lover he's lost, a little sway in his hips. As the falsetto of the chorus comes up, his eyes closed, a hand pressed to his chest, the other arm raised like a beacon, as if to say, to no one but himself, *I am here*.

48.

When I return the next morning, I call out to Pops but the only reply is the echo of my own voice. I go from room to room, looking for any sign or signal of him, finding nothing. As I fill the kettle for a cup of tea, I gaze into the garden, and there he is, nestled between a rose plant and the stalks of tomatoes. He's sat on the bench Ray and he and I tried to build together, many summers ago. That day returns to me as I walk towards him: the three of us had boasted that the bench would be built within the hour; we built a piece of furniture which collapsed the moment Ray tested it; in the end, it had been Mum who oversaw its completion, in exchange for one of Pops's barbecues. That day, we ate until we were full and a little past it, letting music drift from inside the house towards the garden, accompanying our laughter long into the night. I'm about to ask Pops if he remembers that day too, but he speaks before I can.

'Sometimes, I dream of your mother. I used to sit on this bench with her at the end of the day and I dream she's right beside me.'

'What happens? Do you chat to each other?'

'We never needed to,' he says. 'Just needed to be beside each other.' I stand in front of him for a few moments, before walking back up the garden, towards the kitchen, plucking a few mint leaves on my way. Inside, I brew a tea with the leaves, a spoonful of honey too. I return to the bench with a mug for us both and take a seat next to him. I hand him one and he nods his thanks.

'You know, Mum and I were meant to go to Ghana, maybe a few weeks after she passed.' Pops nods and I continue. 'I tried to do all the stuff she had planned. Labadi beach. The castle at Cape Coast. And the gardens at Aburi.'

Pops smiles. 'Her favourite place. When we first moved into

this house, the garden had been filled in with paving and concrete. She made us break it up, get fresh soil, somewhere for things to grow. *A garden is the only place in the world I feel quiet*, she would say.'

We sit together now, in that quiet, as the day gathers itself. Steam rises from our mugs, as I imagine my mother's spirit does, upwards from the earth, rising and rising, to that place where the sounds we make and the life we exhale go to, rising, up above, not gone but now part of the world, outliving us all.

49.

It's mid-afternoon, a few days later, when the doorbell goes. It's Sunday and I have plans to spend a few hours in the kitchen. There are only a few days before I have to go back to work, the time off Femi gave me almost up, and I want to return with some semblance of rhythm, want to know I still hold the same precision.

When I open the door, it's the pastor of my parents' church, Michael, sunshine glowing behind a sweaty Black crown. He greets me warmly and enters with such ease, I almost forget I haven't invited him inside.

'Is your father here?' he asks.

'Is he expecting you?' I know, from what Ray briefly told me, that Pops hasn't been inside a church since Mum passed.

'No, but—'

'Pastor.' Pops appears in the hallway.

'Eric. How are you?' Pops only nods at the question, and beckons Pastor Michael into the kitchen, towards the dining table. I follow them in, pouring them both a glass of water, setting them down but not leaving the room.

'You know, it's been a while and I think I just wanted to check how you were, when you might return.'

Pops gives a shake of his head so small I nearly miss it. He doesn't say anything and he doesn't need to. Pops's belief in anything is crumbling, his faith long gone. He doesn't know where God is or might be, doesn't know how to pray or desire, only to grieve, to silently groan, to make himself a body, like water, a still surface, but beneath this, a ripple, and beneath this, an ebbing tide, and beneath that, a violent, constant tow. And that's where he is right now: an ocean so wide he can't see the beginning or end.

'With the one-year anniversary approaching,' Pastor Michael continues, 'it would be good for the community to see you, and of course, any contribution you provide—'

'Pops, I don't mean to interrupt but we're gonna be late.'

The two men stare at me, forgetting I was there.

'You should get your shoes on.' After a moment, Pops nods and rises. Pastor Michael becomes flustered, stumbling about his own words.

'I didn't – of course, you would . . .'

'Maybe call ahead next time,' I say, my gaze sure and direct.

We leave the house a few minutes later, walking Pastor Michael to a car so new it has its own gleam. The engine barely roars as he pulls away, and I lead my father into the afternoon.

'Thank you,' Pops says.

'That man is a crook. Every month, new car. What happened to Pastor Kwesi? I liked him.'

'Back to Ghana,' Pops says. 'Where are we going?'

'You'll see.'

It's a short walk to the estate, this small city within the city, the air thick with barbecue smoke and summer frenzy. We go by a group holding up the wall in an underpass, an eerie, skittish beat echoing from a tiny speaker into the space, one of them gliding over with vivid lyrics, language as dextrous as water, a swelling solo, but after a turn of phrase I don't catch, the chorus rises, joyful. Out of the short tunnel, towards a patch of green outside a ground-floor flat, where Uncle T stands at his window. Forever dramatic, he holds his chest in shock, his mouth wide open in surprise. He comes round to the door with a flourish.

'Not one, but two! To what do I owe the pleasure?'

As the two embrace one another, memory, image and possibility fold in on each other. The two men hold each other as they would've when they were young, their touch warm and thick with love, a gentle teasing as they compare greys, point to new lines around their eyes and face. I see how they might grow old together, these two men who aren't blood but are certainly brothers, would do anything for one another.

'Haven't seen you in months, Eric!'

'I keep meaning to call back, but . . .' Pops gazes at the ground.

'I know. Come in, come in. Or you have somewhere to be?'

'We're right where we need to be, Uncle T,' I say.

Straight through to his living room, more on the side of lived in than messy, a few house plants drooping on surfaces, an old CD container splayed open on the table like a book. Photos nailed into the wall: a young Uncle T, shirtless on the beach; another grinning beside his late mother; one more of him caught in some joyous motion, all teeth and limbs and glint. In one corner, a shrine to rhythm: a hi-fi system, stacked up high, two speakers on either side. A dub pulses at the walls, at our chests. I recognize the rhythm from the time Uncle T picked me up in his car: *King Tubbys Meets Rockers Uptown*.

'You remember this one, Eric?' He taps at my father's chest, knocking at the cavern as if to conjure something.

'This tune?' Pops raises his eyebrows, a little twinkle in his eye. 'How could I forget?'

'See, Stephen. There was a young lady I met, a sweet one, the kind of woman you have to stop and check yourself for, you know? Anyway, she got me and your father to DJ her party and we had this plan – your father and I knew what to play to get a party moving, what to play to slow it down, and that's when I would make my move—'

'But you didn't stick to the plan,' Pops says, shaking his head.

'I couldn't wait, I had to make my move! Stephen, party is bumping, it's moving and I tell your Pops, *I have to go to talk to her*. So I walk on over to where she stands by the wall, start saying words as sweet as she is.' Uncle T and my father clap hands, click fingers, their familiar handshake. 'She's being all coy, and I'm thinking she's playing hard to get. But that's when someone taps my back, and I'm thinking, who's this disturbing me while I'm doing what I need to? And I turn round to face a man who looks like he ate another man for breakfast. The man had boulders for shoulders. He's looking from me to her, and he doesn't even have to say anything, I already know there's about to be a situation, depending on what I say or do next. But me being me—'

'A drunk,' Pops says.

'I had been drinking, yes, so I was feeling bold, so I say, *is there a problem here?* And Mr Boulder says, *there's about to be.* And you know what, the spirits have me feeling courageous, so I take a step towards him and, out of nowhere, Mr Boulder's friends appear too. And they're as big as him! And look, Stephen, you see me? I'm a fighter. I don't back down. But that day, I chose to be a lover – a lover of my life!' Uncle T slaps his thighs, wheezing at his own joke.

'You had us running out of there so quick,' Pops says.

'*Mi seh*, Eric, leave the records, there's *trouble* coming.' Uncle T leaves the room. I hear his fridge open and close, and he returns with three glasses and a bottle of ginger beer. From a cupboard in the living room, an unopened bottle of dark rum.

'Mind you, if we were together, trouble was never far behind.' He half-fills each glass with ginger beer, then twists open the rum, to which Pops opens his mouth to protest but Uncle T beats him to it.

'We know how this dance go,' Uncle T says. 'I say yes and you say no, we go back and forth and eventually you take the drink. Save us both the time, Eric.'

Pops smiles, knowing he's been defeated, watching as the rum soils the ginger beer from golden to cloudy brown, a little storm in the glass.

'To trouble,' Uncle T says, raising his glass. We join him and drink deeply, the taste sweet and dizzy and familiar.

We get drunk, that kinda sloppy where everything softens and slurs, where it's like your body is climbing a slope, your cheeks blush with warmth and laughter, your spirit dizzy and frenzied and full, joy wobbling from the depths of our bellies, our voices bellowing about the room, time folding in on itself soon, the moon pale and fleshy in the sky, a night as dark as any I've ever seen, Uncle T explaining that if you want starlight, you gotta fly back yard, to Jamaica, where parties start late and finish early, where you drink until you're drunk, that kinda sloppy where everything softens and slurs, and the only remedy is a good meal, something to soak it all up. After consulting Pops, Uncle T sends me to JB's Soul Food with an order so complex I have to write it down. When I arrive, they've locked the door of the shop and a woman is sweeping across the floor. I knock on the window and tell her Uncle T sent me. She asks for the order, and emerges from the back, minutes later, with a plastic bag soiled with grease and goodness.

I stumble back to the flat, where the pair are engaged in a vicious game of cards. My father groans as he loses, saying, '*Again*'; Uncle T's golden grin comes my way as he asks me to play too. They're playing War, which is the only game I know how to play, and because I've been drinking, I'm bold and confident. I catch a little streak and win once, twice, three times. Uncle T dashes his cards away in playful frustration, saying he's not playing any more, but Pops and I celebrate like we've just won the lottery, our arms around each other's shoulders, cheering, both of us instruments of joy, making not just sound but spirit; the room not just filled with music, but feeling too.

I wake, sometime the next morning, sprawled across the sofa, my limbs hanging off the edge. I stand and the room rolls, the drinks I lost count of sloshing about in me. I head upstairs for the toilet, each step more shaky than sure. Coming out, I notice the door to my parents' room is wide open.

My father is on Mum's side of the bed, his eyes open, making the ceiling familiar. He doesn't stir when I enter, nor when I climb on to the bed and lie beside him. It's so quiet. After a few moments, he turns towards me and we mirror each other, our hands underneath our heads like an extra pillow. My gaze asks the questions I want to: Who are you? Who were you? What do you dream of?

Where do you find freedom? Tell me of movement, migration, burden, of having to choose which parts of your life to keep, which to let fall away. Tell me you know this feeling which haunts me sometimes, this sadness on my shoulders.

After a long exhale, Pops opens his mouth to tell me what he can remember, what he cannot forget.

50.

The heat in Accra doesn't care for rainy season, and neither do you, convincing your brothers to make a fourth trip to Labadi beach that month. It's 1985 and the summer is already making light work of time, but at the beach, a day might stretch and stretch. Your brother, Kweku, hits up his closest friend, David, asking if he wants to take the trip, if he still has access to that *tro-tro*, a converted van which might carry their brothers and sisters, some friends, some family, down to the water. David needs little convincing, and soon you're riding upfront, turning the dial of the radio, trying to find some sound in the static. After a few moments, a familiar voice: Bob Marley's 'Waiting in Vain', a song which has everyone singing.

Labadi lives up to its real name of La Pleasure Beach. Many others have had the same idea, the beach congested with families splashing about where the shore breaks, couples taking cover under parasols, and groups of young people, like yourselves, twisting the lids off fizzy drinks, or arguing over what should play on the boombox, staring at the horses clopping through the sand or joining in with the buskers and their drums and guitars.

It's not long after you arrive that a kickabout breaks out, a group of you knocking the ball across a flatter patch of sand. You're one of the youngest here, but you've always found this game easy, leaned into its rhythm, each step and dart and duck like a dance.

You're midway through the game when someone boots the ball away, and you go over to where it's nestled, just short of a group of women huddled around a boombox. One woman – your height and long-limbed, bantu knots twisted across her scalp, her gaze keen and sure – takes a few steps towards the ball, picking it up, holding it out to you. You've never spoken to her but you get the feeling you've met before. You're about to ask when some-one calls your name from behind, tells you to hurry up. You give a quick thank you, your fingers brushing hers as the ball exchanges hands, some electricity, some charge, *something* in the space between you. You want to ask if anyone knows her name, if anyone has seen her before, if anyone knows this *feeling*, but you're pulled back in, the boys eager to continue.

Soon, the game breaks up and you all run towards the ocean, splashing about. Everyone is already knee-deep by the time you're letting the water lap at your ankles. You want to go fur-ther but you're worried the water's endlessness might consume you. You can't swim. You're about to turn back when you feel someone's eyes across your skin; the woman from before is there, just behind you, her gaze upon you once more. You shake off any worry, taking several steps in, past the knee, the chest, the waist. Soon, you're neck-deep, your feet scrabbling for ground where there is none. Quietly, you begin to panic, the water swallowing your thrash and tumble, stealing any energy in your limbs. The woman appears once more, and she's saying, *calm down*. She's saying, *don't panic*. She's saying, *I've got you*. You swim back into the shallows, where you can both stand, and a shyness visits upon you both.

'Thank you,' you say. She only smiles. 'I'm Eric.'

'Joy,' she says.

A few weeks later, you'll be running errands in your father's car, driving from Legon back towards Achimota, the streets a bit quieter than usual for the middle of the day, when you pass Joy in the street, her walk languorous, unhurried. A U-turn, and you pull up, slowing down to a crawl to match her pace.

'Whose car are you driving?'

'My father's. Where are you going?'

She points to nowhere in particular. You gesture for her to get in. She hesitates; you can see she's fighting her desire to accept your offer with the fact that you're still a stranger to her. You stop the car, so that she does too, and pop open the door from the inside so she can get in. She's a little flushed from the heat, her hair pulled into a tight, neat bun, bringing her features forward, eyes ocean-deep, a little glint in them both, as if on the edge of mischief. She raises her eyebrows and you realize you're staring, putting the car into gear before she can question you.

'Where to?' you ask.

'I was just walking.'

'So let's just drive.' You fiddle with the stereo, pushing in the bootleg Bob Marley tape you bartered your brother for, skipping forward to 'Waiting in Vain'. The bassline shakes the vehicle, and Joy shakes her head, but it's not without a smile on her face.

'I know your brother and my brother are in a band together, but do you play any instruments?' she asks.

'No, but I'll learn someday. The guitar, I think. Then I'll move to London—'

'To London?'

'My eldest brother, Victor, is already there.'

'Those are some big dreams,' Joy says.

'Anything's possible.'

'I didn't say impossible, I said big.' You hold up one hand in apology. 'What will you do when you get there?'

'I'll start a band,' you say. 'Maybe open a club. My brother says it's hard there but there's opportunity. More than here, anyway.' Joy makes a short, sharp sound, agreeing. 'He does say there's nowhere for him or people that look like us to dance, and since dancing is the one thing which might solve our problems, I'm gonna open a club.'

'You seem to have it figured out.'

You shrug. 'What about you, Joy?'

She considers. 'I don't know. I might move to London too, since my brother is there.'

'Maybe we'll move together,' you say.

'Maybe,' she says, turning her attention away from you, a slight

233

smile on her face, her palm leaning out of the window, as if trying to catch the light.

On the weekend, you're at Nick's place.

Tonight, while the Supremes play, Nick tears open the plastic on a new record and, as the song ends, places it on the turntable, lets the needle drop. Amongst a group of friends of friends, you catch sight of Joy; she stands in a doorway leading outside while some of her friends trail smoke into the night. You signal to her: she should come, she should dance. She playfully waves you away, but you're feeling bold and audacious, making your way to where she stands. You hold out your hand as if you are holding open the door to your car, your heart. You don't have to say anything, this is all the coaxing she needs. A wry smile from her, your soft hands in a tender embrace, you move across the floor and it's like the world is just you two. You don't have to do anything but be in motion, be beautiful, be free.

This becomes your summer, yours and Joy's. You do everything together: returning to the beach often, feet planted where the water breaks, taking in the enormity of the ocean. Sharing an illicit first cigarette, sputtering as smoke pushes at your lungs. Whenever you run errands in your father's car, you arrange to pick her up: the distance between your houses is perhaps fifteen minutes; even if it's a short drive, at least you'll have a few songs' worth of each other's company. You don't know what this feeling is, that has your brothers teasing you for daydreaming of moments spent or moments possible with Joy, but you do know you don't just want them, you need them.

Your families both begin to understand that what's happening with you and Joy is no simple teenage crush. Your father catches snippets from your brothers and begins to stitch them together; he sits you down with your mum to say if you're serious about this, then a proper course of action will need to be taken. There will be introductions and what's known as a *knocking*: where the two families come together, to formally announce the intention to marry. Your face changes at this. *Marry?* Your father tuts, saying, 'Do you think you'll just continue to run around with this woman? That's not how we do things, you know that.'

When, a few days later, you relay the conversation to Joy, she shakes her head and smiles.

'My father had the same conversation with me.' She lowers her voice. *'There is a certain way to do things, Joy, and you're not doing them. Do you want to bring shame on us? You will not kill me today.'* You both fall about laughing in your father's car. Rounding the corner, Joy taps you, pointing to the *kyinkyinga* grilling meat on the side of the road. You pull in, killing the engine, and ask what she wants, but Joy says she'll come too.

'What did your mum say?' you ask, as you wait for your order.

'She said, *we'll just leave it to God*. Which, yes, but we also have to be practical as well.'

'Meaning?'

'We should be given the space to work this out for ourselves. There's no rush.'

You nod. See, the thing you and Joy both loved, and still do, is the freedom to make decisions on your own terms, not just to please others. So you take refuge at Nick's every week, away from the prying eyes of adults, away from the questions about your life: *What are your plans? What are your intentions?* You're both eighteen and asking for the days not to be gone in moments, for nights to last lifetimes. You don't want things between you to end, this freedom, and it doesn't feel like it will, these moments looping round and round, until—

'I can't believe you're going without me,' you say.

It's that time of the day when the sun is leaving the sky. In Accra, this hour stretches into the evening, dousing all outside in a quiet blue. You're parked outside Joy's house, trying to stretch your own time with her until you must break away. Inside, you know her bags are packed and her family are waiting to say their last goodbyes. This has all come together quickly, you think, in the way rain might fall without warning. Last week, it had been a possibility; then, on Monday, a family friend had confirmed Joy could be given an expedited process if she were to move to London on a student visa. There was less guarantee in the long term, but she would be able to work around her schooling. And anyway, this was not an opportunity you spent too long mulling over. In London, there would be more work and better prospects. More than Accra, anyway, where it seemed like you had to know someone to make any kind of move in life, and even that was no sure thing. From what you've heard about London, work comes quick and the money is plentiful, and there are supposed to be systems in place to ensure people don't fall through the cracks.

Arrangements were made: her brother had already found her a room to stay in. As you sit together, you tussle with the conflict of emotions, knowing this is an opportunity you would take too, but also knowing how much you'll miss her.

'I'm not going without you, I'm just going before you. You'll follow me?'

You nod but can't keep your feelings from spilling on to your features.

'Why are you looking at me like that?' she asks.

'You'll remember me, right?'

She shakes her head and undoes her seatbelt, coming across to you, her hand in your lap for balance. Joy leans in, her lips grazing yours for the first time. The kiss is soft, momentary, and she draws away, but still close enough that your vision is filled by her face.

'How could I forget?'

You promised to write, so you do:

Not much has changed. Roosters still compete with the call to prayer in the morning. Sunrise in Accra is still so sudden, like magic. I've been working at a school, as a teaching assistant, which means early days and later nights. But at least I have the weekends. Nick's parties are growing; his father is living in the US now, so he's moved the gatherings into the bigger house. The way music echoes through every room, all of us dancing and dancing, approaching frenzy, it's like we're at church, like we're praying, approaching rapture.

I finally bought a guitar and Kweku has been showing me what he knows, which has been a way to pass the time. He says I'm picking it up quickly, that I could play with the band before long. Otherwise, I'm getting along. I'm dreaming of London, of what you're doing, of the space I might have with you. I miss you. I miss our rhythm, our routine: sundown at the beach, the last dance at Nick's parties, our long drives with no real destination. Even though our time together was short, it's hard to imagine we were once strangers.

You fold the blue airmail paper around a cassette, a mixtape you spent hours making with your older brother's new cassette deck, perched by the turntable mixing the Delfonics into Al Green, making a left towards Fela and following this line, along Pat Thomas and Ebo Taylor and Ebenezer Obey. You're trying to remind her of the sound you shared, while also catching her up on the person you're becoming.

When you receive her reply, it's like you're holding the whole world in your hands:

It's colder here. Even on days the sun is shining, there's always a bite to the air. I live and work in the south-east of the city, near Lewisham, and study here too, a few days a week. I'm doing a secretarial course, hoping I can pick up some admin or clerical work. Balancing life, it's much harder than I imagined. Some days, I feel like I'm in a loop of going to work, coming home, only to go again. But my brother is here, and I've made a friend too, Gloria, who's from Achimota, near you. Funny enough, the week I received your letter, she got me a little

cassette player from our local market and I've been listening to
your mixtape on repeat. It reminds me of home, reminds me
of you.

I miss you too. Miss that look you have when you discover a
new song, the way your hand feels in mine, the warmth of your
cheek when you hug me and I can feel your smile. I miss the
way you make me feel: beautiful and free, like anything is
possible.

I've been praying that your time will come soon.

When it's your turn, it's almost without incident. Several
months into 1986, your brother says he has work for you lined up
in London and the intention is that you'll study too. You spend a
day deciding what you will take with you and what you will leave
behind. You'll take the guitar, but you'll send for the records, it'll
be too expensive to take everything in one go. You pack your
warmest clothes, fearing the cold might touch your bones. You
try to stuff your life into a case which couldn't possibly hold it.
You try to wonder what your new life will look like, how you
might go out into the vastness of the world, but all you can think
of is the shape of the thing between you and Joy. You hope that
the distance and time haven't warped and shifted it beyond recognition; you hope that your rhythm remains, that you might still
be able to get into a car and drive with no destination.

While you pack, your father comes into the room and takes
your hand, speaking to you slowly, quietly, as if praying: 'Be careful when you go. The world is big and endless. You don't want it
to swallow you up. Work hard, stay focused, send money back
home when you can. And please, remember me, always.'

You take a moment to look at him then. He's a little older now,
not just in his face but in his spirit. You're his youngest son and it
feels like the gap between you grows wider every day. Sometimes,
you see a sheen on his eyes like a glimmer, a sad glint, his attention elsewhere. You've never seen him cry, but in those moments
he looks close. Whenever you go to ask what fragment has bled

into his day, what is haunting him, he waves a hand, pushes any notion of closeness away. Despite this, you open your mouth to ask, 'How could I forget you?' when your mum walks in, all youth and glint and smile. She takes your face in her hands, and pulls you close, so you feel her heart thud a melancholy rhythm.

'You know you can come back home whenever?'

'I know, Mum. I know.'

★

It's summer '86, but it's not like any summer you've ever known. The fatigue has seeped past your skin, into your blood and bones, the fourteen-hour shifts in a kitchen in central London beginning to take their toll. Today, you're on shift, dreaming of the languor back home, of the slowness, the opportunity to just take some time and rest. You're in your father's car, driving on the edge of the seat, always on the brink, wanting to see everything. You're in that place where Joy kissed you and for a soft, momentary moment, your spirit loosened. You're anywhere but here, where you're so tired, after being served food which is to be your lunch and dinner, you drop the plate. There's no crack or shatter; the food lands face down with a thud. It takes seconds for you to clean it up, but the despair remains. Sitting on an upturned bucket in the corner of the kitchen, you lean your head into your hands, and breathe deeply, trying to steady yourself.

Around you, the clatter of cutlery, the shouts of orders, quick footsteps, a crackle of hoarse laughter, more footsteps in your direction, a heavy breath. You open your eyes and there's a man extending another plate of food towards you. You've caught a glimpse of this face before, his curious, feline eyes, a quick smile framed by a short set of dreads, but he often works the night shift, where you work in the day. You take it from him, and bump the fist extended in your direction. The man bops away without a word and you cry as you eat, broken by the fatigue, mended by the kindness.

Outside, desperate for a reprieve from the heat in the kitchen, in the narrow alleyway behind the restaurant, you'll see the man again, smoking something scented musk, a smile as wide as a horizon when he sees you. He tells you his name is Tony, but his friends call him T. He's been here for nearly a decade; his mother sent him to live with his grandma in Tottenham, saying she would follow when she could.

'You got anyone here?' T asks.

'Older brother was here but he went back home for a visit. That was six months ago.'

'That man is gone.'

'Yeah,' you sigh. 'He's not coming back. Oh, and Joy,' you say, taking out the tiny passport photo from your wallet.

T's smile is broad once more. 'That's how I know it's love. You take her everywhere you go.'

'T, I don't know about you, but without that woman I think I would've lost my mind by now.'

'Why d'you think I'm smoking this?' You both laugh, until T is doubled over, wheezing. 'It's like they allowed us to come to England so they could finish us off,' he says, shaking his head. 'Cost of living going up, money I'm being paid going down. And if one more bobby stops and searches me, I don't know what I'll do.' He sighs. 'Eric, what brought you here?'

You shrug. 'Work. Opportunities. My brother was already here. You?'

'I didn't have a choice,' he says. 'But your reasons are the reason I stay.'

T stubs out his joint against the wall, crushing it underfoot, leaning his head against the brick, gazing skyward. 'I had this idea,' you say, interrupting the quiet. 'When I got here, I wanted to put on parties.' T listens and, encouraged, you continue. 'My brother says there's nowhere in the city for us to dance, or nowhere he could find. So I wanted to put on parties, weekly things, and eventually open a club. Dancing solves most of our problems, right?'

T's nodding, his eyes wide with possibility.

'Eric, I think I know how we can make this happen.'

After your shift, you ride the bus back home with T, heading towards the place you share with Joy in New Cross, but continue on until you reach T's lock-up in Peckham, a garage tucked underneath an estate block, where another man, Reggie, leans against the shutter, waiting. You bump fists in introduction and greeting, while T fiddles with the lock pinning the shutter to the ground. The padlock gives with a click and you walk in after them both, T flicking on the light switch.

Small towers of records lean about the space. You count eight big speakers, stacked in pairs, holding up the back wall. Several turntables and amplifiers, some intact, some spilling out their insides, accented by long trails of wires, everywhere. T crosses over to one of the turntables, and lets the needle drop on whatever was atop; it's a reggae dub you recognize but can't name.

'Reggie, Eric has an idea.'

Reggie magics a beer into his hand and places it in yours, and after he nods to say he's listening, you begin to speak.

The first party takes place in Brixton – one of Reggie's friends says her family has gone back yard for the summer, and that you can have the place if she gets a cut, and nothing is broken.

On the night, long after you've loaded the equipment into Reggie's work van, long after you've pulled each speaker into the house, trailing wires from room to room so the sound echoes everywhere, long after Joy has dropped off the food she and Gloria spent all day cooking, long after queues of people begin to trail in, more than you could've expected for a word-of-mouth event, long after all this, each room becomes a thrum. You think about how the last time you partied like this was back at Nick's, back when the only immediate worry was which song to mix next, but there was more on the horizon: *What will you do for work? What shape will your life begin to take?* You think about how glad you are you made the move, because even though there's rent to make and bills to be paid, you have work and you can freely spend time with the woman you love. There's none of the pressure to have things worked out, to marry young, to say forever when you're only sure of now. You're both on your own time. You think back to that first conversation with Joy in your father's car, how big your dreams of moving to London seemed. And now your lives are bigger and wider than you could've ever imagined.

But there's barely enough room to consider this before the party really begins to bump. There is barely enough room to move but there is enough space to raise your arms, for people to shift and shake as they sing Kool & the Gang's 'Get Down on It'. There is enough space for Rick James's 'Give It to Me Baby' to send you all into frenzy, towards ecstasy. There is enough space for you to encourage Joy to join you behind the decks while Teddy Pendergrass's 'Love T.K.O.' spins, and the party slows, the mood quietens but doesn't dull, the gleam in her eye as you pull her close, as you make a small world with your motion, your love.

T, Joy, Gloria, Reggie, his girlfriend, Yomi: you're like family, all of you dancing for your joy, making space for freedom. You throw these parties at least once a month, more frequently if you can manage it. Soon, you have friends and friends of friends requesting you throw them parties, requesting Joy makes her jollof rice – *I've never tasted anything as good* – requesting that you and T and Reggie play slow jams into the early hours of the morning. You're due to throw another, in the spring of '87, and thinking about expansion, how you might find a permanent site for freedom, when T rings. You hear the sadness across the phone, his breath heavier than usual. He says it's probably best you come down to the lock-up.

Deliberate, T says. A lock doesn't snap itself, pointing to the padlock blackened by heat, the mechanism itself in two, like two separate arms curving inwards. Inside the garage, the fire destroyed everything, disappeared your whole world in a cloud of smoke. T's still talking but you can only hear the crackle of flames doing away with your motion, your rhythm, music only a memory, records morphed into puddles of burnt vinyl, the smell cutting through the space like a high-pitched whine. There have been other suggestions that perhaps you're not wholly welcome in this country, but they've always been unspoken: you know, when they cross the road in broad daylight, or the stares you attract on the bus, the frequency with which you or T are pulled over, the jobs you apply for and never get. You thought – and maybe you've all thought this, but never said it aloud – that maybe it was just you, or that once you had enough money, the right job, the right accent, all those behaviours towards you would ease.

You didn't expect for it to become worse. You didn't expect this kind of intrusion.

'Come,' T says, ushering you out. He pulls the shutter down but doesn't bother with another lock. There's nothing left to take.

When the parties stop, your life in London loses its gleam. Summer comes by, and rather than the promise of long days and long nights, surrounded by those you love, your life begins to fall in on itself. You lose your job in the kitchen and struggle to find regular work. Not only do you miss the freedom of the dances but the extra income too, the little it was. You and Joy begin to feel the squeeze of a city doing its best to disappear you both. But still, you go on, making meals stretch, hustling in any way you can.

One afternoon, when you're making a decision no one should have to, between you and Joy eating a full meal or you both taking the bus to work, your father calls. It's been months since you've spoken, and you expect he might be checking in, but instead he berates you for forgetting him.

'Where is the money you promised?' he asks. You don't know how to tell him you don't even have enough for yourself. That your spirit is bent to the point of breaking, that it's happening, quickly, quietly, without incident. It feels like the country has intruded on your joy, crumbling you from the inside, making dust of your life. You open your mouth to speak, to tell your father what's on your heart, but he cuts across, saying, 'I don't need you, anyway.' He hangs up the phone, leaving you with silence pressed to your ear.

The fall is easy. The ground is always close. You're late paying your rent by a few days; the next month, by a week. You tell your landlord times are hard. He says, holding the keys to his multiple properties, 'Times are hard for all of us.'

You're usually at work on Sundays but you're between cleaning jobs, so you take the bus with Joy to someone's living room in Peckham, and pray. As the hi-fi plays gospel in a corner, stood on a plush carpet, you pray, speaking your innermost desires. In the quiet, you feel safe asking for anything: to dance again, for regular work, for a place to make a home with Joy. But mostly, you pray for peace.

When the prayers are done, food is dished and served on paper plates, drinks poured, laughter, the music louder now. Someone switches on the TV, a group of footballers running around the screen. Your shoulders lower, your fists unclench, relax. For the first time in a long time, you believe that more might be possible, for you, for Joy, for you all.

A few weeks later, the notice pinned on your door when you and Joy return home from work states *immediate eviction*. You call your landlord to plead but he says he wants you both out, immediately. So you pack your possessions into bags, deciding what you will take, what you will leave behind. You think of where you could go, who you could call. You call T, but the line rings out, he must be at work. Gloria is visiting family in Birmingham. Your brother didn't return to London and Joy's brother moved to Milton Keynes. You want to fall to the ground and crumble, but there's no time for that. Joy's quiet crying becomes panic when the land-lord appears, demanding you leave, *now*.

Outside the home which is no longer yours, you tell Joy it will be OK, even if you don't believe it. You take both your suitcases in hand, and say, again, it will be OK, willing it to be so. You'll just take a long drive, with no destination in mind, just like old times. You walk to the bus stop, sticking out your hand when it comes. Together, you ride the night bus in circles, only getting off at the final destination to hop on another. By the fifth bus, you're exhausted. You say to Joy, 'It's as if we're in England to pay for our sins.'

Quietly, her eyes closed, she says, 'But we're not in England, are we? If you close your eyes,' she opens one to check your eyes are closing too, 'you'll see we're on the way to the beach, in your brother's borrowed van. We're heading to that place where shore meets sea, where the water might lap at our feet. Where we might feel free.' She pauses. 'And on the radio . . . *I don't want to wait in vain for your love . . . I don't want to wait in vain for your love.*' You join in with her, your voices quiet yet sure; her solo becomes chorus; you become each other's comfort.

★

It's a few years before you feel like you're back on your feet. After a year of couch surfing and room sharing, you and Joy save enough to move into your own place, in Peckham. Gloria and T and Reggie and Yomi help you fix up the place; it's a week before you're in the space alone, and when you are, you plug in the turn-table T gives you as a housewarming present, play 'Waiting in Vain'. You slide about your living-room carpet, singing with all you can muster, singing until your voices break, and there are tears. It feels like you can finally breathe again.

You've given up on those dreams of starting a club. T becomes a Tube driver, Reggie starts his own construction business, you take on an administrative role at the local council. Your first son,

Raymond, arrives at the end of '88, your second in the spring of '92. Your life begins to take a certain shape, a regular rhythm, stable and steady.

Sometimes, though, you miss the music. Sometimes, you can be convinced by T to join him in the evenings, you in turn convincing Joy to join you. On these nights, it's double denim and jheri curls and long chains and short afros. It's small fires between fingers, it's the way rum dyes liquids brown, seeping through mixers like a slow promise. It's the one and only time you try Ecstasy and it's nothing like the real thing, more a prolonged high than a swoop in the stomach. It's those songs which go on and on, like the version of 'Brighter Days' on the B-side of the record, with its beautiful synths, its wandering vocal, a beat which knocks so hard you can't help but slap the walls, whoop in disbelief of the moment. You find Joy and sing to the woman you love, the brightness of the song in your voice. These days, these nights, your life is beautiful; as the song says, there are brighter days ahead.

One Saturday afternoon, Joy wakes up singing a sweet melody and so do you. You suggest walking over to Peckham Rye, to the park, to let the boys run around and have some time for the two of you, together.

Outside is gorgeous and Rye Lane heaves with pedestrians, people making their way to barbershops and salons, or hoping to haggle at butcher's and grocer's, families making the same pilgrimage to a flat patch of grass, lovers doing the dance of longing which precedes separation, young people trying to work out where, tonight, the party will be, aunties and uncles and elders hoping for a visit from family, hoping today they might not feel so lonely.

In the park, you all kick a ball around, encouraging your little ones until they're spent, napping on a blanket, their limbs laid out in the sunshine. Joy lies back on the blanket too, and asks, 'What did you dream of last night?' You look at her, confused, and she says, 'You were talking in your sleep.'

You tell her you were dreaming about when you first met, of the

246

moment she looked at you and it was hard to believe you had ever been strangers. You were dreaming of that moment, stood in front of the vastness of the ocean, your lives opening up ahead of you.

She closes her eyes, smiles, saying, 'We should all go back. Show the boys where they were made.'

You look from Joy to your sons, almost in disbelief that this is now your life. You go to tell her you love the life you're building together, but her breathing has already deepened, already dreaming of freedom.

It's 1995. You've just been promoted and T has insisted he meet you after work to celebrate, but when you get into his car, Reggie's there too. Neither are smiling. T's grip clenches the steering wheel.

'What's going on?' you ask.

'You remember that guy, Wayne? At the *first* party we did, in Brixton? Helped us bring the speakers in.'

'Yeah, man, Wayne's good people.'

'Was. He's dead.'

'What d'you mean?'

'Police got him.' T kisses his teeth. 'I know he was in custody but no one deserves to die.' T slams on the steering wheel, then bites his lip, trying to stem his sadness.

'We're going Brixton police station,' Reggie says, 'to protest. You coming?'

You look from Reggie to T and say, 'Let's go.'

When you arrive, what has started as a peaceful protest is on the precipice of something else, fuelled by the stance of a line of police. They are trying to welcome violence, trying to find a way to enact force, to put the people out here – shouting and chanting, looking for answers – back in their place, which is the unseen, the unheard, unhuman. They're trying to push your anger towards sadness, the line so thin.

They're trying to find ways to kill you too.

And then, you're all pushed over the brink. And then, you're all being battered like drums by sticks and shields. And then, you're seeing a crackle as fires are lit in the seclusion of broad darkness. And then, a brick disappears a glass window, black plumes of smoke rising in the sky, anger happening, everywhere. And then, you, T and Reggie are splitting away down a side street. And then, four police officers give chase. And then, you already know the ending to this story. And then, you're wondering how this doesn't end in your death. That's when Reggie trips, and they swarm. Consume him, whole. You watch his light become dull. You watch a whole life break in the time it takes to make an easy fall. The ground is always so close. You turn to go towards Reggie, but T pulls you away. Reggie shouts for you to go, go; he knows what's happening to him and doesn't want you to meet the same fate. You go, you go, fast, to the car, taking the back roads home. You go, you go, feeling like you left your brother behind to die. You go, you go, until unable to rid the image of Reggie being surrounded, subsumed, all you can do is stop and cry. All you can do is fall to the ground and crumble.

'He came home,' Yomi says to us. It's a week after the protests, and Yomi's standing in your living room. T's there too, on the edge of your sofa, Joy's beside. You and T have been driving round at night all week, hoping the force which subsumed him had spat him back out into the world. But here is Yomi saying, 'He came home last night, with his usual smile, his face unscathed, so I thought, maybe he's OK. But he lifted his shirt and showed me the constellation of bruises starred across his chest. I wanted to run him a bath, but he insisted he would get in and out the shower. He wanted to eat, wanted to sleep. He wanted to be held. There was some corned beef stew in the fridge, and while he showered, I put some rice on the fire. He ate, quietly – I could tell he didn't want to talk much – and got into bed soon after.

'Maybe ten a.m. this morning, there was a knock on the door. I'd heard that knock before, back when I first came to the UK. It's the kind of knock which takes and doesn't give. I began to panic because I've had friends wrenched loose from the grip of their own lives. The knock continued, until it became a thud, until I could hear the slam of an open palm. I heard the door splintered like the snap of a branch, and the immigration officers appeared in the room, and like magic, they disappeared him. They said there would be nothing which could be done. They are sending him back, with no chance of return.'

Yomi stands up then, swallowing, before saying, 'I'd like to be left alone for a while, if that's OK.' She leaves and though she didn't say she blames you, the implication lingers in the air, long after she's gone.

It wasn't your fault, Joy says. First, she'll tell you this, then she'll shout at you, and she's only shouting because you shouted at her, because it's been years and still Reggie haunts you, his absence a permanent spectre. You never heard from him again and yet his voice moves through your mind all the time.

Tonight, you've been drinking again, letting spirits dizzy your blood. You're always drinking of late, down at the Gold Coast bar in Norwood, where you've made a friend, Peter, who's trying not to remember, trying to forget. Tonight, Peter told you his wife had passed in childbirth and he couldn't shake away the image of her, couldn't shake away the guilt of encouraging their move to this country. So really, what you're both saying is you'd rather not feel your grief now, rather not feel it at all. Joy says, it's like you want to abandon your life. Like you want to fly away. You're somewhere between anger and sadness, the line a blur, but you've been drinking, you're feeling dumb and courageous, you're not feeling much, really, because if you were, you wouldn't say what you say to Joy: *I don't need you.* You wouldn't twist the knife you had slid into her in plain sight, saying it again. This is the night when, in her shock and silence, you drag your sons out into the darkness, the moon full, the evening cool and still, intending to take them with you, wherever you're going. When you reach the kerb, they dig their heels into the ground, protesting, sitting on the pavement, and you leave them there, telling them *I don't need you either*. Or maybe it's the night you drive with one of your sons to Yomi's, knowing the way by memory, leaving your youngest son in the car to knock on her door, sitting in her living room, begging for forgiveness. Or maybe that's the night you return to the Gold Coast, drink until your limbs grow stiff, and you're sick, everywhere. You don't know. You can't remember. The lines blur as you briefly forget.

*

Joy doesn't give up on you. She knows who you were, who you are, who you might be. She can see what might be possible for you, even if you can't see for yourself.

You don't argue as much, and soon it's a constant flow of tears. She's always there with a washcloth, with a tender hand atop yours, with her warmth, her love.

You find your voice for long enough to tell her you don't deserve her. You'll tell her you know your silence was killing her too. You'll tell her you're stuck somewhere between your inability to scream and the desire to do so. You'll tell her, every day, every day, you're in pain. But you're trying to go towards it. You're trying to confront what has always scared you: the endlessness of your grief. You're trying to be better.

'I will always love you,' she says, 'but I can only take so much. I need more. They,' she says, pointing in the direction of your sons, 'need more. If you're gonna be better, show me.'

Better means being open. It means allowing yourself to surrender. It means saying things which are honest and true, Godlike even. It means leaning into the quiet, even when it's loud with echoes of the past. It means gathering together on Sundays with others who, like you, have come from Ghana and Nigeria, Senegal and Jamaica, to London, to build a new life. It means making the space for you all to pray, to reach towards your innermost desires; to reach past your beautiful, through your ugly, towards

250

your vulnerable. It means making the space to feel safe enough to ask for anything, and believing what you ask for might be possible.

It means allowing the weight of the love you share with Joy to undo you, to unspool your tightly wound self, in the way love encourages looseness, encourages you to be free. It means sending your sons out of the house with money in hand, so you might have a few hours alone with the woman you love, and on return, embracing them with as much love as you can muster, all of you grinning and laughing. It means asking Joy to marry you, if only to speak aloud what you already know about your love. Better means wiping away your wife's tears when Gloria passes away; Joy's oldest friend holding on until after the wedding. It means giving how you feel voice, rhythm, music, even when you feel like you're always on the brink of disaster, like any moment someone will intrude upon your small world, crumbling your walls, making dust of your foundations.

It means, years later, when your youngest son asks who you are, who you were, what you dream of, where you find freedom, when he asks you to tell him of movement, migration, burden, of having to choose which parts of your life to keep, which to let fall away, you'll tell him that you know this feeling which haunts him sometimes, this sadness on his shoulders. You'll be so overcome, you cannot finish your story. You'll feel like you're rambling. Like you're making no sense. Just a jumble of memories. You'll ask, can I start again? Your son will shake his head. I understand, he says.

You'll tell him, this is how you migrated. This is what you have taken with you, this is what you tried to leave behind. This is the guilt which survived. This is your burden. This is why you struggle to love freely because you feel you lose everything you do. You'll count on your hands: Reggie, Peter, Gloria, your parents, your wife. You expect intrusions. Quietly, without incident, like the way Joy's heart murmured its hurt before giving out. You haven't cried for your wife. You're stuck somewhere between the

251

inability to cry and the desire to do so. You're worried your own body is storing harm in the seclusion of its darkness. You're worried that there's only so much your heart can take. You're worried that your anger and sadness have been echoing through your life, multiplying, misdirecting, finding homes in those closest to you. You're worried that your sons have inherited your haunting and maybe their sons will too. In pain, in pain, every day in pain. Begging for forgiveness. Somewhere between faith and disbelief. No voice, no rhythm, no music. You want to be loose. You want to unspool. You want to answer a door without the fear that you'll be wrenched loose from the grip of your own life. You want to leave your house without the fear you'll be subsumed. You don't want to feel like you're waiting in vain. Are you making sense? Your son nods. He understands.

You'll say, it's been so long since you've known freedom. Maybe you've never been free.

51.

Standing up from the bed, I hold out my hand to my father, telling him to come. I pull him to his feet and hold him steady as he
wobbles, wipe the tears away from his face with my hands, a soft
palm to the face of my kin. 'Get dressed and meet me downstairs,' I say, by the door. He nods and I leave him, quickly blasting
myself with hot water in the shower, some fresh clothes, before
retrieving Pops's flight case of records. I hear the shower go again,
and minutes later Pops comes down the stairs.

'Ready?' I ask. He nods again.

Outside, it's still gorgeous. There's rhythm happening everywhere. The sun is already high in the sky, shade a memory. A pair
of men walk past us slowly, arm in arm, in the depths of conversation, bearing close resemblance to each other; time folds in on
itself; in them, I see who my father and I are, who we might
become.

Onwards. Along Rye Lane, where we bump into Marlon,
always on his way somewhere, always in motion. He crosses the
road to greet us, embracing us both, asking how we are doing,
knowing what it means to lose and to continue to live. Pops nods
and tells Marlon he's doing better, that Marlon must stop by the
house sometime. The smile Marlon gives us is its own shine, and
when he leaves us I notice the way light clasps to Pops's skin at
this hour makes him look beautiful. I want to commit this
moment to memory, so I ask Pops to stop, to give a smile; I pull
out the disposable camera which never leaves my pocket, a click
of the shutter, his grin like light, like a beacon, saying, *I am here*.

We continue walking towards Queens Road, towards Femi's
restaurant, which isn't open today, so I take Pops inside through
the back entrance. I flick on the light and invite Pops to sit at the

counter, asking what he will eat. He puts his head in his hands then, broken by the fatigue, mended by the kindness. I am patient, I wait, as he inhales, exhales, to steady himself. With a smile, he asks for the chef's special, and I set to work quickly, on Femi's favourite of grilled fish atop a bed of sweet peppers and rice, slicing the peppers so they're uniform, paying close attention to the grill, wanting fish that falls apart, wanting a sauce as sharp as it is sweet.

While I cook, I ask him to pick the music. He pops open his flight case, rifling through, crossing over to the turntable in the corner, letting the needle drop on Hugh Masekela's 'Riot'. We both nod our heads in praise, those jubilant horns spilling into the space.

I serve us both a bowl, joining Pops at the counter. We eat in quiet, the clatter of cutlery like percussion. Pops is soon scraping his plate, trying to gather the loose grains of rice.

'There's more if you want it,' I say. He shakes his head, smiling. And since the only thing which might solve our problems is dancing, when we're both finished eating Pops puts on another record, 'Abrentsie' by Gyedu-Blay Ambolley, music which is full and dusty and warm, music from back home, and soon we're sharing the same small motion, a little two-step. Our music is undeniable. I've only ever known myself in song, between notes, in that place where language won't suffice but the drums might, might speak for us, might speak for what is on our hearts, and in this moment, as the music gathers pace, looping round once more, passing frenzy, approaching ecstasy, all my dance moves are my father's. We move like mirrors, haunting the space with our motion, our bodies free and flailing and loose. I'm pulled to tap my father on the shoulder, to try to say to him, *I wish we could always be this open*, but I don't know either of us have the words. So instead, we build each other a small world, our solos swelling, rising like a chorus, forward as he goes back, back as he goes forward, our hands to our chest in reverence, building a church with our rhythm, a place we don't have to explain, a place where we can be honest and true; Godlike, even. A place we can both surrender.

Soon, after the fifth or sixth reload, we both begin to tire. I pour him a glass of water and he drinks deeply, content, a sigh. Soon, he's asking after Del, teasing, mischief a glint in his eye. I tell him every time I see her, it's hard to imagine my life without her, and he nods, knowing, understanding. Soon, he's asking, *where is she now? Call her over!* I'm thinking of where Del might be, of calling her to come by. And my brothers, my family, blood or otherwise: Nam and Vanessa, Jeremiah and Jimmy, Koby and Ife, Uncle T. All of whom knew me from before the loss of my mother, knew me as her son, can help keep the memories of her spirit alive, can ensure, even as I forge new memories, here, now, that Mum will always be part of my world. Maybe I'll even ask Theo and Amma and Robin, with their voices and rhythms and instruments, because I still have dreams of making my own music, and maybe we could get going again, turn the gathering into a party. And maybe, after one song trails into another and another, after our two-steps and tender motions, there will be hugs and embraces, all of us thinking, I didn't know I needed that, all of us needing that *closeness*.

Maybe, maybe, but for now, it's just Pops and me, and I wouldn't have it any other way.

And then, he's asking more questions: *Who are you? What do you dream of?*

Now, I'm sat opposite him, and I'm talking, telling him my dreams: that this place is wonderful, and Femi has been nothing but good to me, shown me all he knows, but I won't be working here forever. One day, I want to have a place for us, a restaurant of my own. On the menu will be food from home: you know, the usual, jollof and red-red, fish grilled in front of you, stew cooked long and slow. Live music on the weekends. I want a place for people to gather, to come together, eat and look good and dance. Just like he wanted.

And he nods, places a tender palm to my forearm, saying, *I believe in you. I believe in you, son. Your mother too, she always did. She would be proud.* And at this, I'm overcome. Maybe this is all we need sometimes, for someone else to believe in the possibilities you see for yourself.

Soon, we're back on our feet. I'm going towards the record player, wondering what we should play next. My father wanders about the space, spreading his arms wide as if he's holding the whole world in his hands. Soft summer light graces his crown as he shakes his head, almost disbelieving of this moment, asking, what would we be if we always had this kind of space? And I tell him, in the quietness of the moment which falls, what I know, what I feel in this moment: free.

Acknowledgements

To Seren Adams: I don't think I'll ever stop thanking you for that first conversation in your office, nor for the encouragement you've always shown. I owe so much of this to you. Thank you for your kind and keen eye, your caring nature and your wonderful friendship.

To Christian Ogunbanjo: I've lost count of the *this year is your year* text messages you've sent me, and I believe it more and more each time. Thank you for believing in me and my vision, for always being on the other end of the phone and the kind of friendship where not much needs to be explained (how lucky I am to have two brilliant agents). I feel so blessed and grateful to have met you when I did.

To Isabel Wall and Katie Raissian: thank you for your patience. For encouraging me to feel my way through this period of writing, and to go deeper where you knew I could. Thank you for making time and space for me to develop and hone my craft. Thank you for encouraging me to dream. Most of all, thank you both for the phone calls and text messages and lunches; thank you both for being such a joyous presence in my life.

Viking Books and Grove Atlantic team: Rosie Safaty, Jane Gentle, Anna Ridley, Alexia Thomaidis, Zoe Coxon, Deb Seager, Kait Astrella. Working with you all has been nothing short of a dream, and I'm so grateful for all you do for me.

To Sarah-Jane Forder: working with you has been a joy, and my writing is better for it. Thank you.

My writing and artistic community: Belinda Zhawi, Yomi Ṣode, Sumia Jama, Kareem Parkins-Brown, Amina Jama, Joanna Glen, Raven Leilani, Nadia Owusu, Nana Kwame Adjei-Brenyah, Dantiel W. Moniz, Katie Kitamura, Abraham Adeyemi, Aniefiok Ekpoudom, Xavier Scott Marshall, Tomisin Adepeju, Natasha Brown, Bolu Babalola, Jasmine Lee Jones, Linton Kwesi Johnson, Zadie Smith, Paapa Essiedu, Legacy Russell, Lemara Lindsay-Prince, Leonie Annor-Owiredu, Sharmaine Lovegrove, Sope Dirisu, Adama Jalloh, Matimba Kabalika, Theo Croker, Bec Evans, Charlotte Jansen, Danielle Vitalis, Justin Marosa, Ronan McKenzie, Campbell Addy – I'm so grateful for the way you all see the world, the work you give to it and the community you share with me.

Candice Carty-Williams: that summer's day in Ruskin Park lives in my mind, rent-free. Thank you for your wisdom and joy and support, and just generally being the best.

Tice Cin: gratitude for the extended conversation, for the late-night walks in New York, for your sensitivity and vision.

Raymond Antrobus: my brother, my family. Gratitude to you, always, for your honesty and brilliance.

Deborah Bankole: fam. Thank you for always trusting and sharing with me, from our first conversation to our last. I'm so grateful for your love and care.

Stuart Ruel: meeting you changed the way I see the world and reframed my artistic practice. I wouldn't be the person I am today without you, so thank you.

To my people, the rest of my Small World: Joe Akinwusi, Krys Osei, Rob Eddon, Niamh Fitzmaurice, Courage Khumalo, Sam Akinwumi, Thomas McGregor, Charlotte Scholten, Nick Ajagbe,

Ife Morgan, Archie Forster, Louise Jesi, Chase Edwards, Nicos Spencer, Steffan Davies, Lex Guelas, Chrisia Borda, Mariam Moalin, Monica Arevalo, Charlie Glen, Diderik Ypma, Cara Baker, Zoe Heiman, Myah Jeffers, Bekah Button, Charles Ashie, Katia Wengraf, Marcelle Akita, Bibi Abdulkadir, Billy Paronia, Ravinder Bhogal, Melissa Thompson, Kristine Formon.

To Sue: you are a light who never fails to make me smile. Thank you for your kindness and care.

To Jumal and Jashel: thank you for always having my back, for your laughter and joy, for your faith, your ambition. Thank you for always being a phone call away and being a constant inspiration.

To Mum and Dad: this one is for you both. For the trips to book-shops and the library, for showing me what love means, for teaching me how to carefully and consciously build community. For all I know that you gave up and all that I don't. For everything. I love you both.

Permissions

'Almeda' words and music by Solange Knowles, Jordan Terrell Carter, John Kirby, Terius Nash, Pharrell Williams © 2019. Reproduced by permission of Sony Music Publishing Ltd. © 2021 2082 Music Publishing (ASCAP). All rights on behalf of 2082 Music Publishing administered by WARNER CHAPPELL NORTH AMERICA LTD. © Published by Kirby Kirbstein Publishing. Administered by Kobalt Music Publishing Limited.

'Heart Attack' words and music by David Orobosa Omoregie, Joe Reeves, James Blake Litherland and Kyle Evans © 2021 WARNER CHAPPELL MUSIC LTD., EMI APRIL MUSIC INC., PULSE GLOBAL, I KEEP CALLING and KYLE EVANS PUBLISHING DESIGNEE. All rights for WARNER CHAPPELL MUSIC LTD. Administered by WC MUSIC CORP. All Rights for EMI APRIL MUSIC INC. Administered by SONY MUSIC PUBLISHING (US) LLC, 424 Church Street, Suite 1200, Nashville, TN 37219. All rights for PULSE GLOBAL and I KEEP CALLING administered by CONCORD GLOBAL MUSIC c/o CONCORD MUSIC PUBLISHING. All Rights Reserved Used by Permission. *Reprinted by Permission of Hal Leonard Europe Ltd.*

'Buy Out Da Bar' by Charmz ©

'Waiting in Vain' words and music by Bob Marley. Copyright © 1977 Fifty-Six Hope Road Music Ltd. and Primary Wave/Blue Mountain. Copyright Renewed. All Rights Administered throughout the world by Blue Mountain Music Ltd. (PRS). All Rights Reserved. *Reprinted by Permission of Hal Leonard Europe Ltd.*

Every effort has been made to trace copyright holders and to obtain their permission for the use of copyright material. The publisher apologizes for any errors or omissions and would be grateful to be notified of any corrections that should be incorporated in future editions of this book.